Where the Stars Cross

by

Dottie Sines

Copyright Notice
This is a work of fiction. Names, characters, places, and incidents are either the product of the author's imagination or are used fictitiously, and any resemblance to actual persons living or dead, business establishments, events, or locales, is entirely coincidental.

Where the Stars Cross

COPYRIGHT © 2024 by Dottie Sines

All rights reserved. No part of this book may be used or reproduced in any manner whatsoever without written permission of the author or The Wild Rose Press, Inc. except in the case of brief quotations embodied in critical articles or reviews.
Contact Information: info@thewildrosepress.com

Cover Art by *The Wild Rose Press, Inc.*

The Wild Rose Press, Inc.
PO Box 708
Adams Basin, NY 14410-0708
Visit us at www.thewildrosepress.com

Publishing History
First Edition, 2024
Trade Paperback ISBN 978-1-5092-5737-9
Digital ISBN 978-1-5092-5738-6

Published in the United States of America

Dedication

For my sons,
who have endlessly cheered me on
and patiently listened
to the many trials, and sprinkling of triumphs,
of my writing journey.
Wanting to make such fine young men proud
of their mother has helped me persevere
through all the rejection, frustration, and editing.
You are among my brightest stars.

Acknowledgments

To Pam Phillips, my sis and fellow writer, thank you for your critique on my novel and for tirelessly talking shop with me.

Bob Adamov, I owe you more than a cup of coffee for generously sharing your publishing and marketing wisdom. (Check out Bob's island-based mystery-adventures.)

Thanks to Anne Fischer for being my first beta reader and a wonderful gal-pal.

Thank you, Irene Herold, for telling me point-blank the good, the bad, and the ugly of the novel's first final version.

Gratitude to my pal Barb Lang for your critique and your leadership of our writers group.

With appreciation to Helen Walkerly for adeptly suggesting my Helen character's dialogue.

A final thank you to Nan Swanson, my editor at The Wild Rose Press, for facilitating my second chance, for your brilliant suggestion to make this novel historical, and for all your hard work on my behalf.

Chapter One

They say you shouldn't make eye contact, you shouldn't show fear. A slight turn of Ellie Todd's head revealed the predator looming in her peripheral vision, still on her trail. She quickened her stride, weaving herself through the swarms of people buzzing along Michigan Avenue. Surely, they would absorb and camouflage her. Her heart boomed against her chest like the foot pedal of a bass drum. Her breath huffed out in shallow puffs.

Anything but afraid of the woman, she simply wanted nothing to do with the termite that had gnawed the axis of her world to a pulp. Especially today, after the heart-crushing morning she'd had. Not to mention the first day of the only vacation she'd taken from her seven-day work week in over two years. It had been tough enough forcing herself out of her house dress and the mundane routine that had gradually become her norm— robotically doing her work, mindlessly reading and napping. Crying.

After straightening her gray felt slouch hat and with a spate of *excuse me*'s tossed over her shoulder, Ellie maneuvered around shabbily attired peddlers selling their apples for a nickel and dark-skinned musicians wailing out the latest blues ode to misery, their saxophone cases poised open to catch the rare toss of a coin. Ellie dodged a stampeding taxicab, bright yellow with a checkered stripe racing along its length, and continued north.

This wasn't the way she used to do Chicago, a place where you needed to give yourself a leisurely pace to fully appreciate its timeless ambiance. A place of towering, venerable stone. A place scented with a blend of French perfumes and earthy lake water, with complex notes of frankfurters smothered in mustard and onions. The way Chicago was before this terrible economic collapse, that is. Now the city was a shadowed place of bread lines stretching around the block, hollow-eyed women begging on street corners, and desperate men turning to crime to feed their families.

Ellie hadn't expected the streets to be so crowded today, but then she hadn't ventured into the city in nearly two years. Maybe FDR's New Deal was having some effect. She hoped things were on the upswing the newspapers claimed they were, for the sake of all these poor souls doing whatever they could to make a dime. For her sake, too. She'd been robbed of too many things, one of which was her beloved city, after Mason's move there transformed it into the place where she might run into him. Or, worse, him and *her*. Today she would take back her cherished city, as decided during last night's insomnia.

Thus, this morning she'd ambled through Grant Park, where she tried to siphon the residual energy of bypassing runners and managed lethargic smiles at mothers as they pushed wicker strollers overflowing with cherubic babies. She'd hoofed the dozen or so blocks up to Marshall Field's, where she honed in on the sleek, silky, bias-cut dresses she would dream about tonight and where she dared try on ethereal hat confections slicked with lustrous ribbons and dripping with alluring netting. But her quick glances at the price tags, even knowing there was no point, had prompted the usual clandestine sighs. So after tucking her golden hair back beneath her late-twenties model and tugging at the dress which had somehow become unfashionably short in the course of a few years—hemlines had coming crashing down along with the stock market—she'd stepped back out into the sunlight streaming through gaps in the skyline and, blessedly, into her mournful soul.

But now the overly embellished figure she'd spotted across the avenue defiled her progress in buoying her mood, especially when the woman charged across to Ellie's side of the street, clipping the shoulders of anyone in her way. Had she seen Ellie? Was she in pursuit of her, or was it a lousy coincidence? Of the countless other footsteps clacking and thumping against the pavement all around Ellie, this person's dominated. Staccato, determined.

Ellie glanced back. At the forefront of the curbside crowd, the woman stood hell-bent and severe, waiting for one of those new pedestrian signals to switch its hand symbol from red to green. Ellie continued her rapid gait, making it to the opposite side of the avenue seconds into the *don't walk* symbol. By now familiar with the footfall, she knew the woman had crossed too. No doubt now that she was in pursuit, having twice altered her course.

A massive shadow simultaneously swelled across the land, charcoal-hued clouds swirling into an ominous formation. No coincidence there. Ellie lowered her face against soft slivers of spring rain. A few more feet to her favorite cafe, and then she could slip inside and her trail would grow cold. Then she could sit and enjoy the rare treat of a hot cup of tea somewhere other than her kitchen, maybe even a slice of sugar milk pie if it didn't cost too much. She needed the pampering today.

"Ellie!"

Are you kidding me? She's actually calling out to me? Ignoring the entreaty, Ellie rounded the next corner and pushed onward.

"Excuse me! Most people are courteous enough to respond when spoken to." The rasp of the words, likely the product of a couple decades of smoking, spewed malice and oppressed the city's honking cars and chattering voices. "Ellie! Are you deaf?"

Ellie halted. If she continued ignoring the woman, there'd likely be an embarrassing scene. The chilly rain began pummeling her skin, but she turned and faced the succubus.

Scarlet zigzags slashed across the blindingly white dress, its skirt flaring from a narrow, high-waisted red belt, and a wrap trimmed in black fur swirled around the woman's shoulders. A small black beret provocatively concealed one eye and tilted seamlessly into long, dark hair rolled into loose, devil-may-care swirls, *à la* any one of the silver screen's most glamorous female motion picture stars. Brows plucked into skeletal arches curved above aloof eyes. Pouty lips were enameled in fire-engine red. Black patent-leather Mary Janes were the only thing to stop the mile-long legs. A fistful of Marshall Field's shopping bags dangled from an arm posed at a right angle. A wax museum figure come to life.

Ellie gave her navy-blue, drop-waisted sack of a dress another tug and pawed at her chin-length, side-parted, Marcel-waved hair. There was a time when she wouldn't have dreamed of coming into the city wearing anything but the latest fashions and looking anything but totally put together.

"Yes?" Ellie pulled in a swig of air, her breathing weighty, her insides like gelatin at finally coming face to face with the titleholder.

"Hmph." The woman snapped her head to the side and back in a well-practiced hair toss. "You know, whatever your problem is, you need to get over it. I'd think by now you'd have the decency to speak to me." Another hair-toss before resuming her mannequin's pose.

Ellie knew Louisa was twelve years younger than she. Knew where she lived, who her friends were, and that her favorite music was anything by any one of the current heart-throb crooners—this self-inflicted knowledge having been acquired through Ellie's inquiring of and listening to anyone who knew that *poor Ellie, her husband has left her for another woman*. She'd then obsessed over it all during those first endless, hellish, sleepless nights, wondering what the woman had that she didn't, until she finally gasped for air and sanity took the reins from self-destruction.

Then she'd seen *the other woman*, prancing with Mason down State Street soon after he moved out. She'd passed for a dozen years younger then. But, wow, up close she looked a lot older than thirty-something. Vertical lines outlined her upper lip like a picket fence. Smoking. Or, more likely, from too much time with countless married men, down on her knees... Ellie felt her face flush at the vile thought. Actually, fine crinkles etched the woman's entire face, like a riverbed in the dry season. Probably too many leisure hours under a hot sun, followed by too many all-nighters in speakeasies, drinking and smoking. And whoring around with married men.

"I'm sorry, I don't believe we've met."

Lou-Easy lit the cigarette she'd fished from her bag. Her face petrified even further. "Oh, I think you know who I am, honey." She blew a long trail of smoke directly toward Ellie's face before producing a mock laugh. "You know, it's no wonder Mason left you. You are one cold bitch."

Ellie waved a hand at the smoke and flinched at the vulgar language, but she was not going to bite at the bait dangling in front of her, and she certainly wasn't going to acknowledge to Lou-Easy that she'd played any role in Mason leaving her. The hag obviously considered herself the winner, having landed herself the grand prize of a man who cheats on his wife, and now she wanted to gloat.

"Is that all you wanted to say? If so, you're wasting my time."

"Like you wasted years of Mason's time, right?" The screechy mock-laugh drowned out the whoosh and whirl and horns of the city. "But I have better things to do with my time, too, and he happens to be waiting at home for me right now." Another suck of the cigarette.

The ugliness of Lou-Easy's words and her gnarled expression obscured the image she tried her darnedest to showcase. She was one of those women you sort of envied because she seemed to have the inside track on all things beauty—the makeup that looks professionally done, the hair that falls impossibly perfectly—but who you disliked without knowing her because you just knew she was a threat to women and a siren to men.

My marriage is none of your business, Ellie wanted to say, but she decided to administer a dose of reality. "I take it you're seeing my former husband. You'll want to get going, then. I'm sure you don't want him out of your sight for long."

Lou-Easy winced. A hint of doubt darted across the painted face. "Oh, my god, for your information, honey, Mason is one hundred percent faithful to me." Cigarette smoke fluttered with her hand motions. "Some women just don't get cheated on. You had him and you blew it." Her face shot toward Ellie's, halting within inches. "He's in love with *me* now. Deal with it."

Ellie's imagination produced a motion picture clip of Mason pounding at Louisa. On a bed dripping with satin sheets. All kinds of panting, grunting, spicy language. The sort of relations she and Mason hadn't ventured in years, if ever. It was such an ancient memory, she barely remembered. She forced her brain to vomit out the sickening images of him with this creature.

Good to learn now that Lou-Easy not only was a lowlife, she also was insecure, petty, and tacky. Any class she tried to project came only from the expensive material goods adorning her severely girdled body. *Enough of this.* Ellie turned toward the door of the cafe. "I'll be sure to tell Mason about our lovely little encounter next time he phones asking to come back to me," she called over her shoulder.

Louisa's eyebrows dipped into a V shape. "Mason is *not* calling you, and you know it. He's happy now, Ellie, so you need to get a life." She flung her smoldering cigarette to the ground, of course not dreaming of tainting her slick shoes by tramping it out. "And tell your needy brats to stop phoning him all the time."

Ellie's hand dropped from the door handle, and she turned, her eyes piercing Louisa's like a welding torch. "Leave my children out of this." Her words emerged in a low rumble, like thunder warning of impending lightning. "Do you understand me?"

Louisa's chin trembled, her eyes widened.

Ellie turned away again.

"I wish to hell you and your annoying urchins would drop dead." Claws clutched at Ellie's head, dislodging her hat, digging into her scalp, snapping her head backward.

Ellie spun around as if on a carousel, pushed into the woman, connecting with a shove or a yank, maybe the swing of a fist. Louisa landed on her bottom with a thud and bounced onto her side. A vague college physics lesson darted through Ellie's mind. The force she'd exerted had resulted in the displacement of Lou-Easy. And the silencing of her mouth.

Good heavens, what had she done? Pushed her? Punched her? She glanced down at the glove on her right hand. No blood on the kid leather, at least, but darn it, another of her cursed impulsive acts. Never in her life had she hit anyone, except for that irritating Leonard punk in the third grade who kept pulling up her dress on the playground. Ellie's stomach surged, her head pounded. She stood paralyzed like a character in one of those ridiculous horror films where the dimwit has the chance to escape but for some inexplicable reason stands there watching the fiendishness unfold.

Lou-Easy's bags had spewed in every direction. A few feet away, a golden perfume box seeped, its bottle shattered into shards, its scent contributing a pleasant aroma to the foul scene, at least. The sole of a two-toned pump peeked from a soggy, overturned shoebox. And the beast lay motionless in a puddle. Then a moan, some muffled incoherency, a little movement.

All right, she's alive. No visible damage, no sign of blood. Only a stunned expression embossed into the leathery face.

Lou-Easy propped herself on an elbow and fished for her displaced belongings.

As the haze of confusion diffused, Ellie scanned her surroundings. Three older women huddled together from a safe distance down the sidewalk, watching from the corners of their eyes and whispering. From across the street, two teenage boys had apparently caught the show. One stared wide eyed, the other grinned and nodded as if in approval. But thankfully nobody seemed to be making a move to apprehend Ellie. No handcuff-toting, uniformed officer approached. *Okay, ma'am, let's take a little ride downtown.*

Lou-Easy shuffled onto her hands and knees. A smudge of blood-red lipstick slashed from her gaping mouth to her chin, and a crimson finger claw nestled in the mussed hair. Staggering to her feet, she rubbed a shoulder, her eyes flitting back and forth. She seemed unaware of her whereabouts, oblivious to Ellie's presence. Did she even know what had happened?

What-ifs flooded Ellie's mind. What if Louisa really were hurt? Or what if she weren't hurt but sent Ellie thousands of dollars in contrived medical bills? Ellie wanted only to get back on that L and disappear back inside her Oak Park home and purge the woman from her mind and her life. She leaned to retrieve her handbag from where it had landed in the melee.

"You bitch!" Lou-Easy grabbed a shard of glass from the pavement and flung it at Ellie. "You're gonna pay for this!"

Ellie had paid all she intended to for this woman's mere existence. She deserved much worse than getting knocked on her behind, and the guilty pleasure of having done the knocking oozed into Ellie's consciousness.

"I don't know what you're talking about. Looks like you've had a little accident," she said before making her escape.

A tirade soared behind Ellie, echoing off the concrete fortress of buildings. "You bitch! You'll regret this! You'd better watch your back, bitch!" *Blah, blah, blah! Screech, screech, screech!*

Chapter Two

"So you beat the tar out of Lou-Easy."

"My goodness, Betty, no." Ellie laughed. "I didn't beat her up. I just…" She flung her arms wide. "I think I pushed her. It was all a blur. I don't know what happened."

Ellie picked up two steaming cups of tea and carried them to her small kitchen table. Placing a cup in front of Betty, she settled onto one of the padded chrome chairs. "What a day." Ellie shook her head. "Listen, thanks for making the trip out."

"Trip? A half-hour train ride from the city? Please."

"I know, but the expense. I just really appreciate your being here."

The two had begun their friendship in their first year of college, and although Betty had reprimanded her for her impulsive decision to move to Chicago after graduation, she'd soon followed. Although the two were the same age, Betty's manner perpetually conveyed advanced wisdom and maturity, a person seasoned in matters of strife, and her voice exuded reassurance. Her staunch presence and the hot tea calmed Ellie's bubbling stomach to a simmer, but the turmoil had left her with a tension headache. She rubbed her forehead with her left hand, her other hand having puffed up like a blowfish.

"I'm going to get you some ice for that hand." Betty marched toward the icebox. "I hate to say it, woman, but

I think you did more than push that harlot."

"I don't know." Ellie smoothed a hand over the speckled, laminated surface of the table. "I suppose I did slug her."

"You need to disinfect any part of your body that came into contact with her. And get a rabies shot." Betty finished wrapping a paper bag of crushed ice in a tea towel, then swathed Ellie's hand in it. "Well, vengeance was long overdue. Gratifying for you, no?"

"Ouch. Vengeance wasn't my intent. There *was* no intent. It just happened. I can't believe I hit someone. When and how did I become capable of something like that, Betty?"

"When she lured your husband away and shattered your family and told you she wished your children were dead." Betty seated herself, picked up her cup, and blew the steam into swirls. "Look, stop beating yourself up. What kind of person says things like that?"

Ellie shrugged and bit into one of the pineapple-pecan cookies Betty had picked up from Ellie's favorite bakery before heading for the L.

"Well, I cannot believe little five-foot-five, hundred-twenty-pound you decked anybody. Details, please."

"Ha. One-twenty. Don't remember the last time I saw that on the scale." Actually, she did remember. It was before she found out about Louisa and before Mason left and before she stereotypically comforted herself with pasta and too many homemade cakes.

"Oh, come on, you've lost what few pounds you might have put on—look at you. And I'm happy you were out doing something. Finally, Ellie. I mean, really."

"I know. I've been a pathetic sloth for so long, it felt

good to get back into the city, and it was such a beautiful day, even though I didn't get my pie. I suppose I have to settle for these awful cookies." She and Betty both laughed as Ellie reached for her second cookie.

"Oh, Betts, I so wanted to buy a new dress. Have you seen the fashions this season?"

"Oh, they're simply darling. I am so sick of wearing old dresses, but you know I can't sew to save my behind."

Ellie's brow furrowed. "I told you I'd make you a dress."

"Thanks, honey, but you work enough hours."

"Gee." Ellie propped her elbows on the table and gazed upward. "Can't remember the last time I bought a new dress."

In the past couple years, she'd functioned barely well enough to pull one of her cotton house dresses over her head. Her unwitting uniform. She'd forgotten how it felt to wear pretty clothes and swirl a little blush onto her face, not to mention visit a salon or even try to keep up with the latest hairstyles. Of course, even if her heart had been into those things, her financial resources had drastically tapered in 1929, like nearly everyone else's in the country, then come to a near standstill when Mason left.

Thank goodness the postman delivered that envelope each month, Mason's familiar all-capital printing on the outside, a twenty-dollar bill and two ones slipped inside. He wouldn't have had to do it; alimony hadn't been granted until this morning's hearing. Without that money, she wouldn't have been able to make the mortgage payment each month. She knew full well that she was always one payment away from sleeping on a cot in one of Oak Park's charitable lodging houses or cobbling together a makeshift home in the shantytown out at the edge of town.

The bronze rays of the afternoon sun breached the mullioned window, lighting the already cheery yellow walls and warming Ellie's shoulders. Between sips of tea, she filled her friend in on the divorce hearing, along with more details about the encounter, with Betty alternating between levity and gravity, her words punctuated by *uh-huh*s *and okay*s.

At the tale's conclusion, Ellie dropped her head back and sighed. "Well, what's the worst that could happen? You'll come visit me in the big house, right?"

"Look, Ellie, nothing is going to come of this. The idiot won't have you arrested, and she isn't going to sue you." Betty shrugged. "Heck, she's so incredibly stupid, she wouldn't be able to spell the word *attorney* to find a listing in the telephone directory. And if she tries to get you for any bogus medical bills, she has no proof you knocked her down."

Betty stood, gathered the cups and plate of cookie crumbs, and headed for the sink. "She isn't worth one more second of your time, so put the whole thing out of your mind," she called back. She rinsed the cups, dried her hands, then returned to Ellie and began kneading her shoulders. "You free tomorrow? We'll do something. We need to counteract the horrible crap you went through today."

"I'm headed to Marietta in the morning."

"You are? When did you decide that? I thought you were going to stay home and relax during your vacation."

Ellie hoisted herself to her feet, stretched, yawned. "I decided just now. I need to get away for a while."

"You decided just now? Ellie…" Betty crossed her arms and aimed stern eyes at her friend from a lowered head.

"Not every snap decision I make turns out bad, Betts."

"I know, I know. But, honey, you cannot make that long drive alone. Isn't there some man who can go along with you? What if your motorcar breaks down? What if a tire goes flat? What if someone—"

"I'll be perfectly fine. I've made the drive alone twice before."

"Fine." Betty raised both hands in a defensive pose. "But be careful. Listen, I'm going to get going so you can pack."

Ellie reached for her handbag. "I'll drive you to the station."

"Don't be silly. It isn't that far."

The story of their lives, most people's lives, these past several years. Walking here, walking there, walking, walking everywhere. Well, it was good exercise, if nothing else. She probably shouldn't be making that drive tomorrow, but she desperately needed to get away, desperately needed to spend a little time in Marietta.

"Now get some rest," Betty said. "You've had a tough day. I suppose this is the perfect time for you to be leaving. This town ain't big enough for both you and that tart. Now, you're going to forget about today, right?"

"Forget about what?"

****

Ellie jolted awake that night, a vague uneasiness clawing at her insides. Probably a bad dream. She blinked to nudge her eyes open, then leaned over and fished for the nightstand clock. Finally grabbing hold of the little burled-walnut clock, she waved it overhead until its sepia-toned face caught a stripe of the platinum moonlight slipping through the plantation shutters. After two a.m. Flopping the clock back down, she shivered and reached for the covers. *What on earth happened here?* Sometimes when she awoke, she'd find herself tucked into the envelope flap of barely disturbed covers. Not this time. The bedspread and top sheet lay twisted and partially puddled on the floor, one pillow amongst them. Must have been some dream. She tidied the mess and untwisted her cotton sack of a nightgown. There was a time when she wore pretty, satin nightgowns to bed, then nothing at all when Mason began keeping her plenty warm.

Mason. Ah, yes, that was the reason for her tossing and turning. She was a divorcee now. As yesterday came into clearer focus, she also recalled the Lou-Easy Incident, the subconscious residuals of which, no doubt, had also disturbed her sleep. She actually had assaulted somebody. *Darn it.* Well, the cops hadn't shown up at her door, although they could yet. But what probably had happened was that Lou-Easy hustled her rear end over to Mason's apartment, spewed out her version of the confrontation, and demanded he phone his attorney, the police, and the United States Army. But Mason wouldn't have complied. He really had been campaigning to get Ellie back, so he no doubt appeased Lou-Easy by fabricating some reason to let the matter drop that the simpleton would buy.

Anger that Ellie thought she'd allayed bubbled back to the surface. How dare Mason involve himself with that terrible woman, putting Ellie through that distress yesterday? The Incident had threatened to split open old wounds, but Ellie knew now that it had instead nudged her across the finish line of recovery. She did not want a man who would associate with someone like Lou-Easy. Time to forget Mason and get on with her life, however it would look now. She tossed her pillow to the cool side and whomped her head onto it to try to force out memories of the whole dreadful day.

Several minutes later, she checked the time again. Two-fifty-two. *How am I going to get up in the morning and make that drive?* She sat up, scribbled her fingernails over her scalp, and let out a moan. The moonlight arced in rhythm with the pear tree swaying outside. How nice it would be if someone were here with her. Someone to take her side after today, to hold her, to see her off on her journey tomorrow.

Ellie climbed from bed, wrapped herself in her robe, and padded out of her bedroom, down the staircase, and out onto the back porch. Maybe some fresh, chilly air would clear her head and prod her back toward drowsiness. She'd lived smack dab in the middle of the city during her first few years in Illinois, but much as she loved Chicago, out here in Oak Park there were no motor vehicles rumbling on streets at all hours or sirens blaring every several minutes.

Out here, a person had all the fresh air her lungs could take in and all the stars visible to the naked eye. Stars she'd been barely able to detect in the city or even in Columbus, where she'd grown up. One place she'd always been able to see them was from the highest hill of Marietta, Ohio, a place where she'd looked to the brightness of the stars when things got dreary. Even more reason to make that drive tomorrow.

For now, Ellie singled out the brightest star and

made a wish on it. A wish to regain her footing and find her place in this new life of hers. A wish for the bluebird of happiness to once again sing to her, like that pretty new song said. And, if it wasn't too much to wish for, perhaps a man might come along and love her forever.

The notion of another man was a first in her lethargic recovery from the death of her marriage. She'd let go, link by slippery link, of the marriage Mason apparently considered a chain, gradually coming to presume she would somehow get through it and emerge all right. But apparently, she hadn't comprehended the desolation left by the strip mining of her life. She'd survived without a single thought of needing or wanting a new man. Until now. And now she longed for him, wished for him. Whoever he was. Wherever he was.

Chapter Three

Ellie peered into the mirror of her bedroom vanity table as she donned her ivory felt bucket hat with the big bow—several seasons old now, but her nicest hat—then dragged her leather suitcase off the bed and wondered again if she should spend the money to drive to Marietta this morning. This vacation was time off without pay, and gasoline was up to nineteen cents now, money that could be added to the stash under the mattress. Funds that she hoped would someday pay for new tires for her motorcar, if they didn't need to be drained again on more pressing necessities. Her tires would probably be just fine for now, but no way would they make it through another winter, little as she drove these days.

The ringing telephone halted the back door's trajectory just as Ellie began swinging it shut. She groaned. After the restless night, she was already leaving later on her long journey than she'd planned, but she'd better see who it was. Dropping her suitcase, she crossed the kitchen, picked up the candlestick telephone, and brought the receiver to her ear. "Hello."

"Ellie. I... How are you?" Mason clearly hadn't expected her to pick up.

Of course. It's a wonder he hadn't phoned before now. The first time he called, about a year ago, she patiently heard him out before responding that no, she could not forgive him and take him back. After his second or third call, she'd asked him not to call again. He'd honored the request for some time but began calling again in recent days.

"Hello, Mason."

"It's good to hear your voice, Ellie. I just... I was headed out for a run and, uh... I'm not interrupting anything, am I?"

"What do you want?"

"Look, uh, Louisa told me about yesterday, and I wanted to apologize. I'm sorry you had to go through that, and I...I wanted you to know that nobody is going to press any charges."

"You're sorry I had to go through *that*." Not sorry she'd had to go through the hell he inflicted on her when he took up with his tramp and destroyed their family.

"Ellie, I—"

"You know what, Mason? I don't need you to protect me. If your girlfriend wants to press charges, let her. I'll take whatever comes my way. I assaulted her. I knocked her sickening rear end down after she told me she wishes our children were dead. Did she happen to mention that detail, Mason?"

He exhaled a guttural sigh. "No, she didn't. Ellie, I wish I'd never—"

"What you *should* do, Mason, instead of assuring me that I won't be hauled off to jail, is think about why you're hanging around with someone who wishes your children were dead. You need to think about why you're running around with a person who...who goes to bed with someone else's husband. That's what you *should* be doing, not making some hogwash declaration about protecting me. I'm no longer your concern. We're divorced now, or didn't you know that?"

She'd thought they both had to appear at the Cook County courthouse yesterday morning for the final hearing, until Mason didn't show up and she asked her attorney how the divorce could go through without both parties present and she discovered that neither was required to appear but it was highly unusual that they didn't give enough of a hoot to.

"I'm sorry. I...I just couldn't come to the hearing. It killed me, the thought of it being over."

Killed *him*. "Our marriage was over long before yesterday, and you ended it."

"I know. I messed up. Big time. I was a real sap. I wish it had never happened. And I'm sorry for all the pain I've caused you. Honey, I...I still love you."

Dammit. Why did his words still pierce her heart like this? Why did his oh-so-familiar voice soften her hard-headed attitude, however justified, toward him? *No.* She would not let him get to her. Not after all these months and weeks and days and hours and minutes and seconds of excruciating recovery, dammit.

"That makes no difference now."

"I have loved you since the day I saw you walking across the quad our freshman year."

"I need to go."

"Look, I...I don't blame you for wanting nothing to do with me. But I ended things with her today. Can we talk? Please, Ellie, just... I really want to talk to you."

Ellie let his words deflect off her like raindrops off a waxed automobile. Did he really think his words could speak louder than his actions? She'd considered him the love of her life, thought they'd die in each other's arms. Believed he'd felt the same about her. Then he stopped touching her. Stopped looking at her, talking with her.

Heck, stopped kissing her. She'd known there was someone else when he stopped kissing her. And when she'd finally asked him if he was seeing someone else, he seemed relieved at the opportunity to get his ugly secret off his chest. After all, the two of them had always shared everything. So he'd shared his secret, and then she told him to move out.

"No, we can't talk. I have to go."

"Ellie, it's killing me, being away from you. I will regret what I did to you until the day I die. Please just tell me we can talk."

He seemed genuinely tortured, but so had she been, and *her* pain hadn't been self-inflicted.

"We're not getting back together, Mason. I spent over two decades of my life with you, and you threw me away. You didn't want to talk when you took up with that…that piece of rotting garbage. My words didn't matter to you then, my tears didn't matter to you. I didn't matter to you then, so don't let me matter to you now. Goodbye, Mason."

****

To Ellie, the gray highway curving away from Chicago had always seemed a portal of sorts. The bridge over the south branch of the Chicago River ushered thousands of wayfarers each day into the towers and tumult of the city, then away later out into the rest of the world. Away from the urban incandescence, the stellar dots of the city glimmered a silent farewell in her rearview mirror. To the east, a tie-dye of orange, pink, and lavender whorled across the lower third of the sky. Oncoming headlights formed a glittering necklace leading into the city.

Ten hours ahead of her, if she could keep the vehicle

up to fifty miles per hour. Ten and a half with fuel stops. The long drive meant plenty of time to think, but after yesterday, she no longer needed to put herself through the agony. Finally, the butchered slab of raw meat that had been her heart had begun to really heal. She would waste no more time analyzing why Mason did what he did and whether she'd done the right thing in divorcing him.

She reached out and switched on the radio knob, then twisted the other knob left and right until a station came in clearly. Might as well enjoy the music while she could. The long stretches between towns would soon mean nothing but static. Ellie hummed along to the top pop hit du jour.

Once the sun gathered enough energy to burn away the morning dew, Ellie shed her hat and her driving gloves and wound down the window. The wind rustled against her face and whisked her hair into a tangle, evoking the way sheets pinned to a clothesline must feel. The landscape eased into more and more rural serenity the farther Ellie drove. Here a crisp, yellow chewing tobacco advertisement on the side of a bright red barn. There an abandoned one-room schoolhouse, nearly obscured by brazen weeds and parasitic vines. More and more of the old schools seemed to fall by the wayside all the time.

She'd traveled all over the States, as well as to Paris during college. But Marietta, Ohio, was her favorite place in the whole world. Marietta felt as much like home as Oak Park did, and she needed the little town now. She needed its people and its river and its refuge.

Chapter Four

Ellie's shoulders relaxed as she drove into Marietta. Nestled in the rolling Ohio Valley at the southeastern tip of the state, at the confluence of the Ohio River and the Muskingum, this was small-town America, a place conspicuously serene but garnished with an undercurrent of grit. Ellie yawned as her gaze gravitated to the dusky river, flowing at the speed of molasses this evening. Although two rivers wound through and around the town, they were always referred to by the locals as one entity—the river.

Downtown, motorcars and people made their way, in no hurry, to wherever they needed to be. A whole world away from Chicago in every possible way. Marietta's tallest building might rival the city's shortest. Everything here, including time, it seemed, moved at a mellow pace. Marietta was a lovely old town whose streets and structures whispered of its past.

Ellie parked in front of the five-and-dime store, recalling having watched, as a child, the construction of the building from her aunt's back yard, atop nearby Harmar Hill. Occupying the enviable corner of Front and Greene Streets, overlooking the river, the ornate, sand-colored brick structure dripped in lavish frieze work and corbels, like an iced cake. Every conceivable notion filled its glass display cases.

Climbing from her automobile, Ellie ambled around

to the sidewalk, where she tipped herself onto her toes to stretch her legs and flung out her arms with a moan, promptly smacking a hand into what felt like a human. She pivoted.

"Oh, my goodness, I'm so..." The "sorry" came a heartbeat or two later, followed by, "Are you all right?" even though there was no way this man wasn't okay.

Tall and sturdy enough to survive much more than a little whack in the chest, his faded blue-and-white pinstriped shirt, tan leather vest, and well-worn trousers did nothing to detract from the toned lines of his body. A sampling of gray wove through the hair peeking out from beneath his newsboy cap. Slightly wavy, sandy blond hair, which on anyone else would need a good trimming but suited him fine. He hadn't shaved in a day or two.

"Lengthy drive, I take it?" His mouth curved into a half smile, crinkling the corners of soft, hazel eyes.

Ellie met his very direct gaze. "Yes, as a matter of fact. The only time I beat up on random pedestrians is after a long journey."

His eyes caught hers in an intense stare, pitching her heart into arrhythmia, and his lips widened into a full-on smile. "Nothing like a good punch to work out the kinks, huh, Slugger?"

Ellie drew in her lips. A laugh didn't seem appropriate right now, but the two men accompanying her victim apparently couldn't resist.

"How's it feel getting KO'd by a little lady?" The younger man hopped around, jabbing the air with his fists.

"I'll show you if you don't shut up," the blond man told him.

Rivermen, no doubt, given their denim trousers,

newsboy caps, and sun-kissed faces. So he probably wasn't from around here, darn it.

The clock atop the nearby courthouse began chiming, reminding Ellie that she had someplace to be before closing time.

"Really, I am very sorry," Ellie said. "You are all right, aren't you?"

"I think I'll be fine," he said with a nod and a languid blink of those captivating eyes. "Ma'am," he said with a tip of his cap before he and his comrades continued toward the river.

Ellie's feet felt their way to the door of the five-and-dime. Wowee, did that bloke look better from the front or the back? Biting her bottom lip, she reached for the door handle.

Inside, the cornsilk-haired proprietor stood in the hardware section, pointing out nuts and bolts to a customer. At the clanging of the bell above the door, she looked up with watercolor-blue eyes, excused herself from the customer, and hurried to Ellie.

"Ellie! When did you get into town? Let me get this customer, and then we can catch up. Have you eaten yet?" Charlene's voice retained the same feathery serenity as when she was a little girl.

After the satisfied patron left clutching his paper bag full of hardware, Charlene called out, "Noreen, I'll be back in an hour to close up."

The two friends clip-clopped across the brick street and headed down the bank toward the river.

"So, when did you get here?"

"Just now. I decided last night to come down, just for a few days. How are you doing?"

"You decided just last night to come?" Charlene's

lips curved into a smile. "No surprise there. I'm fine. Business is picking up again, with spring here. You know there's always that slump after the holidays. I hope you're hungry. I heard Marv got some nice, fat chickens in," she said as they approached the door of the Levee House Cafe.

The place smelled terrific, as always, the air filled with the aroma of roasting meats, simmering soups, and baking breads. Marv, owner of the restaurant, had left a few minutes ago, the hostess told them. Well, Ellie would stop in to see him another day.

After settling in at their table, Ellie and Charlene caught up on the latest news of mutual friends, things going on around town, the divorce. The rosemary-crusted chicken was indeed delicious. Ellie probably shouldn't have splurged on meat, but it soothed her growling stomach. Not many patrons in the place this evening, but it was a bit later than the usual dinner hour. Ellie delighted in the familiar clink of flatware on earthenware plates and the lively chatter echoing off the lofty tin ceiling.

"When will you be coming back down again?" Charlene asked.

"I don't know. I would love to come back sometime this summer," Ellie said. "Hey, we should have a slumber party with Deb and Anita. It's been so long. Oh, we'll fill up on all sorts of desserts and we'll talk for hours. It would be so much fun."

"Oh, Ellie, that sounds simply keen."

"I'm not sure yet that I'll be able to swing more days off work. The bills never take any time off. You know how that goes." Ellie rolled her eyes. "But it'll be a long summer if I can't come down. The children both have plans for the summer, so they won't be coming home." She shrugged. "Not too happy about it, but that's what happens when they grow up, and I'm glad they're independent and thriving."

Charlene reached out and grasped Ellie's hand. "I sure hope you can come back down soon. You don't deserve spending all summer alone. And even though you've never complained, I can only imagine how hot that factory gets."

Suffocatingly hot, actually, and the thought of doing little all summer but working smothered Ellie even more. It was spring, a time for coming out of hibernation, but until the country's economic woes eased, she had no choice but to stay put at home and continue working nearly around the clock. Working and sleeping, working and sleeping. Alone.

****

Back at the shop, Charlene began reconciling the day's sales on her ledger while Noreen restocked the shelves. Ellie yawned, pulled the broom from its closet, and got to work on the wooden floor.

An hour later, streetlights shone trapezoids of illumination for her walk to her motorcar. The squeaky chirp of crickets suffused the otherwise still night. Ellie yawned again as her vehicle auto-piloted itself up Harmar Hill, more familiar to her than any other place in the world.

She'd met Charlene on that hill one lazy summer afternoon long ago. Visiting from Columbus, Ellie sat on the concrete steps of her aunt's place, watching the little blonde girl and a dark-haired girl play hopscotch two doors away. When the dark-haired girl noticed Ellie, she skipped over. "My name's Anita. I live around the block.

Come on, play with us." From that moment, the three were inseparable whenever Ellie came to town.

Soon after, Debbie moved in down the street and waited for nobody to invite her over. Debbie was the loud, daring one. The initiator of the jumping off the swing set and the scraping of knees, of the forbidden leaving of the block and, in their teens, of the sneaking out at night and the brief, cough-filled trial of smoking. They'd never done anything horrible, but Debbie—or Deb, as she announced at the age of fourteen she'd henceforth be called—had always masterminded any deviation from the straight and narrow.

Soon, Aunt Lillian's home came into view. The old mansion stood at the highest point of Harmar Hill, visible from nearly everywhere in Marietta. The north star of the valley. The pale-yellow Queen Anne was held aloft by the sturdy slope of the hill, like Cleopatra borne by servants on her palanquin. Endless turrets and dormers embellished the house, and white columns framed the entry to the wraparound front porch. Ancient oak trees shaded the property on hot days and provided a sumptuous backdrop for the iconic estate.

The iron pendant light cast its usual welcoming beam across the front porch, and the glowing beveled glass sidelights of the massive oak door invited Ellie inside. After a quick knock, she opened the door to the sound of swift footsteps on the marble tiles of the foyer.

"*Meine Güte*, missy, you are here." Hanne all but dragged Ellie into the house, scooping her into her arms. Those privy to one of her hugs would always remark at its robustness, coming from such a diminutive person, but Hanne was sturdy and solid. And Ellie had learned at a young age she would just have to give up breathing for the few seconds the hug lasted.

"Hi, Hanne." Ellie kissed her cheek. "It's so good to be back. How are you?"

"Oh, I am fine, I am all right, but you are worn out. Here." Hanne took Ellie's suitcase and tucked it beside the staircase.

That Hanne served as the cook, and once the housekeeper, had long ago been forgotten by everyone. She'd arrived with her husband, now deceased. Vernon had returned from the Great War with his dream of starting a construction business in Parkersburg shattered by an arm injury. And that wasn't all he'd brought back from Germany. A young Hanne had delivered smiles along with his meals while he was in the field hospital, so *I talked her into coming home with me*, he'd always said. Soon after, he saw the newspaper ad for a groundskeeper, and Lillian and Edward Blaylock—now also gone—hired him, along with his bride to take care of the house. These days, hired companies took care of the housework and the grounds, but Hanne and Vernon had lived here with Aunt Lillian and Uncle Edward since shortly after the newlyweds purchased the home, and the two women had soon become best friends.

Scents of hot tea and cinnamon hailed Ellie, and Aunt Lillian's voice glided from the kitchen. "I hope you've left room for dessert, Eleanor."

Aunt Lillian's green eyes shimmered at the sight of her niece. She returned the teakettle to the stove and took Ellie's face in her hands. Of course her favorite aunt, her father's older sister, would be waiting up for her no matter how late the hour. Aunt Lillian kept late hours regardless, having always declared sleeping more than five or six hours wasteful when there was so much to be done and experienced and discovered.

Ellie had always considered her aunt refined and classy, but also fun-loving. Despite her elegance, she had a playfulness, a twinkle in her eye. And Lillian Blaylock's vital gaze and confident smile conveyed both a keen interest in and a warm sensitivity to those lucky enough to know her.

"Oh, Aunt Lillian." Ellie hugged her. "I missed you. How are you?"

"I'm fine, darling, but come. You're tired." Aunt Lillian handed her a cup of tea and led her to the sitting room at the back of the house. "Decaffeinated. I'm sure you're ready for a good night's sleep."

Wrapped in a silk robe and matching turban, her aunt settled onto the olive-green velvet settee, her usual spot, next to a fluttering fire framed by a carved mantel. This was Ellie's favorite room in the house, the room where many talks with her aunt and countless hours of play with her friends had taken place over the years. Truthfully, the entire house embraced a person with its gleaming wood flooring, exquisite marble, and elaborate trim work. The crystal pendants of chandeliers glinted against encroaching sunbeams during the day and lit the spaces at night.

Ellie went to the floor-to-ceiling mullioned French doors that wrapped around three sides of the sitting room. Rectangles of stained glass, each depicting a different riverboat, filled several of the panes.

"Oh, I enjoy those panels so much," Aunt Lillian said. "I can't tell you how many hours I've spent just gazing at them. You know how I love riverboats."

Aunt Lillian had joyfully accepted the first panel Ellie presented her as a Christmas gift many years ago, and Ellie had added a panel to the collection each year. She'd designed them based on actual riverboats that once glided along the Ohio and Mississippi Rivers, having researched and located photos or drawings of them. Strolling past the panels depicting the *Princess*, the *New Orleans*, the *Vesuvius*, Ellie recalled the many hours she'd put into each panel, but she'd loved every moment of the intricate work.

Hanne joined them carrying a tray of china plates bearing something that smelled divine. Aunt Lillian always wanted her best china, crystal, and linens used regularly, not just for special occasions, and she held the same philosophy on jewelry, clothing, everything. "We shouldn't enjoy our best things only on certain days," she would say.

Ellie dropped into an overstuffed chair, loosened her shoestrings, and kicked off her oxfords. She sank her toes into the thick floral carpet and spooned off a bite of rhubarb kuchen topped with whipped cream and cinnamon, a dessert of Hanne's German heritage.

"Oh, my goodness, Hanne, one of my favorites. Thank you."

"How are those adorable children, Eleanor?" Hanne dropped a sugar cube into her steaming tea, then stirred it into submission.

"They're doing great. Benny is in his final year of college, you know."

"Oh, *mein*, I cannot believe that. What are his plans after *gradutation*?" Hanne hadn't yet completely mastered the English language.

Ellie curled her legs onto the chair. "He wants to put his engineering degree to work. But for now, he's been lucky to have his gig out on that farm. Poor kid, has to get up before dawn, hitchhike out to the farm, and put in a few hours before classes, then go back out afterward and work several more hours. Jessie hasn't declared a major yet. She's been working as a seamstress at the uniform factory, but during her summer break, she has a job lined up in Myrtle Beach, at a saltwater taffy shop. I worry about her being able to afford to live, but three other girls are going, so they'll all be sharing one room in a boarding house."

Ellie sighed. "So I won't be seeing much of either of them this summer." She took another bite of her cake. "I'm so glad they're at the same college. They don't see each other very often. They're both busy, they have lots of friends. But it's nice to know they're near each other, and it makes it easy when I visit them. I miss them like crazy, though."

"I miss those sweet babies, too," Aunt Lillian said. "I will never forget little Jessie playing hide-and-seek all over this place, and I would see her big brown eyes peeking out from under a chair or a table." She dabbed at her mouth with a linen napkin. "And Benny, you couldn't keep him in the house. That boy loved anything and everything to do with the river."

"They miss coming down. We've spent so much time here, so many summers, especially." Ellie smiled at Aunt Lillian. "But you know, once they started high school, it got too tough to get down here much, between football practice, summer jobs, girlfriends, boyfriends."

Then, of course, after Mason moved out, even Ellie's trips to Marietta dwindled. They had always come to Marietta as a family, but the prospect of making the long drive alone had frightened Ellie. Finally, she simply climbed into her automobile one day and did it. It was either that or rarely seeing her aunt and Hanne from then on.

"Well, you tell them to get their little behinds down here for a visit pretty soon, or your aunt and I will be coming up there." Hanne shook a finger at Ellie. "We know how to get to Columbus, don't we, Lillian? And I know how to embarrass them."

Ellie laughed. "I'll tell them. I know they miss both of you too."

The vast differences between the two women always amused Ellie. While Aunt Lillian conducted herself with diplomacy, sensitivity, and a calm demeanor, Hanne's peppy straightforwardness was not always tempered by subtlety. The two complemented each other, Hanne the practical broadcloth to Aunt Lillian's lustrous silk.

"And how is your work going?" Aunt Lillian asked.

"Just fine," Ellie said. "I still weld mostly reapers, but occasionally I'm put on the thresher line. Not much difference, really."

"And you're still working ten-hour days? You know you wouldn't have to, dear."

Ellie nodded. "I know, Aunt Lillian, and I appreciate that. But please don't worry. The work isn't difficult, and it's actually quite liberating wearing dungarees and leaving the girdle at home. Plus, a lot of the men have finally accepted me. In fact, I consider a few of them good friends."

Aunt Lillian would never know how hot, dirty, and tiresome welding really was, would never know Ellie stood hunched over for hours and endured constant burns to her skin and clothing from spewing sparks. Not wanting to distress her aunt, Ellie attributed the tiny burns her aunt did notice to stained-glass soldering.

Fortunate to have been affected very little by the economic depression, Aunt Lillian had offered more than once to channel funds Ellie's way when her stained-glass repair work dried up as abruptly as the stock market had crashed. But Ellie could never bring herself to accept her aunt's money. So she'd taken on clothes mending, then began baking and selling loaves of bread. While those endeavors, along with Mason's contribution of twenty-two dollars per month, covered the bills, Ellie fell farther and farther behind in trying to keep the children in college. They both worked nearly full time to contribute to their expenses, and both offered to drop out of school until the economic situation improved. But Ellie wouldn't hear of it.

That's when welding occurred to her. It paid more than the typical female occupations of cleaning woman or girl Friday. Of course, she was soundly and humiliatingly rejected by the first two companies she approached, but she was able to convince the personnel manager at a farm machinery manufacturer just outside Chicago to hire her, given her expertise at the similar trade of soldering.

"All right," he'd said. "I'll give you a try, but only because we need people who know what they're doing, and you being divorced, well, I imagine you'll be able to hold your own."

Ellie found out what he'd meant by that last supposition on her first day of work, her co-workers having held nothing back in the language department. Had she been a young maiden, the manager surely would have considered her too delicate for such an environment. So for two years now, Ellie had put in her ten-hour shift, then spent several more hours per day continuing with her mending and baking work—a detail she hadn't shared with Aunt Lillian—and the children were able to stay in college.

After another hour and a half of catching up and laughter, Hanne stood and gathered their serving ware onto the tray.

"Let's get an early start in the morning, Hanne," Aunt Lillian said.

"Where are you going?" Ellie asked.

"You'll recall the juried art show held in Parkersburg each spring. You've gone with me before. Well, the show hasn't been held since the economic collapse, and this year they're reinstating it but doing something different. The show will feature the artwork and handicrafts of anyone who would like to set up a booth. It's a marvelous way for people to earn a little extra money and display their talents. Would you like to go with us?"

"Thanks, but I don't think so. I'd like to take a stroll around town, see what's new." Ellie craved a long walk, alone, with the murmur of the river the only sound.

Aunt Lillian stood and kissed Ellie on the forehead. "You'll find everything you need in your suite."

Ellie hugged her aunt and kissed her cheek. "Thanks, Aunt Lillian. Sleep well. I'll see you probably tomorrow afternoon. I think I'll sleep in, and I'm sure you'll be gone by the time I drag myself downstairs."

After Aunt Lillian left, Ellie swung open one of the French doors and stepped onto the balcony. This was what she needed after the day she'd had yesterday. Her aunt, this house, Marietta. Down in the valley, under a bright moon, the violet river flowed in solitude except for a couple boats making their way downstream.

Where were the voyagers headed? Who had they left behind? Did someone wait for them on some distant bank? Ellie stretched and drew in a breath of night air. Where was she headed? Did someone wait for her, somewhere? She stepped inside, fastened the door, and headed to bed.

Chapter Five

Ellie ambled along the brick walkway spanning parallel to the levee. You never walked fast along the river unless serious exercise was the intent. The languid setting wouldn't support it.

In the distance, a chain of barges churned from downstream, heaped with crates of cargo and nudged along by a weather-worn black-and-white towboat. Ellie could almost picture the barges of long ago, lumbering along at the pace of the horses or cattle that trod alongside on the banks, connected to the tows by cables. The blue-green river flowed at an accommodating pace, winding through land garnished with pitch pine, bigleaf magnolia with huge white blossoms, and scarlet sourwood, through banks lush with an undergrowth of sassafras, golden witch-hazel, and dogwood.

Ellie climbed the bank and crossed Ohio Street, taking care not to catch her heel in a trolley rail. Such a shame the economic collapse had propelled the interurban trolleys into extinction. Ellie missed the ever-present rumbling and the friendly waves of the capped conductors.

On Front Street, a shopkeeper sporting a polka-dotted bow tie greeted Ellie before cranking up his green-and-white-striped awning, opening the eyes of his well-rested shop. Across the street, a young, uniformed bellhop made a couple half-hearted swipes with a broom over the sidewalk in front of the Bellevue Hotel. The grand hotel drew visitors from all around the world and was even said to house a permanent guest or two—from the other side.

Ellie strolled past the businesses lining Front Street. Brass plaques commemorated a handful of buildings for their roles in the Underground Railroad network. By virtue of its riverfront location, the town had played a major role in helping slaves escape to the north. Ellie's eyes scanned the granite monuments and bronze statues honoring the town's beginnings nearly one hundred fifty years before, when French explorers claimed land once inhabited by the Shawnee tribe and then named their new home for Queen Marie Antoinette. Boards crisscrossed the dark windows of the old stone bank that had long dominated a prominent corner—another victim of the depression.

Next, Ellie's feet led her into one of the town's many antique shops, this one in a building lavished with cornices and moldings and probably older than many of the antiques it housed. Inside, the timeworn wood floors, tarnished light fixtures, and mustiness contributed to the atmosphere. She bought an ivory handkerchief trimmed in lace for Hanne and a tortoiseshell hair comb accented by burgundy crystals and black onyx stones for her aunt, who collected combs and wore one tucked into her side-parted, silver chignon every day. Occasionally picking up small gifts for Aunt Lillian and Hanne, or the children, was the only splurging Ellie did these days.

By one o'clock, she found herself back at the riverfront and her stomach grumbling, so she headed for the Levee House Cafe. The russet-red brick building's riverfront location had ensured its importance to

Marietta's commerce for over a century. At various times, the three-story edifice had housed a dry goods store, a hardware, a saloon, a hotel and, of course, the token house of ill repute. Now it was the only one left of a string of Federalist-style buildings that once lined the riverfront. Marv had purchased it years ago from a group of men who told him they'd won the building in a game of cards. True or not, the legend added to the intrigue of the structure.

Marv glanced up from the cash register as Ellie swung the door open. "Miss Eleanor. Good lord, you come here."

Ellie hurried over. Marv's stuffed-bear arms wrapped around her, and he extended a cheek for her kiss, a long-time ritual. Good old Marv. The same cherubic-cheeked smile, salt-and-pepper hair, bow tie and vest, the same wry demeanor. A long-time friend of Aunt Lillian and Uncle Edward, Marv had supplied Ellie and her friends with gallons of free ice cream when they were children and had always served as beloved sage and faithful ally to Ellie.

"Charlene and I came by for dinner last night," Ellie told him. "It seems we just missed you."

"Ahh, left a bit early. The grandson had a baseball scrimmage." He patted Ellie's face. "You hungry?" Marv took her hand and led her to a small table beneath a window. "We have some new things." He handed her the thick menu. "Get whatever you want. It's on the house."

"Aww, thank you, Marv. How have you been?"

"Can't complain, can't complain. How long you in town?"

"Just a couple days."

"Well, enjoy your down time, sweetie. Ruby'll be over to get your order."

Luxuriating in the aromas drifting from the kitchen, Ellie peered out the window. The pleasure crafts weren't out and about much this early in the spring, and, really, they'd nearly become a thing of the past since this darned depression began. Towboats were just about the only boats you saw anymore, pushing linked-together barges, moving like slumberous, silent trains.

Ruby promptly arrived to take Ellie's order of mushroom soup and sourdough bread. All Marv's food was made in-house and delicious. Most of the recipes went back decades, but once in a while, Marv would add a seasonal item, sometimes featuring tomatoes or peppers from his own garden.

Streams of natural light filtered through trees, passing through the many oversized windows and flitting about the dining room like a fairy and her trail of shimmery dust. The Levee House Cafe hadn't changed much over the years. Nobody could accuse the place of being fancy, but it was in good repair and received a good scrubbing behind its ears on a daily basis.

When the bell mounted above the door announced the arrival of more patrons, Ellie glanced over. *Good heavens.* One of them was the blond man she'd slugged last night. The three men took seats on the shiny blue leather-and-chrome stools at the counter and accepted Marv's offer of coffee. While Marv and the men talked about the price of something or other and its short supply, Ruby refilled Ellie's glass. With her eyes fixed on the blond guy, Ellie dumped a spoonful of sugar onto the table, then stirred her iced tea. He seemed the leader type. Probably the captain.

Once Ellie's soup arrived, she tore off a chunk of bread and tried to focus on the boats, the pedestrians passing by, the card in the metal holder advertising Marv's specials, but her eyes kept returning to that man. By the end of her meal, which she didn't remember eating, she'd inspected his every feature, at least his back and side features. The powerful arms. The defined muscles of his back. The stubbled face. How would it feel brushing against hers? Ellie took a long swig of her iced tea.

The men ate quickly and talked in relaxed, low tones, interjecting a laugh here and there. The blond man's laugh was spirited, friendly.

"What else can I get you, Eleanor? I think there's a slice of coconut cream pie left in the kitchen." Ruby's smoky voice forced Ellie out of her reverie.

"No, thank you, Ruby. Everything was delicious." She placed a tip on the table, slipped her billfold back into her handbag, and donned her kidskin gloves. She needed to get herself out of there, and now. This was a riverman, for heaven's sake, never in one place for long, not a good prospect for a romantic relationship. But one more look wouldn't hurt anything.

Well, darn. He'd caught her checking him out. His eyes bore into hers, sending her heart slamming against her chest and goosebumps inching across her skin. Quite a smile, the man had, and she thought she reciprocated but wasn't sure.

He approached the ornate cash register and paid the bill. "Thanks, Marv. Great lunch as usual." The two shook hands. "See you next time, buddy."

"Hey, you fellas take care now," Marv said. "Don't take so long coming back around next time."

Before he and his entourage exited the Levee House, the man projected another smile Ellie's way and another Cupid's arrow through her heart. Then he was gone.

Ellie propped her elbows on the table, something she'd been taught never to do, dropped her head into her hands, and let out an exasperated sigh. *What on earth was that? Chicago is full of good-looking men, but I go into cardiac arrest when this guy looks at me.*

She must not have impressed him the same way, or he didn't remember her from last night. He hadn't tossed her a single word on his way out. At the counter, Ellie thanked Marv and asked, casually she hoped, who the men were.

"Good fellas. Tow crew. Been coming through here for years."

"So they're not from the area?"

"Oh, no, no. You know these river men, they're from nowhere and they're from everywhere."

Marv reached for the check that a patron handed him and began ringing it up. "How was your lunch?"

After finishing the transaction, he focused again on Ellie. "Where were we, sweetie pie? Oh, yes, the tow crew. From somewhere down south." Marv pursed his lips, squinted at the ceiling, shook his head. "Can't recall where. I'm sure I knew at one time, but you know." Marv pointed at his head.

Down south. That could mean as near as West Virginia or as far as the Gulf of Mexico. Well, this was all she was going to find out. With no gracious way to dig further, she thanked Marv and went on her way.

Outside, Ellie focused on the riverbank. A lonesome green fishing boat hugged the dock. Nearby, a towboat connected to a line of barges heaped with massive cargo idled. Probably the tow she'd seen on her way into the cafe. Maybe *his* tow. Several men busied themselves on deck, but the blond man wasn't among them. And Ellie hadn't taken enough notice of the other two men in the restaurant to recognize them now.

She stepped across the Levee House's ancient brick patio and down the bank, her eyes scanning left, then right. Just before the bend, another towboat pushed its barges upstream, plowing the river into furrows, silently and willfully gliding away. *Well, there he goes.* She turned and made her way up the bank, negotiating rocks and tree roots.

"I hope you iced that hand last night."

She turned to the source of the robust voice and knew this time that she smiled.

Chapter Six

His eyes made a fleeting roundtrip over her body and back to her eyes, although the speedy inspection didn't come across as leering. Appreciation, maybe? The way he probably would size up a shiny new towboat.

Ellie crossed one shoe, the one with the worst scuffing, behind the other. Her hand raced to cover the faded place on her dress where she'd scrubbed a spot clean a couple years ago. Hopefully it wasn't too noticeable. "My hand is perfectly fine, thank you. But I hope you got that chest x-rayed."

He removed his cap. "Oh, absolutely. Went straight to the hospital. Got a few cracked ribs. You really did a number on me."

The extended syllables and molasses pace of his words revealed that he did indeed come from the South, somewhere far south. He seemed even taller than he had before. Somewhere around six foot, with shoulders able to withstand the hardships of life on the river. He stood firm, like an oak tree, hands on his hips. A breeze meandered through his hair, and those eyes fixed onto hers. Clouds parted, music swelled.

Why was this man having such an effect on her?

"Wyatt Dare." He offered a hand.

"Wyatt as in Earp? And everyone asks you that, right?"

His hand blanketed hers, firm, warm. "Actually,

you're the very first person who's ever asked me that." His sly grin told her that was a lie.

"Wow, I feel really special. So what's the answer?"

"Actually, my favorite uncle suggested the name when my mother was carrying me. He was sure I was gonna be a boy, and he'd always admired Wyatt Earp's quiet courage, so I apparently have a lot to live up to. And you are...?"

"Ellie."

"So, Ellie, how was that soup?"

This man didn't miss a thing. When had he noticed she had soup for lunch? She'd barely taken her eyes off him the entire time and never saw him turn around.

"Everything at the Levee House is delicious," she said. "Marv's an old family friend."

"Marv knows what he's doing, for sure."

This man had been placed directly in front of Ellie twice now, and maybe placed himself there this time, and nobody but the two of them seemed to exist in the world. This was a man who commanded attention.

He crossed his arms and tilted his head at an alluring angle. "Well, Ellie, do you need to be somewhere right now?" His black velvet voice pillaged with its virility.

Here. I need to be here. "Yes, my aunt is expecting me." A blatant lie, but it seemed the thing to say. Did he expect her to readily accept whatever sort of invitation he had in mind?

"Well, that's a shame. I've been hostage to that tow for days, and it's been a while since I've spent any time in Marietta. I wouldn't mind having a look around. No time for a little walk?"

He smiled with his penetrating eyes as much as with his perfect mouth. His demeanor was approachable and friendly, sure, but was it all a siren song luring Ellie across dark, stormy seas? Across dark, stormy rivers? Rivers fraught with jagged rocks and whirling rapids and piranhas. This man was, after all, a stranger. Probably married, too, with a long-suffering wife back at home and a ready, willing, and able girlfriend in every port. A versed lothario of all unsuspecting women unfortunate enough to lie in his path.

She would have to cut back on the romance novels she'd been reading. She glanced around. Why, she wasn't sure, other than maybe to check that there were people around, their presence a deterrent to anything improper this fellow might have in mind. Witnesses.

"I suppose I have a few minutes." The man had been cooped up on a boat. He needed her.

With that, he grinned, turned, and led the way. They maneuvered their way along the riverbank, saying nothing for a good amount of time. Amazing that no words seemed necessary. A lesson from a long-ago college elective came to Ellie's mind. What was the maximum length of silence psychologists deemed comfortable between two strangers before awkwardness set in? Four seconds? This walk shot that theory sky high.

A breeze stirred the warm air into velvety swirls against Ellie's skin as they took in the sleek azure river and the afternoon's pearlescent sunshine. They moved slow and easy, weaving higher, then lower to maintain their foothold, following the dirt pathway long ago worn into the crest of the bank. Heels weren't the ideal footwear for an impromptu hike, but Ellie's old black-and-white saddle shoes had finally withered earlier in the year beyond all possible functionality.

"I thought you wanted to look around."

"I am looking around," he said.

"You're looking at me."

"I'm most certainly looking around." He rotated his head left and right and nodded as if expressing regard for the scenery, before looking back at her with a dazzling smile. "See?"

Ellie rolled her eyes and stifled a smile. "Are you always such a smart aleck?"

Wyatt's head tilted back and he laughed, then laughed again when Ellie repeated the eye roll.

"Where'd you come from, Ellie?"

Ellie's gaze tracked a soaring Louisiana Waterthrush, which she'd learned from Aunt Lillian to identify by its speckled chest and descending song.

"You're the one who came in off some boat. I should be asking you that. I mean, I don't know that you came off some boat. I just thought..." *Just shut up, Ellie.*

"I did actually come off some boat. That one." Wyatt pointed to the crisp white towboat at the dock, distinct in that it was trimmed in a metallic gold stripe, when most towboats were plain white or trimmed in red or blue. "We're up from the Gulf, headed to Pittsburgh. We'll drop off our freight there, pick up a load, then head back down."

The Gulf. Could he be from any farther away? "Is that your usual route?"

"It varies. Depends on the supply, the demand. I never know from week to week where I'll be."

"Your work must keep you on the river most of the time. Does it get lonely out there?" Translation—*Is there anyone back home you're missing?*

"I'm out there most of the time, sure. But I try to get

home as often as possible."

So someone did wait for his return. Of course. A man like this? Yet he wore no ring. But he wouldn't wear it while he worked, right? Too dangerous, with all the things he probably had to do. But he'd wear it sometimes, right? And there was no white cheater's circle on the ring finger of his left hand.

"And as for lonely? Uh, no. The guys make sure of that. Lord, they never shut up." Wyatt leaned to pick up a small, flat rock, then skipped it across the water.

"The other crew members?"

"The *motley* crew members. Depending on the size of the tow I'm working at the time, I have anywhere from eight to twelve men. The crew changes, they come and go. Some discover the life isn't for them, some would rather be sitting in some bar, and I wind up having to send them up the hill."

So he *was* the captain. "Send them up the hill?"

"Fire them. Off the boat and up the bank they go." He gestured with a thumb. "I always hate to do it, but I need good, reliable men who show up and show up sober."

They continued along the dirt path.

"But some of the fellas have been with me forever. There's old Graser, there's Frank. Frank's had some drinking problems in the past, but he's straightened out now. And my first mate, my buddy, that's Hoopie. Hoopie's been with me from the start. He knows more about the river than anybody. Oh, and there's Pickle, our cook. Pickle's been onboard forever, too."

"Interesting names. Pickle, Hoopie."

"I always wondered when I was a kid why so many river dudes seemed to be called Hoopie. Eventually I found out that's what old river guys were called, especially those from Kentucky and West Virginia. Hoopie's from Louisville. He's an old codger but he's gonna outlive us all. That old geezer has more energy than all the others combined. Puts the younger men to shame. And Pickle, I can't remember how he got stuck with that name. Hell, I don't remember anymore what his real name is. I tell you, Ellie, I couldn't do what I do without those fellas."

"Do you enjoy your work?"

Wyatt nodded. "It's in my blood, I guess. You thirsty? I'm thirsty." He extended an arm around her, his hand lightly guiding her up the bank.

Jolts of electricity zinged through her body. What was it about this man? His vitality defibrillated her heart. He probably could maneuver his tow with his own horsepower. And was that a chorus of angels singing?

For heaven's sake, take it down a notch, woman. He's just some guy, not Poseidon, god of the waters.

He led her toward a small, old clapboard store embedded on a flat stretch of land at the edge of the bank. Inside, they picked up a couple bottles of soda pop, then headed back outside. Ellie led the way to a bench, where they sat and sipped their pop while gazing at and commenting on the river. As the liquid foundation stone of Marietta and its people, the focal point, the spice that flavored the town, the river never ceased to provide fodder for conversation and introspection. It seemed to drive everything and everybody.

Now here was this fellow, carried to town by the river, and he was wreaking havoc on every one of Ellie's senses. Such a beautiful day, but she found it tough to look anywhere but at this man sitting beside her, completely unaware that his pheromones were shooting into her and pulsating through her body.

How old am I, thirteen? She recalled her infatuation as a young teen with a dashing stage actor. Aunt Lillian had taken her to a theater in Columbus, and his appearance onstage had set Ellie's heart racing. And when his first motion picture came out, she made Mason take her. Oh, but that wavy hair, the regal nose, those searing eyes. Eyes that had to, and darned well could, say everything, in that era before the talkies came out. But how could she be having that reaction now, at her age and presumed maturity?

After a few minutes, they continued their stroll.

"Ahh, I love this bridge. Come on." Wyatt again placed a supportive hand on her back as they climbed the iron steps of the old Harmar Bridge, an imposing structure of massive lacy black steelwork, supported by enormous sandstone piers worn smooth by decades of flowing river.

A plaque mounted on the iron support explained that the structure originated in 1856 as a covered bridge linking Marietta and its tiny suburb, Harmar Village. Built for horse-drawn vehicles, it was later converted to a swinging bridge, to allow tall boats to pass underneath, and fitted with railroad tracks. It now hosted trains steaming and chugging across its surface, and the wood-planked pedestrian walkway added later remained.

Wyatt leaned against the wooden railing of the walkway. "So, back to you, Miss Ellie. Do I get to know more about you, or do you plan on keeping me wondering?"

How to not blurt out all there was to tell, getting it out of the way so they could proceed into eternity as a couple? "Well, let's see. I'm visiting from the Windy City."

Did she only imagine his chest deflate?

"Do you mean to tell me that yesterday when I saw you stepping from your auto, you had driven from Chicago?"

Ellie nodded.

"By yourself?"

Another nod.

"But that's a good ten-hour drive. Nobody came with you?"

"*By myself* pretty much means nobody came with me." Ellie's lips curved into a sly smile. "And ten-and-a-half hours. I live in one of the western suburbs."

"Well, I'll be…" Wyatt's grin evolved into a slow, dumbfounded shake of his head. "How long are you here, the remarkable Miss Ellie?"

"A few days." *Actually, forever, now that you're here.*

"Do you visit here often?"

"I've always tried to get down to see my aunt a few times a year. Not so much since the economic collapse happened, or the Great Depression, as they're calling it these days." She leaned against the rail opposite Wyatt. Her eyes fixed on the motorcars and freight trucks crossing the distant Williamstown bridge linking Ohio and West Virginia. "And where is home for you?"

A shadow of pensiveness crossed his face. "Biloxi was home all my life. Now, well, it's pretty much the river now. I'm in the process of a divorce."

So he *was* married. But getting a divorce. But not yet divorced. But probably soon.

He explained that he'd moved out of the marital

home last summer, that he thought the divorce would be final by now but the proceedings dragged on.

Was he being square with her? My goodness, Mason had turned her into such a skeptic. "I'm sorry to hear that."

"Thanks. But it's for the best. We were two very different people, which didn't seem important in the beginning, but it just became intolerable. She hated anything related to the river. I wasn't a fan of dressing up for all her social events. But I did it, I tried to please her."

"Any children?"

"Oh, I have a great son." A smile lit his face. "He's, let's see, twenty-one now. Eddie. He operates a tow on the lower end of the Mississippi. He's recently married, so he makes short runs. I get back to see him when I can. He lives in Biloxi. Good kid. Pretty much grew up on the river with his dad."

"It sounds like the two of you are pretty close."

"Oh, sure. He's my boy." He pointed at a chain of barges being silently nudged downstream by a towboat. "That tow is coming out of Pittsburgh. See the steel?"

"What do you usually haul?"

"How does this conversation keep getting turned back around to me? You're not telling me anything about you. You running from the law or something? You're not part of that Ma Barker clan, are you?"

Ellie laughed and proceeded across the bridge. "My clan consists only of my two children, both in college. I'm recently divorced. And for a living, I repair old stained-glass panels. Or did. There isn't a lot of demand for it these days."

"Wow. I've never given stained glass much

thought."

"I love my work. And sometimes I make new pieces, but repairing the old ones is especially fulfilling. I like the process of restoring them as closely as I can to their original appearance."

"That has to involve some serious skill."

"Well, it's been a blessing. The soldering involved is similar to welding, so I've been able to work in that trade for the past couple years."

Wyatt halted, his mouth dropped open. "Excuse me?"

"Hmm?"

"Did you say you've been welding?"

She nodded.

"That's incredible. How does a little thing like you withstand a tough job like that?"

"It isn't so bad. A person gets used to it."

He shook his head, and they continued floating across the bridge in a mist of sunbeams and angel's breath.

Snap out of it, Ellie. You don't even know this person. How many near misses, almost meeting this man, their paths almost crossing over the years? Not that it mattered. She was married then. So was he, probably. Still was.

They continued their trek across the bridge, down the steps at the other end, and into Harmar Village. When would he need to leave? Ellie pushed the thought from her mind.

"You like ice cream?" Wyatt asked.

Ellie followed Wyatt's gaze to the pharmacy housed in the white clapboard building just ahead.

"Well, sure, but you've already bought me a pop."

"Come on."

A couple minutes later, Wyatt placed their sundaes on a small iron table teetering on uneven bricks and sprouting a dainty black-and-white-striped shade umbrella more Belle Époque than practical. Tourists passed by on their way into or out of the shops lining the main street.

"Tell me more about your work," Ellie said.

"Well, they say you have to be crazy to work a tow, but you can't beat working outdoors, the travel, the adventure. You never know what you'll encounter. Fog, ice, high winds. It can be dangerous, so it's important the crew is well trained. The days are long, the work is tough. You're wet, you're cold, sunburned, exhausted. It's pretty much a great time." Wyatt grinned.

Was his kiss as spectacular as his smile?

Dappled sunlight flitted across their skin, a breeze lapped at their hair, ice cream relented under sweltry hot fudge. An extraordinary moment on this early spring day along the river. Ellie willed the bliss to never end. But she'd told him her aunt awaited her. She gathered their empty glass sundae dishes and returned them to the pharmacy.

Back outside, Ellie aimed a smile at Wyatt. "I need to go. Thank you for the ice cream. And the pop." She headed for the bridge.

"Ellie."

She turned.

He took a few steps, then stopped squarely before her. "I'd like to see you again." His eyes bore into hers with determination.

A wave of emotion rolled inside her chest like a tsunami. Why? She'd known the man for all of a couple hours.

"Do you think someday I'll be lucky enough to get that chance?" Not a muscle of his entire being moved.

This man seemed terrific, but that was the point—he *seemed* terrific. But he was married. And a riverman. A man whose office was the wheelhouse of a boat, whose nine-to-five translated in river time to twenty-four-seven. But she couldn't dismiss whatever was happening between them. *Was* something happening between them? Or was it just that he was stunningly handsome and virile and she'd gone without hot fudge for too long?

"I live in Illinois, remember?"

"I know how to get to Illinois. Look, Ellie, the final divorce hearing is scheduled for August, the first week. I don't remember the exact date. May I see you after that? If you don't feel comfortable with me coming there, meet me here, meet me anywhere, I don't care." He stepped closer. "How about," he pointed, "right up there on that bridge on the tenth of August at four o'clock?"

He won't show up. His intentions may be sincere, but by August? Come on, that was four months away. The long stretch of life's business and endless river and parching summer days will have crowded her out of his mind by then. She could think about him for months, anticipate his return, then there would be no sign of him. Or worse, he'd come back and she'd find out that he hadn't gone through with the divorce or that he was a drinker or a gambler. Or a killer.

Ellie's eyes skimmed over the baroque building peaks of Marietta, to the vaporous horizon of the river, to the distant, blue-gray Allegheny Mountains. It all looked different now. Always distantly lovely, it all surged now to vivid, three-dimensional life.

"Look, I'd like to ask you for your telephone number, but I'm still married, and I don't want to complicate your life, and I know you wouldn't give it to me anyway." His smile was tender. "But I would love to see you again. I had a good time today."

Ellie climbed the steps and started across the bridge. His footfall trailed her. His question prodded.

"Ellie."

She turned.

He stood solid. His eyes held hers for a long moment. "I know it's tough to trust some random guy making promises for four months from now. But I'm serious. Tell me you'll be here."

Has this man ever heard the word no from any woman? She looked from his earnest eyes to the hand he extended toward her. Her own hand ventured to his, but he didn't grasp it into an ensnarement of fingers. Instead, he touched his fingertips to hers, fleetingly as a feather, then grazed her hand with his own, fanning the flame that had flickered between them all afternoon.

Chapter Seven

"Ohmygod." Deb signaled the waiter, then swigged the last of her beer. "You went out with that scoundrel Phil Taylor?"

Anita glared at her. "That's what I said, Deb. Do you have a problem with it?"

"No, but *you* should have a problem with it. Are you not aware of his reputation? The man can't keep it in his trousers, and he's a narcissistic asshole. But then, he *is* rich, right?"

"Look, the fact that I see him has nothing to do with his dough. He treats me well. We have a good time together."

Deb shrugged. "Does it not bother you that you're one in a long string of little side interests for him or that he's cheating on his girlfriend with you? He's been with her forever, you know."

Anita slammed her wine glass onto the table, splashing the checkered plastic tablecloth. "The man isn't married. He can do whatever he wants. And who *I* date is none of your business."

"Then quit boring us all the time with your sordid tales about sneaking around with unavailable men," Deb said. "And every one of them has been, ohmygod, simply the bee's knees."

Anita did corner the market on drama, always seeming to function in some realm of urgency and gravity, whether she was raving about a fantastic shoe sale in Parkersburg or spouting a soliloquy on her latest dating escapades. And her face regularly carried an almost tortured expression, a hybrid of angst and annoyance.

Anita's lips thinned into a tense crease, her chin jutted as her eyes pierced Deb's. "If you didn't wanna hear about my life, you should've stayed home."

"Oh look, Anita." Deb pointed across the room. "There's a sharp-looking fella. Maybe he's married or in a long-term relationship."

Thankfully, the waiter interrupted the seething spat with a second round of drinks. Anita downed her remaining wine, then lit a cigarette.

Charlene had declined meeting Ellie and the other two at the Low Falutin that night, preferring to stay home with her husband, with whom she was madly in love. Although Alan was a laid-back man who never minded her going out, Charlene had urged her friends, "You single gals go have some fun."

Ellie and her friends enjoyed an occasional night out at the longtime honky-tonk nestled into the riverbank at the southernmost edge of town. Its weathered clapboard and corrugated tin roof blended seamlessly into the river's craggy edge. Over the years, ownership of the Low Falutin had changed a few times, but with every update and minor renovation, each proprietor had taken care to preserve the ambiance of the much-loved watering hole. Nobody dreamed of touching the original wood-plank flooring, weathered brick walls, and battered bar that went on forever. The Low Falutin's menu cover featured a painting of an old steamboat and a saucy explanation of the origin of the establishment's name:

Y'all know that size matters, and the steamboats of yore were no exception. The taller the smokestack, the less likely flaming embers would spew onto the deck and set off a raging fire. Each steamboat tried to outdo the next with fancy steel fluting bedecking their smokestacks. Folks called these boats "highfalutin."

Well, here at the Low Falutin, we don't claim to be big or fancy, but we do guarantee a good time will be had by all. So why don't y'all come down and see us sometime?

On the stage, two bearded twenty-somethings tuned their guitars. A young gal and another young man flurried around placing microphones and stringing cords into place. Soon the lights dimmed, and the band began to play. The young lady turned out to possess a resonant, woebegone country voice, and soon couples and groups of women hit the dance floor for some spirited two-stepping, their fringe flying and their boots scuffling.

"How 'bout it, sweetheart?" A thirty-something man in tattered denim trousers and a cowboy hat extended a hand toward Ellie, beaming a wide smile.

Ellie returned his smile. She'd always loved dancing but wasn't quite ready to take to the floor. How long had it been since she'd cut a rug? "Not just yet, but thank you."

"I gotcha, Tex." Anita mashed her cigarette in the ashtray while leaping to her feet. "Come on, let's hit it." She grabbed the poor, unsuspecting soul's hand with a "yeee-hawww" and dragged him to the dance floor.

Ellie grinned at Anita's exaggerated, awkward steps that didn't quite sync with the rhythm. Not a fan of country music, Anita had nevertheless agreed to come out tonight since Ellie was in town.

"For cryin' out loud, he's twelve years old. Look at her." Deb rolled her eyes and stood. "I'm going to the ladies' room, probably to vomit."

Ellie sat back and enjoyed the music, sipping her beer. The honkytonk's screen door continually creaked open and banged shut, welcoming newcomers into the smoke-fogged establishment, letting out patrons to cool off in the crisp night air. In a few weeks, with the onset of summer, the place would really be hopping. Ellie especially loved the Low Falutin in the warm months, when the doors were flung open to the patio, the music filtered out into the balmy night air, and the white bulbs strung overhead reflected off the river.

Deb returned to the table. "You let the beer dry up, Ells. What the hell?"

"I'm only half finished with mine," Ellie retorted. "Jeez, not everyone sucks 'em down like they just spent a month in the Sahara, girlfriend."

"For cryin' out loud, how the hell do you get served around here?" Deb left the table in search of more suds.

Ellie glanced around for the waiter, then gasped.

He was leaning against the far wall, long legs crossed at the ankles, taking the occasional swallow of beer, keeping a vigilant eye on the dancers. Darn it, the place was so dimly lit, and smoky on top of that. Ellie strained her eyes at each flash of the cobalt blue neon sign on the wall above his head but still couldn't tell. Could it be? Was that Wyatt?

How could he be Wyatt? He'd told her, after their afternoon together two days ago, that he was pulling out of town that day. He'd seemed like an upfront person, but who really knew? Ellie squinted. Definitely Wyatt.

Her heart thumped around inside her chest like an out-of-balance washing machine. It all had been a lie.

When another song started up, a young redhead in cowboy boots and a calico dress barely covering her bosom accosted him, hands on hips, head cocked to one side. He promptly took her hand, deposited his beer on a waitress's tray, and followed the girl to the congested dance floor.

Ellie leaned this way and that to catch glimpses of the two grinding against each other, then clambered to her feet. She needed to get to the restroom, needed to splash some water on her face, maybe follow Deb's lead and vomit. She glanced over again as she made her way across the room. The scoundrel couldn't take his eyes off the girl's bulging cleavage. Darn it. He'd seemed so sincere.

The song ended, and couples unwound themselves from each other. Before ducking into the restroom, Ellie endured one more look. He and the girl remained on the floor, locked in a disgusting French kiss. His hands grasped at her bottom. "Get a room," someone yelled. When they finally broke apart and he came up for air, his eyes landed on Ellie's. He grinned and winked at her.

He wasn't Wyatt.

Ellie touched a hand to her chest to calm her two-stepping heart. Thank goodness. But what was it about Wyatt that caused these intense reactions in her? She returned to the table and sank onto her chair, weary at the havoc her insides had just gone through. Anita and Deb had found their way back to their seats, and the band hit the ground running with a lively number.

"Who's ready for a ripsnortin' time?" Anita jumped up again and motioned to Ellie and Deb to follow.

"Come on, gals, I'll show you how it's done."
"Right behind you," Ellie said.
Deb followed. "Oh, why the hell not?"

Chapter Eight

"Tell me, Eleanor, what's going on in your life? Have you thought about allowing yourself a date yet?"

Aunt Lillian knew how to get to the point without piercing a person with its sharpness. Ellie had had her opportunities, and Aunt Lillian knew that. But rather than reprimanding Ellie for routinely turning down the frequent overtures, she'd wisely presented dating as something Ellie would be doing for herself.

The two had strolled the sidewalks of Harmar Hill this evening after dinner, a tradition they'd shared since Ellie was a little girl. They chatted about old times in the neighborhood, new residents, and happenings around Harmar Village and Marietta. Now they relaxed on Aunt Lillian's stone patio behind the house. Ellie drew pure joy from every moment they spent together, and she knew her aunt did too.

This morning, Ellie had cleaned her aunt's wrought-iron furniture, brought the chair cushions out from storage, and swept the patio. Temperatures weren't quite warm enough for the patio's spring debut, but Ellie wanted to prepare it so Aunt Lillian and Hanne wouldn't have to in a few weeks.

"I really haven't felt like being with anyone yet," Ellie said. "I needed this time to get past it all. I needed to be sure to land on my feet."

More than that, she felt as damaged as the stained-glass panels she'd so lovingly refurbished. Restoring herself was proving harder than she'd anticipated. How did a person muster the "lovingly" part when she felt so unlovable?

"And I'm fine. Now I just want to be there for the children."

"Who are no longer children. Who both are in college now. More tea?" At Ellie's nod, Aunt Lillian filled her cup.

"I know." Ellie bit into one of the warm walnut coconut bars Hanne had baked during their walk. "But I like to think they still need me."

"Oh, they will always need their mama. But they're self-sufficient now. And now you can make your life whatever you want to make it."

Ellie contemplated the valley. The burnished hues of the sinking sun spread across the sky like melting candle wax. Was she heading into her own sunset? With the children grown and her husband gone, had she fulfilled her purpose? Were her best years behind her? "I'm not sure what I want my life to be," she said. "It's changed so much. I just don't know."

"Life is an ever-changing journey, my dear," Aunt Lillian said. "We make some of those changes, and others happen to us. The thing is to find peace and be happy. And if that isn't happening where we are, we find the place where it does happen."

"I'm not sure where I am, that's the problem. I don't know where my place is anymore. On this journey called life, where am I, where am I headed? That's what I don't know."

"I understand, darling. I've been in your shoes, somewhat."

"You mean when Uncle Edward died?"

"That and..." Aunt Lillian stirred the tea she'd already stirred. "Yes, when your Uncle Edward died, I wasn't sure if I should stay in this house, wasn't entirely sure of my role in life. I understand your feelings of uncertainty, of being at a crossroads. But you're strong, and you need to trust your internal compass in navigating your journey."

"I'm afraid my compass is askew." Ellie laughed.

Aunt Lillian pressed a hand on Ellie's knee. "No. You just need to pay closer attention to it." She stood and nodded toward the house. "Do you remember all those nights when your Uncle Edward would look at the night skies through his telescope?"

Ellie regarded the balcony of the sitting room. Uncle Edward's telescope had been mounted on a tripod at those French doors, and he spent many hours viewing the moon, the stars, and the planets, as well as the comings and goings on the river.

"I sure do." Ellie smiled. "Sometimes he would call me over and point out whatever had caught his eye that night."

Aunt Lillian folded her arms and directed her gaze skyward. "I didn't know your uncle when he was in the Navy, but he would tell me how he and his fellow sailors depended on celestial navigation to determine their ship's location. They would utilize the North Star or the Southern Cross, depending which hemisphere they were in, and sometimes they would reference the constellations."

Seating herself back on her chaise, Aunt Lillian leaned back and crossed an elegant leg over the other. "At other times, they would use what he called the navigational star chart. First, they would look for the three brightest stars in the sky. Then, on the star chart, they would locate those three stars and draw a circle around each of them, large enough that the circles touched each other. The point where those three circles intersected was the location of their ship, directly below on Earth." Aunt Lillian's lips curved into a smile. "Your uncle brought that up often in life. He would say that whenever he wasn't sure about things or what to do, he would look for the three brightest stars in the sky and he would know his place."

"That's a lovely notion," Ellie said.

"It's often inspired me as well," Aunt Lillian said. "And you, my darling, must determine what your three brightest stars are. What are the things most important to you, your passions? You'll discover that where those three things intersect is where you need to be in life. Where those stars cross is your place."

Ellie nodded. "Well, obviously, my brightest star is my children," she said. "They may not need me quite as much as they used to, but they will always be more important to me than anything else in the universe. And the other two stars… I'm not sure. Maybe one of them… I don't know." Ellie swirled her tea in her cup. "I would like to have a man in my life again someday. I'd like to find love again." She shrugged. "Maybe that's one of my stars."

Aunt Lillian nodded ever so slightly, her lips curved in silent agreement.

"And actually," Ellie said. "I did meet a man a couple days ago, in town."

Her aunt's head tilted, her eyebrows lifted. "Well, tell me about this fellow."

It all spilled out. How she and Wyatt had met, how they walked and talked, that they planned to meet again in August, following his divorce.

Aunt Lillian reached over and squeezed Ellie's hand.

Ellie's heart warmed. Having her aunt's wise support had always been so important. "I couldn't believe the way I felt about him. I've never had such a strong and instant reaction to a man before."

Aunt Lillian nodded. "I think I understand how you felt."

Ellie tucked her legs beside her on her cushioned chaise. "Did you feel that way when you met Uncle Edward?"

"I cared very much for your uncle." Aunt Lillian's eyes lowered.

Her aunt had sidestepped the question. Why?

Aunt Lillian glanced at Ellie. "Your uncle treated me very well. He was a hard worker, respectful, considerate. We enjoyed a pleasing marriage."

A pleasing marriage? That made the marriage sound more like a utilitarian arrangement than a loving relationship. Where was the passion? Ellie couldn't remember affection ever being apparent between her aunt and uncle, at least not that she'd observed. Respect and consideration, sure. But had they been in love? Uncle Edward had often seemed a rather remote presence, reading in his leather wing chair in his library, legs crossed, wire-rimmed spectacles perched on his nose; or standing at the far edge of the back yard, surveying the valley and river, when not merged with his telescope. A quiet man, the sort who seemed content with his own thoughts, politely interacting when necessary, but otherwise primarily moving parallel to every other mortal. Uncle Edward of the fine Cuban cigars, leather-bound books, and endless newspaper subscriptions.

"Uncle Edward was such a good man. The two of you were married a long time."

"Thirty-four years. And I do miss him very much. But before your uncle..." Her eyes focused past Ellie as if searching for some elusive image, trying to bring it into focus. "A long time ago, there was another man."

My goodness. Ellie had never viewed her aunt as anything but a married woman, then a widow. Faded photographs she'd seen of her revealed an exquisite young lady with high cheekbones and an alluring smile, her dark curls piled high atop her head and cascading down her back, in the style of the late Victorian era. Of course there would have been other men in her young life. After all, she'd met Uncle Edward in her late twenties. But this man obviously had been someone special.

"Who was he?"

"His name was..." Aunt Lillian sighed. "His name was James. Oh, he was something. Tall, dark haired, with a handsome mustache. He had such a confident air about him. More than anything else, I remember the way he looked at me. The way he always looked at me." She stood, pulled her cardigan closer, and stepped toward the back of the yard.

Ellie followed, waiting for her aunt to continue. A robin fluttered with a warble into a silver maple. From farther away, the honk of a towboat drifted up with the evening breeze.

"It was the fourth of July. Two of my friends and I

went to the celebration at the levee. We were sitting on a blanket, waiting for the music to begin." Aunt Lillian pointed. "Right about there, between the Levee House building and where the Bellevue Hotel stands now. Boats were docked along the bank. This was 1879. A hot night and, oh, it was a marvelous time. We laughed, drank lemonade. And I remember seeing him for the first time, on a boat with his comrades. He was leaning on the railing, and he was staring at me. And his expression was..." Aunt Lillian squinted as if trying to conjure an accurate recollection. "Well, it was determined, dead serious."

The way Wyatt looked at me.

Ellie could almost see her aunt as that young woman on a blanket on the riverbank on a hot summer night. Probably wearing white, a high-necked, long-sleeved bodice draped elegantly well below the hip, over a floor-length skirt ending in ruffles.

"And of course I was not going to stare back, so I went about my business. Then I heard the clearing of a throat and an *Excuse me, ma'am*. And that bold young man was standing there in front of me, and he asked me to dance, right there on the riverbank. And nobody else was dancing, mind you."

"I hope you said yes." Ellie tucked her hands into the pockets of her dress and kicked at a dried walnut pod.

"Absolutely." Aunt Lillian giggled. "There was a small combo playing, a banjo and a dulcimer, and perhaps a fiddle. A lively tune, and yes, I took his hand and we danced. Then James asked me to take a walk with him and, well, my friends were horrified and tried to talk some sense into me, but I didn't care. I went with him. And we walked and we talked. I'm telling you, Eleanor, it was as if we had always known each other."

They stood in silence for a minute or two, watching lights flick on, one by one, down in the valley. Aunt Lillian leaned, picked a tiny mauve wildflower, lifted it to her nose.

"We were standing on Harmar Bridge when the fireworks began. There wasn't much traffic on the bridge at that point, so we were quite tucked away. And then… then he kissed me, and he told me that he and I belonged together."

After a moment, Aunt Lillian's eyes shot to Ellie's, her hand went to her mouth. "I've never told anyone any of this. Not a soul. Running off with a stranger at night, letting him kiss me, it was all very risqué for the late seventies."

"But you did nothing wrong. It's a beautiful story."

Aunt Lillian nodded, and her hand went to her chest. "Well, he asked me to meet him there, on the bridge, the next day. At this point, I didn't even reply. As much as I liked that young man, he was a little too smooth. I simply ran away, back to my friends. And I prided myself on having some common sense, on not having allowed myself to fall for his slick talk."

How similar were Aunt Lillian's story and what had happened to Ellie. They'd both met men who came in off the river, spent an enchanted moment of stilled time with them, and ended up on the old railroad bridge. Both women had instantly felt something for these strangers, and both men had asked to meet again.

"Did you ever see him again?"

"The very next day!" Aunt Lillian laughed. "Somehow, I found myself back on that bridge. It wasn't even a conscious effort. I simply was there." Aunt Lillian rubbed her arms. "Oh, the look in that man's eyes when he looked at me. As if I were the means to his very survival."

Ellie's mind generated a slew of questions. Her aunt's memories of James were so vivid, he must have played an important role in her life. Why hadn't Ellie heard of him before this? What had happened to him?

"And so it began," Aunt Lillian continued. "Oh, I loved him. I thought there would never be another man in my life. I never wanted any other man. But then…"

"Eleanor, there is a long-distance telephone call for you." Hanne leaned out between the French doors. "It is that sweet daughter of yours."

"Excuse me, please, Aunt Lillian."

By the time Ellie finished talking with Jessie, Aunt Lillian had returned to the house and gone upstairs for the night. What had happened with James? *But then*, Aunt Lillian had said. But then what?

Chapter Nine

Ellie wound her automobile around the southwestern perimeter of Chicago on her way back to Oak Park. The city's rigid concrete and congested traffic posed a startling contrast to the tranquil river and drifting boats of Marietta. Like it always did when she returned to Illinois, the little town seemed a dream now. Wyatt seemed a dream now. Had she really met him?

After unpacking, she bathed and slipped into her polka-dotted house dress. Downstairs, she filled her teakettle and set it to warming on the stove, then sawed off a couple slices of bread and slathered them with jam. A bit stale and not much of a dinner, but there wasn't much else in the house right now to eat. Settling in at the kitchen table, she bit into her bread and surveyed the room. If she was going to get on with her life, maybe some changes were warranted. The walls and cabinets could use a fresh coat of paint, but that would have to wait until better economic times. The kitchen was still pretty, though, with its black-and-ivory checkerboard floor, cast iron stove finished in pale yellow porcelain enamel, and the cheery curtains Ellie had recently made from a worn-out floral dress.

After a quick clean-up of the kitchen, she refilled her teacup, meandered into the parlor, and switched on her burled-walnut radio. She really should be in bed. She had to work in the morning, and six o'clock would come soon. But she was too wound up from the Marietta trip. How she longed to talk with Wyatt, but of course she hadn't given him her telephone number, and he hadn't asked for it. Honorable, that he wouldn't try to reach her until after his divorce. More than one man hadn't let a wedding ring stand in the way of hitting on her. And Ellie already missed her aunt. She hadn't asked Aunt Lillian this morning to continue her story about James, having sensed the subject was closed, and Ellie had been eager to get on the road.

Swaying to the woodwinds and brass of one her favorite sentimental jazz tunes, she ambled from the parlor to the dining room, then to the sunroom. She'd put together some pleasant spaces over the years, rooms full of things to provide comfort and beauty for her family. Plump sofas and soft area rugs, gleaming wooden side tables and antique cabinets. Why did these rooms now seem staged for a lifetime cut short? Like a bride left standing at the altar. Ellie and her family had lived happily in the big old house for many years. It had always been the four of them in a seemingly endless age of love and vibrancy, an age which had then faltered and floundered and funneled away into emptiness and silence. Now, those years seemed from a past life. Years whose shadows now formed, loomed, crept closer. Incomprehension stabbed at Ellie's heart. What happened to her life? Where was her family? Was this how she would be living from now on? Alone?

She rushed to the foyer, flung open the door, and seized a lungful of fresh air. Stepping onto the porch, the glow of downtown drew her gaze to the white lights strung above the brick streets, to the striped awning of a restaurant, to the grand façade of a hotel. To couples clutching each other's hands as they strolled together, pleased as punch, out for a night on the town. Her life felt as empty as the chasm expanding in her chest. Tears drizzled onto her face, and she averted her eyes from the downtown revelers. Why this meltdown all of a sudden? Maybe meeting Wyatt and not knowing if she'd ever see him again had nudged her loneliness to front and center. Swiping at her face with a sleeve, she seated herself with a thud on the top step of the porch.

She was on her own for the first time in two decades. She could go anywhere she wanted, do anything she wanted. But where did she want to go? What did she want to do with her life? Why did she feel like a ship on endless seas, with no port to call home?

****

"I'm really going to miss you. How can you run off and abandon me all summer like this?"

The waitress brought their orders. Ellie had met Betty at their favorite Chicago cafe, a downtown art deco establishment featuring a glass block facade and the best pies this side of the Mississippi. Ellie would be heading for Marietta in the morning, having recently resigned from her welding job. Miraculously, a large stained-glass job had landed in her lap, a blessing after several years of virtually no demand for her services. The panels in need were from an 1830s-era church on Michigan Avenue and were in such dire condition that their repair could not be put off any longer. While the job would require months of all-day work, it would pay well upon completion, in addition to the advance the church had provided. And with Benny now graduated from college, Ellie's financial load had substantially lightened. Thank goodness she was able to leave the arduous work at the farm machinery company behind. And because a contractor's removal of the stained-glass panels would take several weeks, hello summer in Marietta!

"Why don't you come down, Betts? Take some time off work. Come hang out with the girls and me."

"Oh, sure, I'm just dying to see Anita again."

Ellie laughed. "I know the two of you have always butted heads. You're both strong-willed and outspoken."

"Translation: she and I both are shrews, right?" Betty feigned agitation.

"Your words, not mine."

"Hey, I know I'm mouthy, but Anita butts heads with pretty much everyone. And whatever is going on in *that* head is totally foreign to me." Betty tapped a finger against her temple.

"Well, come down anyway. I'll referee. I'll keep the two of you in opposite corners."

"Mmm, maybe," Betty said through a mouthful of lemon meringue pie. "But I'm not sure I'll be able to get away from the station. We're starting that new comedy series this summer, and I'm buried up to my nose with work." Betty worked as senior producer at a local radio station.

"Yes, I can't wait to listen to it when I get back." Ellie took a sip of her tea, then dug into her heavenly, long-awaited sugar milk pie. "You guys won't be getting rid of the swing hour, will you?"

"Not a chance." Betty shook her head, then dabbed at her lips with a napkin. "So, Ellie. Gregory Barnes, the president of Brian's company." She paused, apparently for dramatic effect. "You met him at that art exhibit a couple years ago." Brian was a frequent companion of Betty's.

"Sure, I remember him."

"Well, get this. Gregory is transferring to the Chicago office."

Receiving no reaction from Ellie during her second dramatic pause of the conversation, Betty raised her eyebrows, thrust her head toward Ellie, and turned palms upward. "Did you hear what I said?"

"I heard you. Gregory Barnes is moving to Chicago. And?"

"*And* he asked Brian about you. He heard you're divorced now, and, Ellie, he wants to see you."

"I don't know. He seemed nice, but I don't know if I'd be interested in him." The truth was she'd had no reaction to Gregory when they met. Of course, Mason had recently left at the time and the last thing she'd been thinking about was another man, but absolutely no spark with Gregory. Nothing like every time she'd encountered or thought of the man named Wyatt Dare.

"You don't know? What happened to impetuous Ellie? The man is gorgeous, rich, and single. Come on. Do you know how rare a creature he is? A guy like him won't be alone for long. By the time you figure out if you're interested, I guarantee he'll be off the market."

"So you're saying I should grab him before somebody else does?"

"That's exactly what I'm saying." Betty huffed out an exaggerated sigh. "Eleanor Helene Todd, this man is amazing. And you've been alone for, what, two years now? Come on. You'll be glad you said yes."

Ellie's explanation would have to do. No way was she going to tell her about Wyatt. Betty was far too pragmatic to understand Ellie's feelings for some man she'd known for only a few hours. She would roll her eyes and summarize why she thought Ellie was being idealistic. *The man isn't here now*, she would say, *move on. Besides, what kind of money can a riverman possibly make?*

"I appreciate your watching out for me, Betts." Ellie directed a warm smile at her friend. "But I don't need talked into anything. When I'm ready to date, I'll date." She tamped her fork down over every last crumb on her plate, then popped it into her mouth. "Thanks for the pie, sweetie pie."

****

Half a dozen motorcars filled Aunt Lillian's driveway the following evening. Three things were always a certainty at Aunt Lillian's—warm welcomes from her and Hanne, good food in the kitchen, and something interesting going on.

"We're in the sitting room, Eleanor," came her aunt's voice.

Ellie hugged her, then greeted Hanne and the other women, who perched on various chairs and sipped from icy glasses or steaming cups and jotted on notepads.

"We're making plans for the gala," Aunt Lillian told Ellie.

"It's terrific that the event is finally being reinstated after, what, a six-year absence? May I help?"

"Absolutely," one of the women said. "If we're going to do grand on a budget, it's all hands on deck."

"I'll be right back, then. I'm just going to get settled in first."

After depositing her things in her room and pouring herself a glass of iced tea, Ellie joined the women. "Give me my assignments." She grabbed a notepad and pen from the pile and plopped onto the floor.

"There's plenty to do. We've already lined up a terrific swing band out of Columbus. And let's see…" Aunt Lillian consulted her notepad. "We've rented the venue and booked the caterer, but we need to decide on the flowers and other decorations. We think this will be the most successful fundraiser ever for the children's home."

"Eleanor," one of the ladies said, "your aunt tells us you made these beautiful stained-glass panels." She swept a hand toward the French doors. "We could use someone as creative as you to help with the decorations."

Ellie readily accepted her appointment as decorations chair and scribbled notes on the various ideas the women spewed.

In the next few weeks, Ellie, her aunt, and Hanne spent many hours talking and laughing, eating some variety of Hanne's cookies, pies, and German delicacies. Aunt Lillian would play a theatrical piece or something from the Great American Songbook on the ivory-colored grand piano in the parlor at the front of the house. In the evenings, they dined and lounged on the patio, chatting and laughing. And Ellie jumped right in with the knitting of blankets, baking of bread, and collecting of clothing to aid in the local economic relief efforts. So relaxing, so soothing, being in Marietta, with Aunt Lillian and Hanne. Ellie would eventually find her footing again in Oak Park, solo as her new pathway was. But these balmy, breezy summer days with these two dynamic, disparate, delightful ladies were just what she needed right now.

Chapter Ten

This was much more than a mere slumber party. This was a twenty-four-hour production, planned with the precision of a military maneuver. First, Ellie, Charlene, and Deb met at Anita's home at ten hundred hours to drop off their rucksacks. They then infiltrated the corner grocery store to stock up on their traditional slumber party rations, including chocolate, ice cream, and wine—beer for Deb. The four of them then proceeded to the mess hall, AKA the Levee House Cafe, for lunch. Having been alerted to expect the hungry troops, Marv had promised them a special feast, and he didn't disappoint. Creamed chipped beef on toast, sweet potato pie, bean soup, and black raspberry pie with ice cream would provide the sustenance needed for their busy day. This was no time for counting calories.

At fourteen hundred hours, they deployed for an afternoon of shopping in downtown Parkersburg. Well, not so much shopping as browsing, their bygone shopping binges having fallen by the wayside in recent years. But the foray did yield a few affordable necessities for the women—a brassiere, some shoe polish, a set of hosiery or two—and a daring pair of shoes for Anita, who swore they were essential.

For dinner, they chipped in on a large pizza and took it to the Parkersburg city park, where they enjoyed an evening of big band music at the bandshell. Finally, they gratefully advanced to Anita's at close to twenty-one hundred for the sleepover. Busy lives and tough times had interrupted the tradition for the past three years. But Ellie had declared it time to reinstate the *Slumber Party* campaign.

Anita hadn't worked since marrying a successful businessman a few years ago, her third marriage. Having received a generous settlement in the subsequent divorce, she'd been able to keep the spacious house. Her only child, a son, lived in Philadelphia.

"Keep 'em coming, Anita," Deb commanded.

"This is all I've got. How many can you possibly need?" Anita flung another pile of blankets onto the floor.

"Hey, we're not twenty anymore." Deb unfurled one of the blankets and layered it on top of the others. "And when did you get rid of your carpeting? For cryin' out loud, I'm gonna need a walking cane in the morning, after sleeping on these hardwood floors."

By then, the women had changed into their nightgowns, set their hair in pin curls, smeared on facial creams, and settled onto the floor of Anita's huge living room with wine—beer for Deb—and assorted chocolates.

"My feet are killing me as it is," Deb said. "Nobody in their right mind spends as much time shopping as you broads. And speaking of feet, let me see those shoes, Anita."

Anita shuffled through her shopping bags and tossed Deb one of her black patent leather pumps featuring precariously high heels and a peep toe.

"Damn, woman, these shoes are insane, even for you." Deb stared at Anita, her mouth gaping. "They're streetwalker shoes. What the hell were you thinking?"

With her usual insouciant attitude, Anita propped her feet on the coffee table. "You wouldn't know the latest style if it bit you in the ass, Deb." Anita fished out the other shoe and hugged it to her cheek. "These shoes are the cat's pajamas. And I'm not catching many flies with honey. It's time to take things up a notch."

Ellie wasn't sure there was another notch for the flamboyant Anita to take it up to. But jet-black hair and just-this-side of too much makeup somehow worked on her, and she could rock a low-cut dress without looking like a tart. Her expensive clothing and impeccable grooming tempered her spicy style.

"Flies? Girl, the only creatures you're gonna catch with these contraptions are crabs."

"They're just shoes, Deb," Anita shot back.

"Why does everyone think they need a man to be happy?" asked Deb. "Is that our sole purpose in life? Pun intended." She pointed at the sole of the shoe. "To find a man?"

"I don't need a man to make me happy." Anita raised her eyebrows. "I just need one to keep me warm at night."

"Oh, Anita." Charlene blushed.

"What happened to Phil Taylor?" asked Deb. "I mean Phil-anderer. Too busy keeping everyone else warm at night?"

Ellie jumped in to change the subject when Deb's mouth opened in reaction to Anita's silence. "Deb, you're going to break your ankle."

Deb was limping around the living room, her foot stuck halfway into Anita's shoe. "So where you gonna wear these to? The Depot?" She referred to one of

Parkersburg's oldest, roughest bars. "That'll get you a quality fella."

"I've always worn high heels. These are just a little higher." *And would you get your gargantuan foot out of my shoe, Sasquatch? You're gonna stretch it out."*

"You know, Deb," Charlene said, "even though you don't need a man to be happy, I think someday the right one will come along, and you'll never want to be without him."

Deb paused. "When did this become about me? I have no desire to date." She waved a dismissive hand and resumed her hobbling. "And there is no such thing as *the one*." Deb gestured air quotes, then kerplunked onto the ottoman, pulled off the shoe, and tossed it to Anita. "How the hell do you wear these monstrosities? Contrary to what all of you seem to believe, there is no such thing as soulmates."

"I don't think it's about finding the perfect man or some soulmate," Ellie said. "But I hope there's someone out there for everyone."

"Look." Deb took a swig of her beer, then directed a pointed finger at each of her friends. "You girls have been seeing too many moving pictures. There is nobody out there waiting to meet us, fall madly in love with us, screw up and piss us off, then climb the highest mountain—even though he's deathly afraid of heights by the way—and beg us to take him back. I'm sorry, but I'm not wasting my time hoping some unrealistic dream personified comes along."

"Oh, come on. Nobody said life is like the films." Anita popped a chocolate into her mouth. "But you can't tell me you have absolutely *no* interest in men."

"None. And the sooner you all realize there is no

eyes meeting, hearts pounding, running in slow motion toward each other on the beach, the better off you'll be. It's all Hollywood motion picture shit, and I've never felt anything remotely like it."

"Even with Vinnie?" Ellie asked.

Deb stood and forged her way to the kitchen. "Vinnie was fine," she yelled. "We had a good time. But I never felt like I was in love, whatever the hell that means." She returned carrying another beer.

"Then why'd you marry him?" Anita asked.

Deb had married Vinnie, a stocky Italian fellow, a decade ago after knowing him for three months. Easily bored, she despised routine and predictability in general, and that soon extended to her marriage. After two years, she'd told her husband she wanted out.

Deb shrugged. "I don't know. It's what you did. You got married. But it wasn't for me. I don't understand the whole marriage thing. I'm happier on my own and not always worrying about someone else's baloney."

"Vinnie seemed to always treat you well," Charlene said.

"Sure. He did. I'm just not cut out for marriage. I can eat what I want, go where I want. Besides, after a long day at the store, all I want to do is get the hell away from people."

Deb managed the housewares floor of a large department store in downtown Parkersburg. Very bright, she'd rapidly moved up the ladder at two smaller shops before landing her current position.

"Well there's more to life than work, and really, I mean, that's all you do, Deb, is work." Anita rolled from her stomach to her side, propping her head on a hand.

"I have a lot of responsibility. My department

doesn't run itself, you know."

"Well, you don't try anymore. I mean, really. You look the same whether you're at work, out for dinner, or pulling weeds. Do you even own anything other than sailor pants? Most men don't agree with women wearing trousers, you know."

Uh oh, this is going to get ugly. Ellie jumped to her feet and headed for the radio. "Who's ready for a little music?"

Deb plopped onto a chair and glared at Anita. "This coming from the queen of fire-engine-red lipstick and sequins."

"At least I care about how I look." Anita rolled onto her back and propped an ankle over a bent knee. "I fix up. I make the effort. You could be attractive if you wanted to. You just don't try."

Ellie rotated the radio knob through various levels of static, settling on an upbeat melody. "Lindy Hop, anyone? We may not have any cats here tonight and we may look like something the cat dragged in, but hey, we've got each other." She began exaggeratingly hopping and twirling around the room.

Charlene burst into laughter and joined Ellie, but Ellie's humorous attempt at a ceasefire went ignored by the adversaries.

"I *could be* attractive?" Deb sprang to her feet and paced the room. "Well, I am not going to paint myself up and prance my feathers all over the place, the way you do to land men." Deb paused in front of Anita. "I suppose you want me to bleach my hair and expose my bosom like that buxom Brooklyn broad from the moving pictures. Well, I've got news for you, honey. How I look is none of your business."

"Well, maybe you should make it *your* business." Anita propped herself on an elbow. "My word, Deb. Do you even own a full-length mirror?"

"Shut up, Anita, okay? Just shut up." Deb sliced her hands through the air in rhythm to her staccato words.

"Oh, don't blow your wig." Anita shook her head and hoisted her arms outward as she boosted herself to her feet. "She starts these things, then gets mad when someone gives their opinion. Anyone else ready for some cheesecake?"

Ellie and Charlene glanced at each other. Thankfully, the exchange hadn't escalated into an evening-wrecking all-out war.

Midnight approached when Anita uncorked another bottle of wine and found a bit more tranquil music on the radio. "So Ellie, what's going on with you? You still living the life of a nun? There must be some decent fellows in Chicago."

Ellie lay on her stomach, hands under her chin. Influenced by thoughts of Wyatt and, no doubt, by her two-going-on-three glasses of wine, "I met a man" slipped out.

Deb bolted upright. "You met someone? Where? Who is he? And when the hell were you going to tell us, bitch?"

Anita and Charlene dissolved into laughter, as did Ellie.

"I met him when I was here in the spring. I met him downtown. He's a tow captain and he seemed like a good person."

"Oh, Ellie, that's just swell," Charlene said. "Have you seen him since then?"

Ellie flipped onto her back and propped her head on

her linked fingers. "No. He lives in Biloxi. And he... he's going through a divorce, but by August it should be final. He's coming back then." Hearing herself say the words almost cheapened the whole thing and didn't begin to convey how she'd felt that day.

"What's he look like?" Anita asked.

"Tall, blond. An interesting fellow, very engaging."

"I believe you're stuck on him, sweetie." Charlene reached over and patted Ellie's knee.

"Wait a minute. Hold the presses." Deb raised up, crawled over Charlene and perched cross-legged next to Ellie, having by now out-drunk the other three women, as usual.

Ellie rolled her eyes. *Oh, boy, here it comes.*

"Let me get this straight, Ells." Deb squared off with Ellie. "You spend a grand total of an hour and a half with some total stranger off the river. Who, by the way, is married. Oh, but he's getting a divorce, and we're sure that's true because he said so. And he promises to come back to a gal he spent all of three hours with, and—"

"Wait, was it an hour and a half or three?" Anita asked.

"Never mind that." Deb waved an arm in Anita's direction, then focused again on Ellie. "So you meet some random guy, he admits he's married but, oh, he's madly in love with you, so the two of you are going to paddle off down the river in his rowboat. Into the sunset." Deb proceeded on her beer-fueled roll, leaning into Ellie. "Girlfriend, has it crossed your mind that your lover boy might have a woman in every port?"

By now, tears of laughter rolled down Ellie's cheeks. "Look, I have no expectations," she said after composing herself. "I met a man who I felt something for, who seemed nice, who asked to see me again. That's all. If it leads to something, great. If not, fine."

Deb swiped a hand across Ellie's face, slurred out a mere "okay," and swallowed another gulp of beer.

"What will you do when you need to go back to Chicago? If you really like him and want to pursue this thing, I mean?" Charlene yawned and sank deeper into her blanket.

"Oh, I haven't thought that far ahead. But I can pretty much make my own schedule. Who knows? He might not even come back."

"He'll come back," Charlene assured her. "And you spend every minute with him you can. Don't worry about the future. Just enjoy your time with him. He sounds simply keen."

By two-thirty in the morning, sleep had silenced Ellie's friends. She lay on her side, head propped on a hand, staring into the misty possibilities of the future. Did Wyatt lie awake somewhere thinking of her? Or was he cuddling with his wife, with no intention of getting a divorce? And how many other women waited for him along the banks of the Mississippi and Ohio Rivers?

Chapter Eleven

"Such a lovely evening." Aunt Lillian flashed her brilliant smile. "What a shame Hanne couldn't come with us."

Hanne had stayed home, recovering from a pulled tooth, but insisted that Ellie and her aunt carry on with their plans to come to the Parkersburg city park to listen to big band music at the bandshell. Everyone else seemed to have had the same idea, with every bench on the grounds full and people clustered on blankets to the sides of those. Glowing lanterns dripped from trees, and a subtle current of sultry air harmonized with the band.

Aunt Lillian swiveled toward Ellie on the bench. "How are you feeling about tomorrow?"

The tenth of August. The day she was to meet Wyatt on the bridge. "Nervous. And trying not to get too excited."

"In case he doesn't show up." Aunt Lillian fanned herself with her mother-of-pearl and lace fan.

Ellie nodded. "And if he doesn't show up, it won't be the end of the world."

At Aunt Lillian's silence, Ellie glanced up. Her aunt's eyes fixed somewhere across the crowd, her fanning halted, her furrowed brow the only disruption to her usual placid demeanor.

Standing at the periphery of the seating area, arms folded, an imposing older man, tall and silver-haired, stared unabashedly at Aunt Lillian. Ellie looked back to her aunt, whose gaze didn't waver. Her chest visibly rose and fell. This man was having quite some effect on her. Her eyes shimmered, seemingly sparked from long-ago memories. Ardent memories contained but obviously never extinguished.

Clearing her throat, Aunt Lillian turned back to focus on the band and continued fanning herself. Ellie peered her way a couple of times, to find a soft tension in the contours of her lovely, refined face. She wore a white chiffon dress sprinkled with small clusters of violets. In her elegant chignon, beneath her small beribboned and netted hat, she'd placed a platinum comb accented by amethysts and topaz. But the light in her eyes when she looked back to the man far eclipsed the luster of the jewels. And when an aching Gershwin tune began, she stood and excused herself.

He uncrossed his arms and seemed to steel himself as she made her way to him. Carrying himself elegantly, he removed his straw Homburg hat, stepped forward, and reached out a hand for her. He leaned and touched his lips to Aunt Lillian's hands, one, then the other, before leading her to a bench across the lawn, next to a grove of trees. A nearby lantern cast an ethereal aurora around the two. Turning toward Aunt Lillian, he propped his forearms on his thighs, hands clasped, and leaned close to her.

Ellie forced her eyes away. She couldn't sit there and stare at them, could she? But, good heavens, there was something powerful between these two people. Another sentimental tune glided from the bandshell. Bordering the park, mounds of lilacs, yellow honeysuckle, and magenta English roses lent their sensuous scents to the ambience. The darkening sky provided a dramatic backdrop for the flaming colors of tonight's sunset. Lightning bugs performed a free-form dance, their tiny amber flashlights flicking on and off at hypnotic intervals.

Ellie's survey of the setting included periodic, inescapable glances at her aunt and James. Who else could this man be but James? The only man who could induce this reaction from Lillian Blaylock. He spoke in earnest, she responded gently, a mutual secret, it seemed, having been roused from the past and silently conveyed between them. The two shared an outright aura and emotion so strong that it remained after all the years. A wave of melancholy swelling in Ellie's chest nudged tears into her eyes.

After the orchestra played its last note and the conductor bid the audience goodnight, James stood and gathered Aunt Lillian to her feet, then seemed to say farewell with a touch of his lips to her forehead and a tender but heart-crushing embrace. As he led her back toward the seating area, Ellie stood and worked her way toward them.

A fragile smile curved Aunt Lillian's lips when she spotted Ellie. "James, this is my niece, Eleanor Todd. Eleanor, this is…this is an old friend, James Farlow."

"It's very nice meeting you, Mr. Farlow." Had that come out a bit too enthusiastic?

"James, please." He tipped his hat and leaned to kiss Ellie's hand. "My pleasure, Eleanor."

With his height, silver hair, and the tailored, light-colored linen suit he wore with a silk necktie, his allure was powerful.

"It was wonderful seeing you, James." When Aunt

Lillian slipped her arm from the crook of James's elbow, her foothold seemed tremulous and her green eyes brimmed with pure grief.

Ellie took hold of her arm. "Would you like to sit for a while, Aunt Lillian?"

She shook her head. "If you don't mind, may we head home?"

Ellie nodded, then looked away as James took her aunt's hands and bid her a whispered goodbye.

On their way home, Ellie didn't ask a thing, and aside from quiet small talk, her aunt offered no words.

****

With a rivulet of light separating the curtain panels and making its way to Ellie's eyelids, she awoke earlier than she would have wanted the next morning. After flipping and plumping her pillow, she dropped her head back onto it. She stretched, rearranged the covers, and burrowed under them. Never having been one to spring out of bed at the moment of awakening, she usually needed a bit of time to shake off the inertia. After a few minutes, she emerged from bed, shuffled across the floor to the French doors, and stepped onto the balcony. Overhead, swirls of baby-blue and yellow preceded the sun's debut. The water below hosted a few boats, their lights glowing through the low mist of dawn on the river.

Ellie's eyes went to the place where the river wound around the bend, into the horizon. If only she had a telescope like Uncle Edward had, only with a periscope feature, to twist and turn and provide views all the way down the Ohio and beyond to the Mississippi, to see if Wyatt was on his way. Had he remembered? And if he had, would he show up on the bridge this afternoon? Four months had passed. If he did come, would the same feeling be there, for both of them? Or would the passing of time have diluted the initial intoxication? Ellie's gaze moved to Harmar Bridge. Her stomach or heart, she wasn't sure which, tumbled and rolled, nearly bursting with anxiety or excitement, she wasn't sure which. So much for not getting too worked up.

Only the hum of the house's systems and the creaking of floorboards accompanied the sounds of Ellie's morning routine. Aunt Lillian and Hanne had left early for a Depression relief committee meeting in Marietta. After throwing on a cotton dress, Ellie pulled her straw cloche hat over her droopy hair. She hadn't mustered enough interest to marcel it since coming to Marietta, and it was covered by a hat anytime she went out, anyway. After squeezing out a glass of orange juice and downing it, she went for a walk on Harmar Hill.

Another hot day. A neighborhood man greeted Ellie, his dog sniffing toward her until tugged back by its master. Across the street, a teenaged boy tossed the daily newspaper onto, or at least toward, one porch after another. Harmar Hill brimmed with large, old houses wrapped in spindle-trimmed porches and graced with beveled windows and rich histories. Many of the homes had been built by investors who made a fortune when oil was found shortly before the Civil War broke out. No doubt, some of these houses harbored the memories of broken hearts, while others had played supporting roles in realized dreams. Having grown up in Columbus, then having lived for many years in or near one of the world's most vibrant cities, Ellie had always felt well suited to the urban life. But inhabiting one of these lovely, old houses would be quite amazing.

After a bath and some breakfast, Ellie chose a book

from Uncle Edward's library and headed for the sitting room. She had intended to browse the shops of Marietta before going to meet Wyatt, but today's humidity prompted her to cage herself inside for as long as possible. She tried to supplant wondering whether Wyatt would show up with the book and a glass of iced tea. But when she could no longer absorb a sentence without reading it three times, she clapped the book shut and went to see Charlene at the store. Her friend's tranquil nature would help calm the tempest going on inside her.

Several minutes later, Ellie's jaw dropped open as she shut the door of the five-and-dime behind her. "Deb! Furthermore, Deb holding a box of paper dolls! What on earth?"

"I know, me with dolls. Something you never thought you'd see, right? Hell has frozen over." Deb placed the box on a shelf.

"Hi, Ellie. Deb is helping stock the shelves." Charlene finished breaking down a cardboard carton.

"Isn't this the day you're meeting that river guy?" Deb asked.

"In a few minutes. If he shows up."

"He'll be there," Charlene said.

"When did you get into the paper doll business, Deb?" Ellie grabbed a carton and began breaking it down.

"It's my day off." Deb shrugged. "What else do I have to do?"

"She's been helping me for a while now," Charlene said. "Ever since she and…" Charlene's hand went to her mouth.

"Say it," Deb said. "Ever since Vinnie and I split. It's no big deal. It's not like I'm pining away for the guy or anything."

"I had no idea you helped out here." Ellie patted Deb on the back. "How sweet of you."

"Please. Sweet?" Deb rolled her eyes.

"Well, I just popped in to say hello. It's almost four. I guess I'll head over to the bridge."

"Go meet your man," Charlene said. "And phone me tomorrow with all the details."

Chapter Twelve

Ellie scaled the steps of Harmar Bridge. Neither Wyatt nor his tow were anywhere to be seen, but there was plenty to entertain her eyes as she leaned against the railing during her wait. A constant convoy of motorcars and trailer trucks crisscrossed the distant, towering Williamstown Bridge. The sleepy silver-blue river sparkled in the afternoon sun, and a lone motorboat cruised beneath Harmar Bridge and glided on its way, animated voices and laughter trailing from it. Only a couple of pedestrians crossed the bridge. Even though the economy was easing a bit, people still shopped primarily only for necessities, most of which were found in Marietta. Hopefully the restaurants and quaint specialty shops of Harmar Village would continue holding on for dear life.

Ellie had borrowed an antique hair comb, gold and pewter inlaid with mother-of-pearl, from Aunt Lillian to tuck low into the side of her waved hair, where it peeked from beneath her straw cloche. A breeze billowed through her plain, A-line dress with its dreadfully out-of-date baby-doll collar, its turquoise fabric having faded to seafoam green. If only the wind would blow the darned thing away and whisk a more fashionable dress in and drop it over her head. One of those lovely, slender, bias-cut numbers.

Several minutes later, Ellie checked the time. Nearly

four-thirty. *He's coming all the way from the Gulf of Mexico. Give the man a break.* She ambled across the bridge, then back.

"Well, that's that," she said as five *dong*s of the courthouse clock reverberated through the treetops. She turned and made her way with lengthy, heavy paces back across the bridge. A feverish flush arose from her chest and washed over her face. What an idiot she'd been to think those few hours with some random man meant anything, that he would remember her or care about his promise. He was a smooth talker who collected women all up and down the river, and he was a cad to have not shown up. Obviously a man of no integrity. As Ellie hurtled down the steps from the bridge, a lovely white gull swooped near, then fluttered away downstream and disappeared around the bend.

****

"I'll be back in the spring to help with the last-minute preparations for the gala. Will that be all right?"

Except for the past few lean years, Ellie had visited Marietta nearly every autumn of her life, when the leaves of the valley's oak, maple, and cypress trees displayed the warm spectrum of the color wheel. But now, coming back that soon held no appeal. She just wanted to fling herself back to the reassuring hum of Chicago, where the river bore no resemblance to this one and prompted no reminder of *him*.

"You come anytime you want, darling," Aunt Lillian said. "This is always your home. You know that."

"It's always difficult leaving this place. This house, Marietta, most of all you. But…" Ellie shrugged.

Aunt Lillian patted Ellie's cheek and lowered herself to the brocade bench at the foot of Ellie's bed.

"He didn't show up yesterday, did he?"

After Ellie left the bridge yesterday, she'd lumbered along the riverside pathway for a bitter while. In case he showed up? To recover from the disappointment? Heck, she didn't know. She had simply walked, her heart leaden, her mind in neutral. And when she returned home, she'd grabbed a glass of water, told Aunt Lillian she wasn't hungry, and bolted upstairs.

Ellie finished flinging clothes into her suitcase. The mattress springs yelped when she lobbed herself onto the bed and dropped her forehead into her hands.

"No, he didn't show up."

"You're disappointed, of course," Aunt Lillian said. "And you may never know the reason he didn't come. If you do one day learn why, it will be either a good reason or a lousy excuse. And it may be because of something you'd rather not have known about." She nudged a lock of Ellie's blonde hair aside. "Whatever the case, you will be fine."

Ellie appreciated not being subjected to the usual well-meaning platitudes that other people might offer in such a situation. *I'm sure he'll come back. It's his loss.* Those things wouldn't be true, anyway. If the man had wanted to see her, he would have made sure to be there. Ellie's aunt knew how to comfort in a healthy way, without sugar-coating the issue.

Ellie nodded. "I know I'll be fine. It was very disappointing, but the fact is he wasn't there and my life won't include him," she said with a shrug. She inched herself off the bed and went to peer out the French doors for about the hundredth time this morning. Why? To see if Wyatt's tow was docked down there somewhere? To revisit the scene of the humiliation?

"And it isn't even so much that some guy stood me up. I mean, I really liked him, but jeez, I barely knew the man. It's just that I felt, when I met him and let myself hope to see him again, I felt as if that was some progress in moving on with my life. Like it was a positive step in figuring out what my life might look like." Ellie turned back toward her aunt. "But just because he wasn't one of my three stars doesn't mean someone else can't be."

"I admire your attitude, Eleanor."

"You inspired my attitude, about a lot of things. Do you know that?" Ellie returned and flung herself back onto the bed. "Aunt Lillian, I want to be you when I grow up."

Their laughter mingled in a beam of sunlight slashing across Ellie's bedroom.

Aunt Lillian stood and clapped her hands together. "Are you ready to go to lunch, dear?"

"Mm-hmm. But may I ask you something first? Something personal?"

"Of course." Aunt Lillian folded her arms and focused on her niece.

"It's not my business, but I wondered…" Ellie grazed a hand over the swirly pattern of the plush chenille bedspread. "I just wondered, do you plan to see Mr. Farlow again? The two of you seem to have quite a connection, and he seems very nice."

Aunt Lillian hadn't mentioned James since they'd seen him that evening in Parkersburg, and Ellie had resisted bringing him up. But now that she was leaving, she just had to say something, for her aunt's sake. She and James obviously belonged together. Why weren't they together?

Aunt Lillian smiled sweetly. "No. I won't be seeing

James again."

"But... I'm sorry. It's none of my business. I just want you to be happy."

"I am happy, but my days with James are in the past. It wasn't meant to last any longer than it did."

"Hey, you two, come." Hanne's voice carried up the stairs. "I am starving, and the restaurant will give away our table if we don't get going."

Aunt Lillian took Ellie's hand and led her toward the doorway, then paused. "Thank you for caring so much, dear. James is a very good, very special man. But things are as they should be. Now let's go have a nice lunch."

****

Ellie's farewell fetes continued that evening. Her friends had planned one last gathering of the summer, after-dinner drinks on the patio of the Levee House.

"It doesn't matter," Ellie said.

"Well, it's pretty crummy of him to stand you up and not call you or anything."

"I told you, Deb, he didn't have my telephone number. Bottom line, the man didn't want to come back. Or he forgot. Either way, it doesn't matter. It's in the past. Can we stop talking about it now?"

The sinking sun cast platinum beams over the valley like searchlights at a Hollywood moving picture premiere. The river rippled and blushed in reflected shades of rose and amethyst. As evening turned into dusk, the glow of turquoise and lime-green bulbs strung around the striped patio awning intensified. Ruby arrived with a tray bearing stemware and two bottles of wine. On an evening like this, Ellie couldn't feel too down. Things didn't get much better than throwing on a cool dress and meeting your gal pals for drinks along the river on a warm summer night.

"I'm sure he had a good reason for not being there," Charlene said. "And he would have contacted you if he could have."

Ellie smiled at sweet Charlene, always so optimistic.

"Hmph. I guess he wasn't the perfect guy you thought he was." Anita's mouth curved into a grin as she lit up a cigarette.

"Pretty sure I never said he was perfect, Anita. I said he seemed nice and I wanted to see him again, that's all. The subject is now closed." Ellie filled her glass from the bottle of white wine at table center.

"Good old Anita. We can always count on you to be happy when someone else's love life is on the rocks," Deb said.

Anita shrugged and took a long drag from her cigarette.

Charlene raised her wine glass. "Here's to Ellie on her last night in town."

My last night in town. It's just as well.

Chapter Thirteen

"Finally, you're home."

"Betty?" Ellie flipped onto her back and rubbed her eyes.

"Did I wake you?"

"It's probably time I got up." Ellie forced open her eyes enough to see that the night hadn't yet completely surrendered to dawn.

"Listen, I'm really sorry I couldn't make it down to Marietta over the summer."

"I told you, no need to apologize. I know how busy you've been." Ellie stuffed the extra pillow beneath her head.

"Well, let's get together later this week. I want to hear all about your summer."

"Yes, of course. It was terrific. Lots of good times." Ellie stretched, making no attempt to get up and deprive herself of her warm bed. She'd gotten home late last night, having stayed and talked with Aunt Lillian and Hanne longer than she'd intended. She always had a tough time tearing herself away from the two of them.

"You don't have plans for Saturday, do you?" Betty always rapid-fired her words, but where did the woman get her energy so early in the morning?

"Well-let-me-check-my-social-calendar-no-amazingly-Saturday-is-wide-open," Ellie replied in nearly one syllable. "Why?"

"Gregory Barnes wants to take you to dinner, along with Sam and me. You'll go, right?"

The suggestion of dating landed with a thud in Ellie's chest. Her one attempt had been a major fail. "Ugh. Come on, Betty, I already told you—"

"Just tell me why not."

"I have a lot of catching up to do. I was gone all summer, remember? And who's Sam?"

"You have all the time in the world to catch up with things. I'm talking Gregory Barnes here. You know, the handsome, rich, intelligent hunk? He keeps asking about you."

Ellie pushed herself upright and propped the pillows against the wrought-iron headboard. "What happened to Brian? And who's Sam?"

"Some guy. Are you even listening to what I'm saying?"

"So how was your summer, Betty?"

"Come on, Ellie. You have completely eradicated the effects of the divorce. Why won't you give this an opportunity?"

"I am not going out with Gregory Barnes or anyone else right now." Ellie enunciated each word.

"Hmph. Okay, I won't say another word about it. Phone me later."

Ellie plunked the bell-shaped receiver back on its hook, then parted the slats of the plantation shutters behind her bed. The brightening sky promised a sunny day. *Why? What was the point?* Rain would better match her mood.

During the next several weeks, Ellie worked on the stained-glass project and devoted time to designing a new riverboat panel to give to Aunt Lillian for

Christmas. This panel would be of the *Anne*, a riverboat launched in New Orleans in the nineteenth century and named for Anne of Brittany, who became queen consort of France in the fifteenth century. Ellie had laid out the design and selected the glass, including the perfect shade of Provincial blue for the boat's upper quarter.

She also spent way too much time thinking of Wyatt, in spite of efforts to barricade him from her mind. That day on the bridge with him seemed surreal now. Meeting her had meant nothing to him. No doubt, he'd moved promptly on to the next woman, the way his towboat moved from port to port. Darn it, why did that man infiltrate her mind like this?

"It's about time you came to your senses," Betty said when Ellie telephoned her a couple weeks later saying she would go out with Gregory Barnes if he was still interested. "What changed your mind?"

"Fall is almost over, I'll be housebound most of the winter, working on that big project. I just woke up this morning in the mood to go out." And maybe she could finally push what's-his-name completely from her mind.

On Saturday evening, Betty and Sam picked up Ellie for the drive to the Oak Park restaurant where they would meet Gregory. Sam seemed like a good fellow, but so had Brian, and so had most of the men before him. How long would Sam last before being humanely but abruptly nudged out of Betty's orbit? Betty had never married, had never wanted to. Although her supply of men to date seemed endless, she was self-sufficient to the point that a man constantly in her life would be more a hindrance than a pleasure.

Ellie laughed throughout the evening and appreciated the stimulating conversation, not to mention the restaurant meal, a rarity these days. Gregory's vital dark eyes and energetic personality implied something interesting always going on around him. And had he been this strikingly handsome when she'd first met him? Dark, wavy auburn hair and spiffy in his wide-shouldered, double-breasted suit and sapphire-blue necktie.

"For a while there, I thought we would end up married, but I couldn't get past her suspicious nature and her moodiness," Gregory told Ellie. "I ended things with her several months ago."

The four of them had decided on a stroll through downtown Oak Park after dinner. Betty and Sam had dropped farther and farther behind, on purpose, Ellie knew.

"I'm sorry. I'm aware that talking about another woman on a first date is ill advised."

Ellie laughed. "I suppose it's good to know a little bit about each other's sordid pasts."

"A little, yes. But you're the only woman I want to talk about now." A biting breeze whooshed at them. "Are you cold?" He made a move to extend an arm around her.

Ellie found herself leaning away. "I'm fine, thank you." Gregory was attractive and fun, but she didn't want his arm around her. This was not about romance, only an evening out.

"Well, I want to hear more about you. Tell me everything." Gregory made a person feel like his priority.

Ellie provided a brief rundown of her life and her career. He seemed to hear and process every word she said, expressing interest, asking questions. A nice feeling. And it really felt good to get out and socialize.

Back at Sam's car later, Gregory touched his lips to

one side of Ellie's face, then the other. "May I phone you?"

"I enjoyed myself very much. But I'm not looking for anything serious."

Why wasn't she more interested in him? After all, she'd realized that night in bed after The Lou-Easy Incident that she wanted a man in her life, and Gregory seemed like a terrific person. Had she shut down emotionally after the Wyatt episode? How pathetic if that were the case. She'd barely known the man.

"Then we'll simply spend some time together here and there," Gregory said. "We'll have a little fun."

That seemed reasonable, getting together once in a while, no expectations. "All right," she said with a smile.

Soon, that *here and there* evolved into once a week, for dinner, dancing at a ballroom, a motion picture. Their only area of conflict was Gregory's push to see her more often and his desire to be alone with her.

"I don't understand it, Ellie," he said one evening. "You can't ever invite me in?"

Ellie unlocked her door. She'd had a nice time, as usual, but her warm flannel nightgown beckoned, and how good it would feel, with the air hinting at winter.

"I enjoy our time together, Gregory. You know that. But I told you from the start I don't want anything serious."

"I take you out all the time. I'd think you'd feel compelled to at least let me past your front door. And heaven forbid you step inside my apartment."

"It isn't about reciprocating, Gregory. This is what I'm comfortable with right now."

"What about what *I'm* comfortable with?" Gregory swung his arms wide.

"I think we *both* need to feel right about how things are going, don't you?"

"You're right," he said. "I'm sorry."

But before long, she did invite him over. He'd been patient and shown his devotion these past few weeks. Maybe she shouldn't keep holding him at arm's length. Why not let it develop and see where it went? So she cooked a nice dinner and baked a pumpkin pie.

"You know I really care for you, don't you?" Gregory pulled her closer on the sofa after dinner and kissed her. He pushed her hair back, his lips moved to her neck.

The kisses and the want deepened. It had been so long since Mason's touch. Would it be so awful if she were to go all the way?

Gregory's kiss hardened and he pressed into her, nudging her backward until her head rested against the arm roll of the couch. "You're so sexy, baby. Tell me you want it."

The stubble of his face clawed at her skin. His body pressed into hers, his knee bore into her thigh, pinning her to the sofa.

"Ouch. Gregory, ow!"

He pulled back. "What's wrong?"

"Your knee was digging into my leg."

"I'm sorry. I didn't realize." He leaned down again, kissing her, pushing against her. "I've waited so long for this," he whispered. "Damn, doll-face, I want you." His lips dominated hers. He pressed harder, his face smashed into hers, his full weight crushing onto her chest.

"Gregory. Gregory, stop."

"Now what's wrong?"

"I can't breathe. I can't move."

He hoisted himself up, then jumped to his feet and ran a hand through his hair.

Ellie sat up. "Maybe I'm not ready for this."

"Not ready? Christ." He paced the floor, then turned back to her. "You seemed ready a minute ago."

"It was just too much. I'm sorry."

Had it been so long that she'd become timid? Or was Gregory's style overly aggressive? All she knew was she'd felt trapped, claustrophobic, dominated.

"Well if *that* was too much, I hate to imagine how you'd react if we actually did something." He propped his hands on his hips. "Look, I'll talk to you later." He grabbed his automobile key from the side table and headed for the foyer. "Sorry if I came on too strong. I'll phone you before I hit the sheets."

But he didn't call that night, nor during the following week and a half. Then a dozen red roses arrived, along with a card. *I'm sorry I was a (insert derogatory sobriquet here). I promise a kinder, gentler Gregory next time. Please let there be a next time.*

Maybe she'd overreacted that night. She couldn't blame him for his frustration at her holding him at arm's length for weeks, then rejecting him when things finally heated up. Next time she would do better.

Chapter Fourteen

"Why can't you see me this weekend?"

"Gregory, what are you doing here?" Ellie's arms shot up to cover her hair, still tightly rolled in curlers.

"What do you have going on this weekend, that you can't see me?" Gregory stepped into her foyer and gave the door a swing behind him.

Ellie flinched at the slamming of the door. "I just want to stay in, get some things done around the house."

"Well, do them during the week." He pinned her with a piercing stare. "I don't get it, Ellie. We used to see each other every weekend."

They *had* been seeing each other every weekend, before the episode on the sofa, but although he'd apologized with the roses, she simply couldn't dredge up any interest in seeing him again so soon. Things had probably moved too fast with them. So when he phoned this morning to ask if he could see her this weekend, she declined with profuse apologies, and now he'd appeared at her door barely after hanging up on her.

She went to the foyer closet, fished out a chiffon scarf, and tied it around her chin. "I'm sorry. I've been very busy with the stained-glass projects, and it's going to be freezing out. I just want to stay in."

"Then I'll come here." He removed his trench coat and flung it onto a chair. "We'll listen to a radio show, have a little wine."

"Gregory, please." Ellie headed toward the kitchen. "Would you like a cup of coffee?"

"Dammit, Ellie, what am I supposed to do this weekend?" He followed her, pacing the kitchen floor, running a hand through his hair.

Ellie began filling the teakettle with water. "I don't want to argue about this. Please respect my wishes and don't give me a hard time when I say I can't see you."

"You're my girl, aren't you?" He came up behind her at the sink, wrapped his arms around her, and pressed into her. Tell me you're my girl."

"Yes…yes, of course."

He kissed her neck and ran his hands over her hips. "You're one beautiful dame, you know that? Some fine curves, great pair of gams. Say you'll see me this weekend. Come on, baby, say it."

His wanting her so intensely would have felt good were it not approaching a possessive level. She twisted out of his grip and turned to face him. "I care for you, Gregory, but I—"

"But you don't want to be with me this weekend. Fine, Ellie. That's fine with me. You have your precious weekend alone, and I'll find something else to do." He headed for the foyer, with Ellie following.

"I'm sorry. How about I make dinner for you next weekend, and—"

"Next weekend," he spat. "Have a nice day, Ellie." After grabbing his trench coat, he fumbled with the door. "How the hell do you open this thing? Damned ancient house."

Ellie reached around him and unlatched the door.

Gregory flung the door open, swinging it directly into Ellie's forehead.

"Ow." Her hand went to her head.

He ignored the collision and her cry of pain. "See you whenever."

"Gregory?"

"What?" He turned, his livid gaze boring through her eyes.

"You hit me with the door. You hurt my head." She rubbed her forehead.

"You're not hurt." He turned back toward the door.

"Are you kidding me?"

"I'm sorry, all right?" He'd barely lobbed the words over his shoulder before making his vexed exit.

****

Four stained-glass panels lay on the padded surface of the table in Ellie's workshop. After sliding her fingers into thin plastic gloves, she brushed a mixture of linseed and bleach onto one panel's crumbled putty, which had begun losing its grip on the colorful pieces of glass. She had become intrigued by the beauty of stained glass in her studies as an art major in college, and after reading a nineteenth-century artist's description of *the art and the lure of stained glass*, she was hooked. Then, during spring break of her senior year, she'd tagged along with a friend to visit her family in Chicago. The moment they stepped off the bus, newsboys shoved copies of *The Chicago Daily Tribune* in their faces, yelling "extra, extra, read all about it," and Ellie and her friend had gasped at the gigantic headline. *LUXURY LINER TITANIC SINKS ON MAIDEN VOYAGE; 1300 DROWNED; 866 SAVED*

Amid the constant radio coverage and daily newspaper headlines screaming out shocking developments related to the tragedy, Ellie and her pal allowed themselves scraps of respite from the heartbreak. Late one morning, they visited the city's Cultural Center, where Ellie feasted her eyes on the largest Tiffany stained-glass dome in the world, the midday sun illuminating it to glorious magnificence. And it seemed that everywhere she went in the city, windows gleamed with the deeply-hued artwork, so she decided then and there to move to Chicago after graduation.

And now she was doing the work she loved. After the four forty-two-inch-by-twelve-inch sidelights flanking the main doors of the church were removed, they'd been delivered to the workroom in the rear of Ellie's home.

Over the years, putty that sealed glass to its lead caming could become brittle and crumble away, allowing air and moisture to weaken the caming and compromise the glass. In addition, over the years, these panels had suffered cracked and chipped glass. Ellie's job was not only to structurally repair these pieces, but to restore their appearance. She waited an hour before applying another coat of the linseed oil and bleach mixture, then waited twenty-four more hours. When the putty became supple, she scraped it away and wiped the panel with a soft cloth dampened with solvent to remove the excess putty. She then mixed glazing putty, linseed oil, and lamp black to the consistency of molasses and brushed it onto the window, pushing it into the caming then cleaned away the excess. The new putty would need several hours to set.

Turning her attention to the damaged glass, she tapped and pulled away the broken pieces with pliers and a lightweight miniature hammer. She always salvaged a the glass she could, for repairing other panels and creating new pieces. The beautiful remnants, no matter how small, were too beautiful, too valuable to discard. Ellie then raised the panel by sliding small blocks of wood under its perimeter. Next, she donned her respirator—which she always thought made her look like a distant cousin of the platypus—and her safety glasses and proceeded to melt the caming with a soldering iron. This involved quick work to avoid overheating the glass.

She then removed the blocks of wood and lowered the panel back to the padded surface before sliding a thin sheet of wood, topped by a piece of white paper, beneath the panel. Using a sharp pencil, she traced the outline of the missing piece of glass and cut out the shape. She traced the shape onto the new glass she'd chosen to match the original, in color and texture, as closely as possible. After scoring the shape with a razor, she used her glass cutters to snap and nip the glass into shape before calling it quits for the evening.

Resuming her work the following day, Ellie wrapped the edges of the glass in copper foil, then brushed flux onto the edges of the panel where the glass would be installed. The flux would help bond the solder wire with the foil. She then steadily soldered the replacement piece into the panel with a length of solder wire clipped from its spool. For each damaged piece of glass, Ellie would repeat the process, seemingly a never-ending task. During the next weeks, she labored each day for hour upon hour, scoring, then snipping at glass, then grinding and polishing the edges of each piece smooth and soldering it in place. She then would turn over the panel and solder the reverse side of each new piece.

When she finally finished the panels, she followed

up with two types of cleansers on the entire panel, then applied patina to age the solder to match the old caming as closely as possible. Finally, another cleaning and a coat of wax to seal and protect the lead, a good buffing, and the pieces were finished. What joy and pride Ellie took in the refurbished panels, their caming smooth and strong, the purple, gold, emerald, and magenta glass once again luminous. The glorious pieces would endure for many more decades.

****

Benny and Jessie both had come home for Christmas, and Ellie's parents flew up from their Naples, Florida, home a few days later. Ellie had invited Aunt Lillian and Hanne, but her aunt had said she felt tired—not something Ellie had heard from her aunt very often—and opted to stay home. So Ellie sent her aunt's completed stained-glass panel with her parents when they left to spend some time with Aunt Lillian before returning to Naples, and her aunt had declared it the loveliest panel yet when she phoned to thank Ellie.

Ellie had also agreed a couple of weeks before Christmas to see Gregory again, having told him after his nocuous departure several weeks ago that she thought it best that they take a break. Not only had she been dismayed at his insensitivity after he flung the door into her head—unintentional as it may have been—she'd craved respite from his intensity, from his demands. She hadn't been sure she wanted to see him again at all. Was his pushing for more from her something to be expected? Had she been unreasonably standoffish with him? She certainly had very little experience with dating. A break would give her time to think, she'd figured. Of course, he hadn't taken the notion well and never ceased pursuing her. Over the weeks, though, his aggressive implorations had softened into tender pleas, and Ellie finally gave in after a candid conversation with him on her expectations for more considerate treatment going forward.

At the first sign of spring, she deemed the weather stable enough to make the drive back to Marietta. Gregory didn't hide his annoyance when she told him she would be gone for two weeks. According to him, she was abandoning him. Since she'd taken him back, he seemed to have reined in his harshness, interacting with her in a more mellow, more sensitive manner. He'd even let up on the physical advances. She simply was not ready for that level of involvement and had made that clear in their December discussion. But after his hostile reaction to her pending trip, she couldn't wait to leave for Marietta.

The day before her trip, the ringing telephone interrupted her packing.

"Eleanor?" The feeble voice quivered.

Chapter Fifteen

"Oh, Eleanor, your aunt… When I came downstairs I found her on the kitchen floor… I think she was passed out… I telephoned for an ambulance and…"

Ellie's thoughts swam. "Hanne, slow down, what happened? What's wrong with Aunt Lillian?"

"I don't know. She was just lying there." Hanne continued through sobs. "I don't know if she was breathing, she was so still, she was just—"

"Is she all right? Hanne, is she…" Ellie couldn't let herself consider the possibility of her aunt having died.

"They say she is stable, but I just don't know. They are not saying much. They are running tests. Oh, *mein*, Eleanor, I don't know what to think. They won't let me see her."

"Where is she, Hanne? Is she okay?" The chaos in Ellie's head surged to her stomach. She paced from her bedroom to the parlor, to the kitchen, back to the bedroom. The knot in her throat strangled the many questions she wanted to ask.

"She is in the hospital. Oh, missy, I know you were going to come down tomorrow, but you must come now."

"Yes. Yes, I'll come right away."

"I am telling you what, Eleanor, I don't know what I will do if—"

"Hanne, don't worry about a thing. I'll be there as

soon as I can."

****

At Ellie's first glimpse of the Ohio River that evening, she steeled herself against memories of that one pointless day with Wyatt. But who cared? She had more important things to think about. Aunt Lillian's big yellow mansion on Harmar Hill soon came into view. How different the house and all of Marietta would feel, bleak and soulless, if something were to happen to her aunt.

Hanne leapt from her chair at the side of Aunt Lillian's bed and rushed to Ellie as soon as she stepped into the hospital room.

"Eleanor!" She clutched Ellie in her arms. "Thank the good Lord you are here."

Ellie gave Hanne a squeeze, then approached her sleeping aunt, clothed in a faded blue hospital gown that did not suit her at all. Ellie had never seen her in anything but sleek, satiny dresses in watercolor shades like peach and rose and platinum, accented by swags of luminous pearls.

"How is she? What happened?"

"They say she had a mild heart attack. They are waiting for some test results. They say her heart is stable now, her blood pressure has lowered. They gave her some pills to sleep."

Ellie leaned close to her aunt. A gray pallor dulled her skin, and was her breathing shallower than it should be? A glance at the chart hanging on the wall above the metal bed told Ellie nothing. The numbers were difficult to discern, and she wouldn't have known what was normal and what wasn't anyway. She would look them up in a volume of Uncle Edward's encyclopedias later.

"You know, she told me around Christmas time that she felt unusually tired. I don't think I'd ever before heard her even hint at being tired." Ellie slipped off her gloves, then removed her hat and placed them on the side table. "I should have told her to see a doctor then."

"I think she was working too hard, with the gala and everything," Hanne said. "Oh, I cannot believe this is happening. A heart attack. How can that be? She has never been in the hospital, not one day of her life, and she always took such good care of herself." Hanne removed her round, black spectacles and pressed at her eyes with the heels of her hands. "Oh, Eleanor, I just don't know—"

"It's all right. She's going to be fine. Here, sit. You look exhausted." Ellie led her back to her chair, as much for Hanne's benefit as for Ellie's sanity. "Have you had anything to eat today?"

"Oh I cannot think about eating." Hanne dismissed the notion with a wave of a hand. Her forehead crinkled, her fingers kneaded the beads of her necklace. Poor thing, she looked so haggard, even in her buttercup-yellow dress with its lacy white collar.

"She has been sleeping for about one hour this time, but it is a miracle anyone can sleep with all the racket going on in this place." Hanne jumped to her feet again, worry lines crinkling her forehead. "I am telling you what, if that witch of a nurse comes in here banging things around one more time, she will hear from me." Hanne's arms flailed in rhythm with her pacing.

"Who? Hanne, what happened?"

"That nurse. I tell her please to be quiet, she says she must get her work done. Horsefeathers! She does not give a damn how much noise she makes."

Ellie's eyes widened. She'd never heard Hanne use such language. "It'll be alright. I'll have a talk with her. And I'm going to take over the gala planning. We'll make Aunt Lillian rest. We'll take care of her. She's going to be fine."

"Yes, yes, she will be fine." Hanne stepped to her friend's bedside and took her hand in her own.

"Hanne, why don't you go on home and get some rest? Here." Ellie fished in her pocketbook for a few coins and handed them to Hanne. "The receptionist downstairs will phone a taxicab for you."

Once Hanne begrudgingly left, Ellie used the bedside telephone, reversing the charges, to tell her father about his sister's heart attack. He and Ellie's mother would try to book flights and be there tomorrow, he said before hanging up. Ellie sat at her aunt's side until she could no longer keep her eyes open.

Two days later, Aunt Lillian was released from the hospital. The cardiologist had said the tests revealed a minor blockage and believed the heart attack was due to that. He felt confident that, with medication to alleviate the blockage and more diligent attention to rest, Aunt Lillian could count on a full return to good health. To Ellie, she seemed as healthy as before, strong and vibrant.

After five days, Ellie's parents returned to Naples. Hanne and Ellie remained diligent, making sure Aunt Lillian didn't lift a finger in spite of her many attempts at cleaning up after meals, watering flowers, and making telephone calls about the gala. Always, one of them intervened, relieving her of whatever task she tried to take on.

Late afternoon nearly three weeks later, Ellie sank

into a chaise on the patio and brought her glass of wine to her lips. Far downstream, the sun would soon sink beneath the water. River traffic used to flow heavily this time of year, not only with towboats but also with private motorboats, houseboats, and canoes. But the economic downturn had left the rivers mostly to the commercial vessels. Because Aunt Lillian's house stood too high for any sounds but the occasional marine horn to reach it, the craft seemed to drift in silence, and their headlights created a horizontal, water-colored display on the rippling water. Further upstream, the *Valley Gem* sternwheeler bobbed forsakenly at its dock, its tourist runs stilled. Before 1929, it could be spotted at any given time, puffing its way downstream, filled to capacity with tourists looking to enter some vortex of time, to be carried back to the era of hooped skirts and showboats and gamblers named *Black Jack*.

Darned river. Would it ever cease to remind her of Wyatt? She pictured his face and what she'd taken for sincerity in his eyes, then banished the image. Why was she still thinking about that man? Thankfully she'd be leaving for home in a couple days. Maybe there she'd be able to finally and completely purge him from her mind.

The double French doors of the house swung open, and Aunt Lillian appeared, carrying a tray bearing two plates of something that smelled divine. After placing the tray on a small table, she lowered herself onto the chaise next to Ellie's.

"Is that bee-sting cake? Oh, my goodness," Ellie said. "Thank you, but you should not be serving me." She luxuriated in her first taste, appreciating the way Hanne always overfilled the two cake layers with the creamiest pudding in the world, and the confection was topped with caramelized almonds. "How are you feeling, Aunt Lillian?"

"I'm feeling like shopping. I was hoping you, my darling, would go downtown with me tomorrow to find a gown for the gala." Aunt Lillian raised her face to the warm sun. Its lazy, late afternoon beams flitted through trees and across her cheekbones. "What do you say?"

"As long as you feel up to it, of course I'll take you." Her aunt looked good—vibrant and healthy. Her cheeks glowed with a rosy tint.

"I'm thinking something in a blush pink. It's always been my favorite color, you know." Aunt Lillian slipped a forkful of the cake into her mouth.

"You look beautiful in that color," Ellie said, "and you could wear your silver comb with the rubies."

After fluttering down from a nearby oak, a robin made a few exuberant skips across the patio. The long wail of a towboat horn surged across the valley. A breeze carried the scent of cherry blossoms from a nearby tree.

"Do you plan to bring Gregory to the gala?"

"Gregory? I don't know." Why hadn't she considered asking him to go with her? "I suppose it would be nice to have someone to dance with." Then, with a smile, "Don't you think so, Aunt Lillian?"

Aunt Lillian's eyes scanned the landscape. "The daffodils look brighter than usual this year." Her head rested against the cushion of the chaise, and she glanced at Ellie with a smile of her own. "You're referring to James."

"Seeing the two of you together that night at the bandshell was like a fairy tale. He seems to really care for you."

"James has always made his feelings for me clear.

And I do… I *did* love that man." Aunt Lillian stood and ambled across the patio. Her eyes squinted toward the peaked horizon, as if seeking images from the past. "He wrote to me many times afterward, after we parted all those years ago. And I wrote back, until the time your Uncle Edward came into my life." She shifted her eyes to Ellie's, shook her head, and raised a finger to emphasize her point. "James was not a man who would disrespect something like marriage. Then, after your uncle passed and James's wife passed two or three years after that, he began to write again."

"Wanting to see you."

Aunt Lillian nodded. "After several letters, I wrote back." She walked to another side of the patio and leaned to pull spent petals from a lavender crocus. "I told him I wished him well but that I was Mrs. Edward Blaylock. And that I couldn't see him."

"But…Uncle Edward was gone. Aunt Lillian, he's been gone almost ten years now."

"But I was his wife. I had my one marriage, ordained in the eyes of God."

Ellie had never seen such melancholy in anyone's eyes. Why did her aunt feel she couldn't be with James? Why this self-imposed separation from him?

"He still lives upriver, in New Matamoras." Aunt Lillian's eyes shifted to where the river curved upstream, around the bend. "When I saw him that evening, with you, I hadn't seen him since…since before your uncle and I married." Her chin trembled. "It was all such a long time ago."

Ellie went to her aunt and took her hand. "I'm sorry. I didn't mean to bring back sad memories for you."

"You didn't, my dear. My memories of James are

always with me." Aunt Lillian's lips pursed. "I know you don't understand why I feel the way I do. But Eleanor, I don't want you to ever lose your belief in love, your hope for love. Keep sight of that star, my dear. Keep sight of that love that I know will come your way soon."

"Alright." Ellie nodded. "I will."

"Promise me you will, and please understand that my situation was very different. James and I were never meant to be. Your Uncle Edward was the man in my life, my husband. And I was his, and only his, wife."

Ellie had taken so much inspiration from her aunt over the years. This was a woman of both boundless inquiry and serene contentment, a quality reflected onto Ellie with the intensity of sun flares but softened by consideration and utter adoration.

Aunt Lillian kissed Ellie's forehead. "I think I'll turn in." She reached for her plate.

"I'll get this." Ellie gathered the plates onto the tray. "Get some rest, Aunt Lillian. We'll have fun tomorrow, and we'll find the perfect pink gown for you."

"We'll leave after breakfast." Aunt Lillian placed another kiss on her niece's forehead. "Good night, dear."

"Good night. Aunt Lillian, may I ask you one more thing?"

Aunt Lillian smiled. "Certainly."

"Was he one of your three stars?"

Without hesitation, "Yes, he was." Aunt Lillian turned and slipped into the house.

And Ellie realized she hadn't made clear to which man she had referred.

Chapter Sixteen

The many visitors calling on the house on Harmar Hill glided like apparitions in Ellie's peripheral consciousness, their words of comfort and hugs of support falling on dulled senses. She wanted only to curl up in her aunt's settee in the sitting room. The world felt desolate, strewn with tumbleweeds blown about by desert winds. Even her parents, who came right away, could do little to soothe the deep wound.

After that last evening on the patio, Aunt Lillian had died in her sleep.

Benny and Jessie had arrived by bus as soon as they could. Deb and Charlene were permanent fixtures during those surreal days that seemed one long, dark night, and Anita came and went a couple times. Hanne managed to help Ellie and her parents plan the services and burial but mostly sat weeping at the table in the kitchen alcove. The speckled laminate table that had arrived at the house all those years ago with Aunt Lillian and Uncle Edward. The table that, despite its dulled chrome edges, nicks, and faded color, nobody had ever dreamed of replacing. The place where Hanne and her oldest, dearest friend had spent many hours over morning cups of tea and homemade pastries, talking, laughing, crying, sharing life. Now, Hanne slumped there with swollen eyes and a drenched handkerchief wadded in her clenched little fist.

The day before the funeral, Ellie drove downtown.

She needed to get away from the houseful of people. She needed some quiet time with Aunt Lillian, to talk to her, to tell her how much she had meant to her for her entire life. To say goodbye. But mostly, Ellie needed to keep her promise to Aunt Lillian. She needed to find the pink dress her aunt had wanted. Her final dress, but she would not be wearing it for the gala she'd worked so hard to plan.

As usual, Marietta brimmed with people. Ellie couldn't fathom their lightheartedness and envied them their routine business, which they went about as if nothing at all had happened. The sun shone but it didn't, robins sang but in sorrow. That the world proceeded as usual seemed a cruel betrayal.

The next morning, Ellie mopped at a ceaseless stream of tears and processed few of the minister's words. Something about Lillian Blaylock's spirit. Her many ways of contributing. Her legacy. The tender melodies and normally comforting lyrics of Aunt Lillian's favorite hymns were no match for Ellie's grief. Dozens of people crammed the pews, with Marv and his wife mourning from the row directly behind the family. The faithful Betty had arrived by train two days ago, and Gregory had driven down yesterday.

Aunt Lillian's exquisite face appeared luminescent against the beautiful blush pink silk dress. After Ellie blotted her tears with her handkerchief and leaned to kiss her aunt one last time, the funeral director approached, offered his final condolences to Ellie, and closed the casket.

The lapping river provided a steady soundtrack during the brief graveside service. The sprawling cemetery next to the river in the flatlands at the edge of town was as old as Marietta itself. Nearly as many trees as tombstones dotted the lawn, and Aunt Lillian's burial site was under the shade of one of the largest oaks.

Ellie averted her eyes at having spotted her aunt's name, which had long ago been inscribed on the headstone shared with her husband. Instead, she scanned the horizon, the skyline of Marietta, the train gliding along the tracks that ran parallel to the river like two strips of silver ribbon trimming a flowing blue gown. Ellie had always loved the sound of the distant train whistle at night, when the sigh of a sleepy breeze would take hold of the clear tenor of steam, twirl it about, and carry it high over the valley. From Aunt Lillian's home, Ellie would squint to make out the people silhouetted in the windows of the passenger trains, inching their way toward their destinies.

Ellie's family and close friends remained after the burial, clustering close to each other, hugging, exchanging words of support in low tones. The peppy Hanne had never been so still, so quiet. How sad to see her wearing bleak black, so oppressive to the vital little soul that on any other day expressed itself with a splash of red, purple, or lime green.

Ellie knelt and touched the cool, freshly turned soil that lay between her and Aunt Lillian. Inconceivably, this six-foot patch of crumbled dirt next to the river was the only place now where she would ever be able to visit her aunt, and the realization drove another dagger into her heart. She pulled a few pink roses from the arrangement that had been placed at the foot of the headstone, but their scent provided little of their intended comfort. Seeming to prod her that it was time to go, a breeze caressed Ellie's face. She forced out a last goodbye, then turned to walk away, trailing the others, who climbed into the funeral home's black motorcars. Before stepping in herself, Ellie turned for one more look at her aunt's grave. And there he stood.

Ellie had wondered if he would know she was gone. She'd wanted to notify him but wasn't sure if she should involve herself in this most private, and certainly painful, aspect of his life. But he was here now. Of course he had somehow known that his Lillian had passed.

Removing his black fedora, he moved close to the burial site and lowered his head.

Ellie needed to say something to him, to connect with him on this day of shared loss. After taking a few steps toward him, she stopped herself. He needed this time with the woman he had loved for nearly his entire life. Ellie waited, watching.

James's head dropped back, his eyes focused far away, as if searching the heavens for his Lillie. More than once, he appeared to wipe away tears. He stood firm where his love now lay, not wanting to walk away or maybe not being able to. After raising a small cluster of flowers to his nose, he leaned and placed them on the base of the stone. His shoulders heaved in what seemed a final, deep sigh. When he turned away, his eyes met Ellie's, and his lips curved into a scant smile.

Ellie swiped at her wet face and went to him.

"I'm so sorry, Eleanor. She was a very special lady." His red-rimmed eyes were kind but shrouded by profound grief.

"Thank you, James. She was the most wonderful aunt. She was my best friend. She was everything. There was nobody else like her." Ellie looked at the flowers James had left at the marker. "Lilies of the valley. Her favorite."

"I always called her my Lillie of the valley." He returned his hat to his head, then tipped it to Ellie. "Take care, Eleanor." He managed a few steps, then turned back. "I loved her. Very much."

Ellie nodded. Then, through tears, "She loved you too."

Should she have let that slip? Was it a betrayal of her aunt?

He nodded. "I shouldn't have taken no for an answer."

What beautiful, sincere brown eyes, set in a face that attested to a long, full life well lived. How could Aunt Lillian have kept from this man all those years?

"Mr. Farlow, why…" Ellie stopped herself. She would not contribute to the many agonizing *what-if*s James likely already dealt with. She pulled a pink rose from the quasi bouquet in her hand and extended it.

He took the blossom, winked at Ellie, and walked away. And he and his Lillie were gone forever from each other's lives.

****

By late afternoon, Hanne had retreated to her room and Ellie's friends had departed or busied themselves elsewhere in the house so Ellie and her family could be alone together. Clustering around the kitchen table, they gratefully sipped strong coffee and picked at cookies and pies brought by friends in the preceding days, and the topic landed upon the man Ellie had spoken with at the cemetery.

"Who was he?" Ellie's mother bit into an icebox cookie.

"His name is James Farlow."

"James Farlow?" Ellie's father straightened from his slump, his eyes shot to Ellie's.

"You know him?"

Her father glanced at Ellie's mother, whose mouth hung open, and took a series of sips from his coffee cup. "I didn't know him well. It was a long time ago." He rubbed the back of his neck.

Ellie looked from her father to her mother and back. "Aunt Lillian and I ran into him at the Parkersburg bandshell last summer. She told me that was the first she'd seen him in years." Ellie sipped her tea. "And she never saw him again after that."

Ellie's father rose, went to the counter, and cut a slice of pie. He tilted his head back toward Ellie's mother. "Margaret, we'll need to get going early in the morning."

"Yes, we have an early flight." Ellie's mother stood and gathered cups and plates. "I'll go see what I can get packed." After a quick trip to the sink, she made an even quicker departure from the room.

"So, who is this guy?" Benny asked of nobody in particular.

"Whoever he was, he seemed really upset about Aunt Lillian," Jessie said. "Did they used to date?"

Ellie's father was taking his time maneuvering his slice of pie to a plate. At the silence that had befallen the kitchen, he glanced at Ellie and his grandchildren, who all focused on him, then shoveled an oversized bite of pie into his mouth. After a bit, he cleared his throat, then coughed. "Good pie. I believe they were old friends. I should give your mother a hand."

Why the secrecy? Her aunt had told Ellie that she and James had been in a relationship, had been in love.

Why had Ellie's parents seemed so uncomfortable with the topic?

Her parents left the next morning, as did Betty, and the children boarded the bus for Columbus late afternoon the following day, both needing to get back to their own lives. Ellie's already bruised heart barely withstood their goodbyes.

Only Gregory remained now, aside from Hanne, who'd emerged from her room in the past couple days only to force down a few bites of the food Ellie pleaded with her to eat. Gregory and the children had interacted politely, superficially, not seeming to connect on any level. Naturally, Benny and Jessie had behaved amiably toward him, but he hadn't seemed to respond with any interest. He hadn't asked them anything about their lives or seemed to care much what they had to say. But Ellie had lacked the energy to try to determine whether it was due to possible nervousness of their first-time meeting or general apathy.

"I need to hit the hay if I'm going to make that drive in the morning." Gregory said after dinner. He stood and began walking out of the kitchen, then paused and returned to her. "Would you like me to stay with you, in your bedroom, tonight?" He ran his hands over her hips, he tapped his lips on hers. "You've been through a lot. I'd like to be there to comfort you."

Stay with her? Dare she consider it? How nice it would feel to be held, and maybe she would even be able to sleep more than an hour or two at a time. "I don't know, Gregory, I—"

"Come on, baby, you don't want to be alone tonight, do you?" His lips brushed alongside her neck, then returned to her mouth. He kissed her hard and nudged her close against him.

Ellie's arms went around his shoulders, and she dissolved into him, letting his lips soothe, his hands comfort.

As soon as she climbed into bed a bit later, he pushed against her, his mouth pressed at hers. He tugged up her nightgown and flung a leg between her legs, nudging them apart. His fingers trailed over her body, his breath heavy, and his tongue rammed into her mouth. "You're gonna get it good, baby." Damp with sweat, his skin pasted itself to hers. A hand restrained her arms against the bed, fingernails dug into her wrist. His nibble on her lips intensified, his teeth digging into them.

"Gregory."

"What?"

"You're hurting me."

"No, baby, it's about to feel really good. Just relax and take it." His words growled low and raw. He tightened his grip around her wrists, his knee rammed into her leg, shoving it out further.

"Stop. Gregory, stop. Get off of me."

"Are you kidding me?" He leapt to his feet, pulled on his boxers, then his trousers. "This is insane, you know that?" He flung his shirt onto his arms and pointed a finger at her face. "You have a problem, woman."

Ellie jumped out of bed, yanking down her nightgown, and grabbed her robe from the floor. "Keep your voice down." Hanne slept, hopefully, just down the hall. "You were too rough."

"For chrissake, Ellie, I didn't know I needed to treat you like a delicate little virgin. Were you such a frigid-assed prude when you were married?"

"I wasn't… I'm not… You were hurting me."

"Oh, for the love of… I don't need this shit."

He didn't need this shit? "You know what, Gregory? A little sensitivity might be a good thing sometimes. I would have liked hearing an *I'm sorry I hurt you*. And you might have first held me in your arms and asked how I'm doing." She tied the belt of her robe. "My aunt just died and you were behaving as if you were in a…in a house of ill repute."

"Oh, for…" He buckled his belt. "Does the whole world have to stop just because your aunt died?" His words spewed like slivers hacked from a block of ice. "She was an old woman. Get over it, Ellie."

She rushed to him, stopping within inches. "Get out of here, Gregory. I never want to see your face again."

His eyes widened, his right hand formed a fist.

Lifting her chin, Ellie fixed resolute eyes on his. Her heart thumped at twice its usual rate, her voice trembled. "Get the hell out of this house."

"Oh, believe me, I'm blowing this joint." He grabbed his billfold and keys from the nightstand and stomped toward the door. Pausing in the doorway, he turned and pierced the space between them with a vile glance. "You're not the only dame in the world, you know. Dames who aren't cold as ice. If it hadn't been for them these past few months, I'd have frozen to death."

Well, that explained why he'd stopped pushing her for physical involvement for that long stretch. As soon as his motorcar screeched away, Ellie ran downstairs and locked the door.

Chapter Seventeen

"I still can't believe she left her house to me. Her home. I mean, this is where she lived her life, and with all the things she was involved with and all the friends she had, she loved being here more than anywhere else. She made this house so beautiful and so special."

Ellie had fixed a lunch of tuna salad sandwiches and sliced peaches. Slumped at the patio table, she and Hanne picked at their food the way robins pecked at dirt in the flower beds. The morning's reading of the will had left them both feeling bruised.

"Of course you should have this house, Eleanor. You *practicably* grew up here, and your aunt was closer to you than anyone else."

Ellie suppressed a smile at Hanne's ragged pronunciation. "You know, the hair combs she left to me mean as much to me as the house."

"She never went a day without wearing one." Hanne dabbed a napkin at her mouth. "But really, Eleanor, I don't feel right taking that money, or those diamond earrings. I am not a jewelry person. You know that. Besides, where will I wear earrings like that?"

"Wear them every day, Hanne. Too many people keep their good jewelry for special occasions. Didn't you learn anything at all from Aunt Lillian?" Ellie laughed. "She wore her diamonds with a house dress. Put those sparklers on and keep them on."

By early evening, Ellie found herself treading along the riverbank, unable to handle another hour in the house, suffocated by boxes and boxes of Aunt Lillian's clothing and shoes and coats. Yet, at the same time, the house seemed empty. The spaces her aunt once vitalized now seemed to silently wail at the desolation.

Ellie's heart slumped in a battered heap inside her chest. How could Aunt Lillian have died? Someone who had thrived on every breath she took, who'd been intrigued by life's smallest offerings, who'd given with all her heart and soul? Ellie felt ready to burst from all she was feeling and all she wished she could say to Aunt Lillian. Talking with *someone* right now would be nice, but the five-and-dime was closed, Deb was working late today, and Anita had gone to visit her son in Philadelphia. Ellie's feet led her to the Levee House Cafe and hopefully a dose of Marv's sturdiness. With a tug of the heavy wooden door, the aromas of dinnertime greeted Ellie's nose, and the sight of Marv lightened her heart.

After a much-needed bear hug, Marv guided her to a stool at the counter. "How's my girl?"

"I don't know, Marv. Everything's changing."

"That's the thing about life, Eleanor. It always changes. What'll you have?"

"I don't know. I don't even know if I'm hungry." Ellie slumped at the counter and propped her head on a fist. With every ding of the bell, she found herself twisting around to see who had arrived. Would she ever again be able to come to the Levee House without thinking of that man?

"You don't know if you're hungry? Horsefeathers." Marv leaned over the counter and covered Ellie's hand with his. "I remember the day when I couldn't keep the food coming fast enough to keep that little tummy full. Especially the ice cream. Hey, how about a big bowl of ice cream, huh?"

Ellie thumped her fingers on the counter. "No, thank you. I don't know. Maybe. What kind do you have?"

"Ruby, make up a banana split for Miss Eleanor, would ya?" Marv yelled toward the kitchen. "Be sure to go heavy on the whipped cream, and I'll have a slice of that peach pie."

"Come on, dear." Marv walked around the counter and led Ellie by the elbow toward the door, away from the swelling supper crowd. Before exiting, he called back, "Bring those outside, would ya, Ruby?"

They sank onto a wooden bench at the side of the building, around the corner from the busy patio. From here, the diners' animated conversation translated into an unintelligible murmur. Ruby soon appeared with their desserts.

"I know losing your Aunt Lillian has been a big blow. She was a great lady. I'm gonna miss her myself. Talk to me." Marv slipped a third of the slice of pie into his mouth with one forkful.

"I just can't believe she's gone. She was my best friend, my rock. It's going to be so hard without her. The house feels so different. Marietta isn't the same."

"Well I'm still here, ya know, so you have to keep coming back down to see good ol' Marv, if nothing else."

"You know I'll always come see you, Marv. I just don't know what to do about the house. Aunt Lillian left it to me."

"Well, bless her heart," Marv said. "And lucky you. Beautiful place."

"Oh, I love the house. It's been my second home my entire life. And I have to say, Marv, inheriting it will lift the financial burden. But I don't know how I would keep it. I wouldn't want it to sit empty most of the time."

"Have you considered relocating? You know, those kids of yours are just a hop, skip, and a jump away from here." Marv nodded at a couple approaching the restaurant. "Evening. Enjoy your meal."

"Yes, I'd be able to see them lots more if I lived here. As long as they live in Columbus, that is. Who knows where my adventurous children will plant themselves after that?" Ellie slipped another spoonful of the banana split into her mouth. "But I don't know if I could live in Aunt Lillian's house without her. It's just so sad there now."

She'd thought and thought about having inherited the house, but no course of action seemed the right one. What had happened to her decisive, impetuous self? She'd never been this wishy-washy about anything.

"I know, sweetie pie. But, you know, it's been my experience that when something sad happens, the sadness eventually moves along. Oh, there will always be some left behind, but it doesn't just sit there." Marv waved a vertical hand from right to left. "It passes through and flows on its way." Marv nodded toward the river. "Just like that river."

Ellie wiped her chin with a wad of napkins. "Good heavens, I think Ruby put half a gallon of ice cream into this banana split. I just… How would I take care of the house from Chicago? How would—"

"Eleanor, Eleanor, listen. You do not have to solve all the problems of the world right now. It'll all work out." He finished off his pie, set his plate on the bricks beneath the bench, and wrapped an arm around her shoulders. "You've been through a lot these past few years. Give yourself some time."

Marv's warm, strong arm felt good around her. After another bite of her treat, she sopped the drips from her dress. Why could she never eat ice cream without making a mess? She sighed and dropped her head onto Marv's shoulder. A pair of sparrows skipped past, jabbing their beaks at the uneven bricks, foraging for stray crumbs, no doubt.

Ellie covertly dabbed at tears before they saturated Marv's shirt. "Marv, do you remember that tow crew that came in here last spring when I was here?"

"Can't say I do. We get quite a few crews come in. Why?"

"I met the captain, Wyatt Dare. I met him after I left here that day."

"Wyatt Dare. Sure. Good man." Marv leaned out, dipped his head toward Ellie, and inspected her eyes. "He isn't one of the reasons for the tears, is he?"

"He shouldn't be. I don't even really know the man. But we spent a few hours together that day, walking along the river, over to Harmar Village. And he was supposed to come back last August. He was in the midst of a divorce when I met him, or so he said, and we planned to meet on the bridge. I thought he was someone I could trust, but he didn't show up."

He didn't show up because he wasn't one of her three stars. Mason had once been, but his betrayal had dimmed his star, in her sky, and thank heaven that brute Gregory never came close to meaning that much to her. Maybe nobody would ever again be one of her stars. Maybe her three stars would never cross because when it came to love, maybe she was star-crossed.

"Well, Wyatt's the best kinda fella there is. If he didn't come back, there's a good reason. Do you know he put a new roof on this place one summer?"

"He put a roof on the Levee House?"

"Eight, nine years ago. The roof was on its last leg. Wyatt took notice of the pans I'd set out around the place to catch the drips when the rains came. I told him I'd bought the shingles, just hadn't gotten around to laying them. Next thing I know, he's hiked himself up there—" Marv twisted around and pointed upward—"Old shingles are dropping like leaves, and three days later I've got a new roof. Completely gobsmacked me. Oh, that was a hot summer. All he asked for was a couple of meals each day. Wouldn't take a dime. And every time he comes in here, I tell him his meal is on the house, and yet he still insists on paying."

"That was nice of him, putting your new roof on. But I don't know why I even brought him up. It doesn't matter now." Ellie's eyes drifted to a couple strolling the river trail, then to another couple, then another, before darting to some other focal point, any other focal point.

"Obviously it does matter, Miss Eleanor." Marv raised his eyebrows. "You like him."

"I *did* like him. But he apparently didn't feel the same."

"Well, sweetie pie, I don't know. All I can say is he must have had a good reason. And next time he comes in here, he's gonna have some explaining to do." Marv stood and gathered their dishes. "You want some more ice cream?"

Ellie laughed. "Are you kidding me? I'll be waddling away as it is." She hugged him. "Thanks for listening, Marv. You always make everything better."

"You know, come to think of it, Wyatt hasn't come around in a long time. A real long time. Now you got me worried. I hope nothing happened to the boy."

He's been enjoying a second honeymoon with his wife, or standing on some other bridge feeding lies to some other unsuspecting woman, that's probably what happened to him.

Chapter Eighteen

Ellie burrowed into Uncle Edward's leather chair with a cup of tea and a novel, something to keep her mind off things. With Hanne having left on the train this morning to spend a week with her only child, a daughter who lived in Wheeling, West Virginia, this was the first Ellie had been alone in the house since her aunt died. The quiet fell heavily around Ellie, like a thick, oppressive blanket. But Mother Nature had selected a torrential downpour for the afternoon, so having spent the morning working in Aunt Lillian's flower gardens, she sank into the comfort of the cozy library.

When tears blurred the words, she tossed the book aside. Apparently, no book was going to lure her thoughts away from the turbulence in her mind, in her heart. She'd decided, while lying awake in the morning's wee hours, to sell the house. Aside from the memories and the sentiment, the culmination of all her debating and agonizing came down to one thing. She simply could not live in this big, empty house with only the remnants of its past incarnation to keep her company. Still, the notion of walking away from the place, and never again coming back to it, killed her.

Whisking a tear off her cheek. Ellie leapt to her feet. She couldn't sit there letting the gloom consume her. She must think practically about all this, she needed to make plans. She would arrange for an auction of Aunt Lillian's belongings and her furniture. All these books, for starters—the county library would love having them. Ellie marched into the parlor, across the foyer, where the grand piano now paused, silenced. Aunt Lillian had taught her as a child where to place her fingers, how to create a few basic chords, and Ellie had taken lessons for several years. But it had been her aunt's touch on the keys that most often filled the house with lovely melodies, and the room resonated with her aunt's spirit. The piano would probably fit into Ellie's parlor back in Oak Park. Maybe she would keep it, along with a few other things.

Striding into the sitting room, she made a snappy inventory of the furnishings, ticking them off in her head. This piece would be auctioned, that item donated, the settee... The settee. Aunt Lillian's, and her, favorite piece. Ellie rubbed her forehead and shuffled to the French doors. Leaning her forehead against a pane, she peered out at the sharp arrows of rain pinging off the yard. Down below, Marietta looked like a looming, massive ghost, shrouded in gauzy white mist.

Her dear aunt was gone forever, the world she had so lovingly created now relegated to a distant era. Wyatt hadn't shown up. Mason had torn apart their family for a nasty tramp, and the only man she had seen since the divorce had revealed himself to be a brute. And now, this beloved house would soon be gone. Was the rain heavy enough to drown out a good scream?

****

The woebegone country song wailing from Harmar Tavern's jukebox suited Ellie's mood, but being with the girls eased the gloom. Deb had planned the outing to help Ellie through her first stretch of solitude in the big yellow house. Although Ellie wasn't in the mood for partying, at least she wouldn't have to spend the evening in oppressive silence, missing her aunt. And Ellie loved Harmar Tavern. It had been a part of Harmar Village forever. In fact, Aunt Lillian had recalled it as a saloon, complete with swinging doors, dirt floors, and a hitching post out front. Now, it was a fun place to take a step back in time for a few drinks and some simple but renowned food, and tonight the place was packed, as usual.

After the bartender slid their beers to them on the slick wooden bar, Ellie told the girls about Gregory. The subject would have come up eventually, she might as well get it over with.

"What an asshole," Deb said. "He'd better never show his face around you again."

Ellie sipped at her beer. "I'm just thankful I didn't completely fall for him. You know, I can almost understand why some women tolerate and justify their abusive relationships. Finding out a man likes to slap around women after falling for him, after being with him for a while, I'm sure it's a lot tougher to walk away. Especially if he's chipped away at her self-esteem and turned the blame on her. I have to say, I almost fell into that trap, justifying Gregory's behavior, questioning my reactions. But his abuse was his fault, not mine."

"Wait a minute. Abuse? So he hit you?" Anita swigged her beer.

"No, he didn't hit me, but he hurt me."

"Well, what you described doesn't sound like abuse to me."

"Hold on, what?" Deb splatted her bottle of beer onto the bar and pinned Anita with a glare. "You're kidding, right?"

Ellie frowned. "Anita, are you serious? So you think that only beating someone with their fists qualifies as abuse?"

Anita shrugged. "Maybe that's just the way he is. Maybe he's just very masculine and comes off as a little rough around the edges." She signaled for the bartender.

"Very masculine? Do you think it's acceptable for him to be physically aggressive toward women because he might be more masculine than the next man?" Ellie asked.

"No, I just think people express themselves in different ways, and maybe that's just his nature."

"Anita, I think you're way off base," Charlene said. "If Ellie was hurt by the things Gregory did, I would call that abuse."

"For crying out loud, ladies, do you know how rare a decent man is?" Anita clasped her head with both fists.

"Gregory Barnes is *not* a decent man," Ellie said. "And whether he intentionally hurt me or he's extremely insensitive and just gets rough, I don't know and I don't care. The thing is, he knew he caused me pain and he didn't give a darn. He's a cruel man."

"Cruel." Anita let out a huff of air. "My word, Ellie, I don't see any bruises."

"You are insane, Anita. Seriously," Deb said. "A real man doesn't rough up his woman, and a real man cares if she's hurt. Vinnie never laid a hand on me."

"Then why did you ditch him?" Anita shouted.

Ellie sometimes wondered whether Anita enjoyed arguing. She seemed to contradict popular opinion on most every topic. Thankfully, when the bartender delivered another round, Deb opted to plunge into her beer rather than zing a retort to Anita.

Anita shrugged and tapped a finger in Ellie's direction. "Good luck ever finding anyone like Gregory again."

"Wish me luck that I don't," Ellie said.

****

After Hanne returned from her daughter's place, she and Ellie began sorting through Aunt Lillian's clothing. What was Ellie going to do with such personal items, items so beautiful, so well made? Probably donate most of it, maybe keep a few of the vintage dresses and the quilted designer pocketbook she'd always loved.

"Oh, missy, I remember this gorgeous thing." Hanne ran her fingers along the neckline of one of the dresses. "I have not seen this in years."

"When did Aunt Lillian wear it? Do you remember?"

"Oh it has been years and years. I am not sure I remember the *occasional*, but I do remember her wearing it. Oh, she looked lovely." Hanne's eyes widened. "Try it on, missy. You would look beautiful in it, with your blonde hair."

A gorgeous dress, probably from the early 1910s. Elegant folds of lustrous black silk overlaid a columned, ankle-length, ivory underskirt. An underlay of ivory lace peeked above the low, draped bodice and extended into fluttery cap sleeves.

When Ellie appeared from behind the dressing screen, Hanne gasped. "Oh, Eleanor, you look just like your aunt. You must wear this dress to the gala. Here." Hanne handed her the pearl-and-crystal dress clips that went with the dress, and Ellie fastened one to each side of the neckline.

****

By midafternoon on the day of the gala, Ellie had slipped into the freshly cleaned dress. She opened one of the jewelry boxes on Aunt Lillian's vanity and glided her fingers over the velvet lining. She'd done the same thing as a little girl, her aunt having always shared her pretty things with her niece. Of course, the finer pieces had been designated off limits, but her aunt always permitted her to pick through some of the boxes and choose sparkling costume necklaces and bracelets for playing dress-up. This was the first Ellie had allowed herself to revisit her aunt's jewelry since inheriting it, and she chose a double strand of luminous pearls and a pair of pearl earrings. In her waved hair, she placed a comb of enameled yellow roses and seed pearls set into black lacquer.

Charlene and Alan arrived at the gala looking adorable. Anita sashayed in, gorgeous in a slinky, low-backed red gown, on the arm of some thirty-something fellow named Tad. Even Deb had fixed up, having stopped short of donning a dress but wearing low heels with her high-waisted, flare-legged pants and coordinating cropped jacket, along with a swipe of pale lipstick. Hanne was, of course, there and fluttering around, fretting about the food, for which she served as committee chair.

Ellie's decorations produced a magical ambience, with strings of glinting lights accenting silky midnight-blue and magenta fabric draped across the ceiling. White linens adorned tables set with glowing votive candles and vases of hydrangeas, pale pink roses, and lilies of the valley in honor of Aunt Lillian. Ellie had been unsure how successful the gala would be, given the economic situation. But with the Depression easing a bit, a substantial profit had been realized, more important than ever for the children's home due to so many children having been placed there in the past few years.

After dinner, the French doors were flung open, extending the room to the stone patio. Pots of white geraniums and strings of blue and white lights continued the romantic theme outside. Serenaded by the swing band, couples merged onto the patio for dancing. Satisfied that the event was exceeding her expectations, Ellie went to the bar for a glass of Riesling.

"There you are." Hanne took hold of Ellie's arm. "Dear, your guest is here."

"My guest?"

"Your gentleman. Very handsome and wearing a tuxedo. He is in the *vestibull*." Hanne crossed her arms, tilted her head, and raised her eyebrows. "And why didn't you tell me you had a date for tonight, missy?"

"I don't have a date for tonight."

The nerve of that cad. Gregory could turn his disgusting behind around and slither right back to whatever hole he crawled out of. After a gulp of wine, Ellie banged her glass onto the bar. *Don't stomp. Not becoming to the vintage dress.*

He stood at the far end of the dim foyer, silhouetted against the wispy light of the crystal chandelier. The nerve of him. Ellie's emotions had taken a long, wild rollercoaster ride these past few years. She was more than ready to finally jump off, to stand on stable ground. No way was Gregory going to extend her turbulent ride.

He began walking the long, wide foyer toward her. Bracing herself, Ellie inched up the rickety track of the rollercoaster, then halted and crossed her arms. The same sort of fearless gesture she'd made in her teens when she flung her arms high on a real rollercoaster. Even now, she didn't need to hold on. She would face this, the way she'd faced everything else these past few years.

As he continued toward her, the rollercoaster crested the hill. Then his face came into view and the cart hurtled downward and knocked the breath from her body.

Chapter Nineteen

He wore a tuxedo, this man who'd told her he didn't care for dressing up. Satin lapels, black pearl studs on his bib shirt, pleated trousers. The man she'd thought she would never see again. He was here and he had gone to the trouble to come to this event and to put on tails, and he looked incredible and he stared directly into her eyes.

He removed his top hat. "Hello, Ellie."

Every thought, every feeling she'd buried for nine months flooded into her mind, but none yielded words.

"You're even more beautiful than I remember." His eyes circled over her dress, her face.

Wyatt. The sight of him deluged her senses, robbed her equilibrium.

"Is there a quiet place where we can talk?"

A moment later, they had seated themselves on a bench on the bank of the river, seeming to have been transported there on some involuntary wavelength. Was this really him, sitting beside her? Her eyes sought the realness and stability of the river. Why was she trembling?

"Are you cold?"

She nudged away the arm he extended toward her shoulder. If she weren't a lady, she'd shove him away. But she also wanted to pull him as close as humanly possible and kiss his mouth and unleash whatever this was that she felt for this man.

"Ellie, I couldn't come back in August. My wife's attorney dragged things out. We weren't divorced until last month. And I had no way of letting you know."

"You found me now."

"I thought about phoning Marv, over at the Levee House. I remember you telling me he's a family friend. But I didn't know how you'd feel about my involving him in your personal business. So I figured I'd be back through here soon enough, for work, and I'd try to find you or get a message to you or something. But this divorce was such a nightmare, so time-consuming I couldn't leave town, for all the court appearances, the endless meetings with attorneys. Finally, I did call Marv, and you'll be happy to know he was very protective of your privacy, but he told me about this event tonight."

Ellie's fingers navigated her necklace, pearl by pearl, her eyes fixed on the river.

Wyatt stood, then kneeled in front of her. "Ellie, look at me." His voice coursed low, almost a whisper. "I'm sorry. I meant to be there that day on the bridge. I never stopped thinking about you."

His words seemed so reassuring. But no matter how handsome he was, no matter how he incinerated her senses, for some reason it had really hurt when he didn't show up. She did not need some man trying to elbow his way into her life when things with him had started off on the wrong foot. She did not need the emotional baggage. She would walk away before he had the chance to hurt her again.

She stood. "It's all right. Things have changed anyway. My aunt died, and as soon as I sell the house, I'm going back to Oak Park. So it doesn't matter." She hurried back toward the gala, the sound of his footsteps trailing.

"Ellie, wait." He took gentle hold of her arm and drew her to a stop. "I had no idea your aunt died. I am so sorry. One impression I took away from our time together that day was how close you and she were."

Ellie studied her shoes. "Thank you."

"But please don't say we don't matter. That day we met, I mean, damn, Ellie, I felt something. That's why I came back. I always meant to come back. Didn't you feel anything at all that day?"

Couples strolled the grounds of the old mansion which had been transformed several years ago into an event venue. Notes from the band carried through the air. Tender, romantic music. *Dammit.*

Wyatt touched a thumb to a tear that had fought its way out of Ellie's eye.

She jerked back. What made him think he could come back after all this time and she would be waiting? Presume she wouldn't have a date tonight? Then ask if she'd felt anything that day? She would not put her heart on the line for some stranger. A just-divorced, unreliable stranger who lived hundreds of miles away.

"That was a long time ago. A lot has happened. We live different lives. It was silly to think anything could come of you and me."

Wyatt ran a hand across the nape of his neck. "Ellie—"

"I need to go." She pulled back from him and in the next moment found herself in the ladies' room.

Deb glanced over from inspecting her teeth in the gilt-framed mirror when Ellie invaded the space. "Well, I have to admit, I wouldn't mind having good old Vinnie around tonight. Everyone's coupled up, and this music is damned good." She did a double-take at Ellie, then turned from the mirror. "Ells, what's wrong? What the hell happened?"

Ellie yanked a tissue from the countertop container, dabbed at her eyes, then rooted through her evening bag. "Wyatt is here. You know, that man I met last year who said he would come back and who didn't come back? He's here. Darn it, why am I being such a crybaby?"

"You have got to be kidding me." Deb's jaw fell open. "So he just showed up?"

"He said his divorce was final just last month. It supposedly took longer than he expected it to." Ellie continued fishing in her bag. "Why now? I thought of nothing but that man for months, finally put him out of my mind, and then he shows up out of the blue." Ellie flung her handbag onto the counter. Her arms thrust outward like an orchestra conductor. "Is this all some big joke on me? Why this luck with men? Did I murder some man in a past life and now karma is getting me?"

Deb stifled a laugh and hiked herself onto the vanity. "What did you tell him?"

After digging out her eyeliner pencil, Ellie leaned close to the mirror and re-lined her eyes. "I don't need any relationship to start out with this much drama. I've had enough drama for one lifetime." She dropped her eyeliner back into her bag, yanked off one of her black opera-length gloves, and rummaged through her bag again. "Darn it, why does the darned lipstick always end up at the darned bottom?" She dumped the bag's contents onto the counter.

"Ellie, calm down. Listen, why not give the man a chance?"

"He had his chance. He's just another player who

jerks women around all up and down the river. He's probably got…got Marybelle in Mississippi, Lorylou in Louisiana, heaven knows who in Kentucky."

"Listen, kid, we both know I'm not an expert on men," Deb said, her legs swinging from the edge of the vanity and a pointed finger jutting toward her friend. "But I'm pretty sure they don't travel hundreds of miles and put on a penguin suit just to try getting fresh. I think this Wyatt bloke's being square with you. Where is he? Is he still here?"

"I don't know and I don't care. I was having a nice, peaceful evening until he showed up. How dare he come to something this important, something so close to my aunt's heart, for crying out loud, and expect me to be available? How can he just waltz in here and wreck my evening like this? Who does he think he is?" Ellie stomped toward the door.

Deb hopped off the counter, stepped into her path, and took her by the shoulders. "Ellie."

"What?" Emphasis on the *tee*.

"The man made a grand gesture. You are going back out there, and you're going to give him a chance."

"Why should I?" Ellie crossed her arms.

"Why shouldn't you? It's only a second chance."

Ellie rolled her eyes.

"Okay, you've thought about it long enough. Come on."

"I didn't think about it. I want nothing to do—"

"Let's go." Deb grabbed Ellie's hand and pulled her out the door, into the foyer.

Wyatt sat on a bench, elbows on his knees, rotating his top hat through his fingers. At the sight of Ellie, he stood and seemed to survey Ellie's face for clues.

"Hi." Deb offered her hand. "You must be Wyatt. You were a smart man to come back."

Ellie introduced them, and Deb made no effort to disguise her inspection of him. "Okay, I get it now."

She would kill Deb later. But had Deb been right, in the ladies' room? Was Ellie being too hard on Wyatt? She really had no basis for not believing him.

"It's a pleasure to meet you, Deb." He extended a hand toward Ellie. "May we talk?"

She let his hand enfold hers and lead her to the patio, where they fell into step with a misty caress of a tune, moving together with the ease of a seasoned, perfectly choreographed highwire act. While his hand wrapped hers in sturdy warmth, his arm around her waist held her near, as candlelight fluttered around them like a million fireflies. He seemed sincere, with gentle eyes that seemed to reflect a soul incapable of telling, or living, a lie, and the tension in Ellie's shoulders relented. Although he wore no cologne, she inhaled his scent like a starving predator. Pulling her closer, his chest rose and fell, and he looked from her eyes to her lips. Her heart pulsated, his heartbeat seeming to pump the blood through her own veins, and he leaned toward her, his lips a whisper away. It was all too much. She broke loose.

"I...I need to check on some things."

"Ellie, don't go." He hurried after her, grasping her hand at the edge of the patio.

Shaking her head, Ellie swiped at tears with both hands. She perused the crowd. Thankfully, nobody seemed to notice their little drama. "This is ridiculous," she said. "This is only a fantasy."

"Ellie, I think we could have something really special." His eyes were those of a man facing down a grizzly bear, knowing that his countenance was paramount to his survival. "Please give this a chance. Please."

How could she know if his words were genuine? If he had told the truth about why he hadn't shown up in August, it was admirable that he hadn't tried to pursue her while he was married. But she'd heard *I'm sorry* and *Please give this a chance* too many times, from too many men, these past few years. She turned away, but not before glimpsing the eyes of a wounded man.

****

Guiding her auto toward the refuge of the house late into the night, she mopped at the tears flooding her cheeks. "Damn you, Wyatt!" she shouted. "You won't break my heart. You won't get the chance. And damn you, Gregory, and damn you, Mason. You all can go to hell!"

She lay awake in the few hours left of the night. Why wouldn't sleep rescue her from this agitation and uncertainty? Images of Wyatt, gorgeous in his tuxedo, dejection in his eyes, glimmered in her mind like bits of hot coals reigniting a fire. Why had she treated him so cruelly? It wasn't the end of the world that this near stranger hadn't come back on that one specific day. He'd gone to some trouble to get to her tonight and had asked only for a chance to get to know her. With anything else in life, she'd jump right in without all this darned analysis. Why was she so firmly closed off when it came to Wyatt Dare? What was wrong with her?

Chapter Twenty

Hanne blotted a tear from her face with a floral linen handkerchief. Hanne always kept a handkerchief tucked in the pocket of one of her petite, jewel-toned dresses or crisp, flowery aprons.

"Eleanor, I know you do not want to think about this, but it is time we went through the rest of your aunt's things." Hanne reinstalled her spectacles on her nose.

"Here, Hanne, sit." Ellie led the frail-looking little woman to a chair and took over slicing cucumbers for salad. Her own eyes were inflamed from all the crying. Could nothing remain constant? When had the ease and contentment of life become such a rare commodity?

"I'm so sorry you have to go through all this," Ellie said. "I know how hard it will be for you to leave the house."

Hanne ran a hand across the speckled laminate tabletop. "Don't you worry, missy, I will be fine." Never immobile for long, she sprang from her chair, scurried to the oven, and peered in at the savory loaf of bread she'd crafted this morning. "Just a few more minutes. I have had many good years here. Vernon and I had many good years here. Hmph. I am telling you what, missy, I sure miss that man."

"I loved Vern. He was never serious for one minute." Ellie laughed. "He was a big part of why I always had so much fun here. You were too." Ellie paused in her cutting. "Have you decided what you're going to do?"

Hanne went to the icebox, pulled out a jar of her homemade salad dressing, and shook it. "My friend Ruth has been trying to talk me into buying a house in her neighborhood. The houses are small there, just what I would need."

"That is a nice neighborhood," Ellie said. "Hanne, will you... Are you all right financially? It's none of my business, but—"

Hanne waved a hand. "Oh, *ja, ja*. Vernon left me a good pension, and of course your aunt left me that money."

"That's good, but if you need anything, just let me know. Aunt Lillian wouldn't want you to endure any hardship as a result of having to move."

"*Nein, nein*. I will be fine."

Ellie and Hanne spent the next few days going through more of Aunt Lillian's things. A difficult task, deciding what to sell, what to donate, what to give away or maybe keep. And Hanne had a tale to tell about nearly every item, filling gaps Ellie didn't know existed in her knowledge of her aunt. Then the task of sorting through all the papers, mementos, and books. She would keep some of her favorite books, a few of them first editions.

Ellie spotted the stained-glass piece of the *Anne* riverboat, her final gift to Aunt Lillian, propped in a door panel in the sitting room. The place, no doubt, where her aunt intended to have it installed. What would Ellie do with it? It seemed a shame not to have it installed in its intended place, but even worse to leave it, and all the other panels she'd crafted, to strangers who likely wouldn't appreciate the sentiment that had gone into them. It seemed a shame to leave the entire place to strangers.

A pang of doubt stopped Ellie in her tracks. Other people would be living here and tainting the place with their sleek, unadorned furnishings and banishing any sign of Art Deco and Victorian decor and bashing out the stained-glass panels because they weren't contemporary enough. Bile rose in Ellie's throat. But no, she'd made her decision. She couldn't worry about what might happen to the place after it sold. Removing the stained-glass piece, she wrapped it in a blanket and took it to her aunt's bedroom.

"Eleanor, come here." Hanne stood in front of Aunt Lillian's closet holding a packet of yellowed, brittle envelopes tied in a faded pink satin ribbon.

Ellie took the stack and fanned through it. The faded name *Lillie Blaylock* and a Marietta address were handwritten on the top envelope, and the ink of a postage cancellation machine rippled across the orangey-red, two-cent, Andrew Jackson stamp.

"I found them in this box." Hanne gestured toward an old hat box. "It was on a closet shelf. And there are more letters. I do not know what they are. I will let you decide what to do with them."

Ellie took the box and peered in at another bundle of envelopes, tied by a frayed white ribbon, resting inside. These letters appeared to have been written by the same person but much more recently, and all the letters had been postmarked from New Matamoras, Ohio.

"What is in there is not my business. I will stick to the clothing." Hanne went to the chest of drawers and pulled open the top drawer. "And listen, Eleanor. I have decided to buy a cottage on Ruth's street."

"You have?" Ellie placed the wrapped stained-glass panel on a closet shelf. "So you found one you like? Do you think you'll be happy there?"

Hanne removed a neat stack of undergarments and placed them on the bed, then focused on Ellie and placed her hands on her hips. "To tell the truth, I would not want to be here without Lillian. It is not the same. I will be happy there, *ja*."

"Good for you, then. I'll help you move and get settled. Ruth is always so active with social engagements. The two of you will probably have lots of fun."

"I am telling you what. I am happy my house is far down the street from her house. I would not get a moment's rest if I lived next door to her. That woman is always on the go, and she is always trying to drag me along. I like to have a little fun, too, but not every second of the day."

Ellie laughed. "You'll probably have to switch off all your lights and pretend you're not home sometimes."

"Don't think I have not already thought of that. I think I will do something with this rat's nest, then see what we have for lunch." Hanne tugged hairpins from her hair on her way out of the room. For as long as Ellie remembered, Hanne had worn her hair pulled back into a low bun.

Still holding the hatbox, Ellie shuffled to the three-sided alcove of her aunt's bedroom and opened one of the French doors to the chirp of a robin constructing a nest in the fork of two tree branches. The budding leaves of a cherry tree fluttered in the late morning breeze. After lowering herself onto the tufted chaise, Ellie raised her face and let the warmth saturate her skin.

She didn't want to pry into her aunt's life, but she couldn't just throw the letters away or place them back in the box, ignoring the significance they obviously held. Her aunt had kept them, tied with ribbons, some for decades. To disregard them didn't seem right. Ellie slid the top envelope from under the white ribbon and pulled out the single-page letter.

Dear Lillie, Seeing you last night after all these years was exceptionally wonderful. It meant everything to me. I think of you every hour of every day and I want more than ever to be with you. Please think about this, Lillie. It's time for us to be together again. Yours with love always, James

The letter was dated soon after Aunt Lillian and Ellie had seen James at the bandshell.

"Oh, James," Ellie whispered. She went to the bathroom for a tissue, grabbed the entire box, and returned. She sat for a few minutes, her head resting against the chaise, remembering how serenely blissful Aunt Lillian had seemed with James that evening, replaying James's words at the cemetery. *I shouldn't have taken no for an answer.*

After placing the letter back in its envelope, Ellie slid it under the ribbon. She picked up the older bundle and eased the folded paper out of the bottom envelope. This letter's handwriting appeared more fundamental than that of the other, its cursive more exactly formed. A glance at the date told Ellie this letter had indeed been written by a much younger James.

October 4, 1879. Dear Lillie, I cannot think of the words to write to tell you how much I miss you. I don't know what to say other than we belong together. I only hope you are not hurting the way I am because this is purgatory. You were my whole life and our time together was the happiest of my life. Lillie we belong together. Please let's make this work. I promise I will take care of you and love you for the rest of your life. Please write back. I love you now and forever. James

Ellie shuffled through the stack and pulled another letter from its envelope.

December 29, 1879. Dear Lillie, I received your letter today. Thank you for writing back. I was afraid you would not receive my letter and I would never hear from you again. I cannot tell you how much it means to know you still love me. I am ever so sorry you are sad and you cry every day for me. Believe me, I feel the same. Christmas was very sad without you. Please let's find a way to be together again. I love you with all my heart and do not want to be without you in the new year. James.

Such sweet, earnest words. Why had he had to plead, when their love was mutual? Ellie wiped her eyes and dropped her third or fourth tissue to the floor. After returning the letter to its envelope, she tidied the stack and placed it on the chaise. Dabbing at her swollen eyes, she glanced outside. The mama robin still darted this way and that, strategically poking twigs into her nest. The buds of the cherry tree swelled with the unfolding day. New beginnings all around. But only an ending for James and his Lillie.

****

The next morning, Ellie drove down into town. She'd needed to get away from the house and the endless sorting and all the reminders of how very much things had changed in her life these past few years. But strolling along the river only brought more memories of the past.

Memories of Wyatt. Why? They would never again lay eyes on each other. She'd ensured that when she walked away from him the night of the gala. Maybe she'd taken it all too seriously. Maybe she should have been more understanding instead of dismissing him so absolutely. Why was she always so annoyingly quick to make her self-righteous, set-in-stone decisions?

An unfamiliar silhouette caught Ellie's eye as she pulled into the driveway of the house on Harmar Hill later in the morning. The auctioneer's sign, sprouting from the lawn. Ellie had known it was coming but glared at the interloper that seemed to have sprung from the ground like a poisonous mushroom.

By early evening, she was ready for the day to be over. Having expended every bit of energy she possessed, she couldn't wait to burrow into bed with the book she'd borrowed from the county library this morning. Everyone was talking about *Gone with the Wind*. Hopefully it lived up to its rave reviews enough to provide the distraction she so needed. Stepping into the hall to flip off the light, she glanced toward Aunt Lillian's room. The letters had raised questions. The answers were none of her business, yet her feet led her to her aunt's room.

July 21, 1880. Dear Lillie, Thank you for writing back. I do not know what else I can say. I respect your decision. That doesn't mean I understand it but I will try to live my life without you. But please try to understand we did nothing wrong, Lillie. Yes we were young but my intentions were honorable. I was prepared to take care of you for the rest of your life. Maybe the guilt you feel isn't because you think what we did was wrong. Maybe other people made you feel guilty. I do not mean to disrespect your parents. I know they love you and they want what is best for you. I know they want you to be married someday. But please believe me when I tell you I intended to spend the rest of my days with you. I respected you then and I respect you now so I will accept your decision. I do not know how I will ever stop loving you but I shall have to try. But you are 18 now and you can make your own decisions now and I know that you still love me.

Ellie gasped at the next sentence James had written.

Chapter Twenty-One

So if you ever change your mind, I will be here waiting with open arms and we shall get married again but this time in a church with your family there, and there will be flowers and a wedding cake, and you will wear a lovely white dress. You will be my wife again and I will love you and take care of you forever. To some people, the annulment meant our marriage never took place but in my heart our vows were made in the eyes of God as much in that little parlor of the justice of the peace as they would have been within the walls of a church. I love you, my Lillie. Yours forever, James

Every cell of Ellie's body chilled. "Wow," she whispered. How sad that the fist of guilt had never loosened its grip on dear Aunt Lillian and that, consequently, she'd deprived herself of James's love for the remainder of her life.

No wonder Ellie's parents had seemed so uncomfortable when James's name came up that day in the kitchen. They'd obviously been guarding Aunt Lillian's secret, and so would Ellie. She would never tell a soul about the letters, about the secret they held.

****

The engine of an automobile shuddered to a stop nearby. A glance confirmed it belonged to nobody Ellie knew. *Good.* She was a mess, with perspiration matting her hair and pasting her dress to her back. This August had broken temperature records for Marietta. The heat wave caused by all that horrible dust out in the Great Plains had brought temperatures in the 100s.

She continued sweeping the sidewalk, having finished the mowing and weeding. Normally, a neighborhood man, hired long ago by Aunt Lillian, took care of those tasks, but he was on vacation this week. Ellie enjoyed the yard work, particularly since the house was so empty and quiet. Hanne had left for Wheeling several days ago, to help out her daughter, who had sprained her ankle.

A door slammed shut, footsteps landed on pavement.

"Can't say I've ever seen such a pretty landscaper."

She spun toward the voice. The broom slipped from her hands, clattering to the pavement, and she slogged back matted strands of hair from her face. She gasped, her lungs seeming to have stopped pulling in oxygen.

"You have a way of finding me, don't you? Let me guess. Marv at the Levee House."

"Marv at the Levee House did give me your address," Wyatt said. "I'm sorry if that was an unwelcome intrusion for you. I was desperate."

She'd seen this expression before on his face. *I'm serious about this. Damned serious.* The man was persistent. He surely had endless opportunities with other women in his travels, but he wouldn't give up on her. Maybe his feelings really were genuine.

"I'd ask if you're busy, but it's pretty obvious you are."

Ellie swiped at her hair again and plucked the fabric of her dress away from her drenched body. "Just finishing up, actually."

"Can we talk? Now, or maybe a little later?"

When I'm not a sweaty mess, right? He had to pick this moment to come see her. And there he was, looking incredible in his tweed jacket and tilted porkpie hat that only made his eyes more devastatingly gorgeous. Well, this was how she looked right now, take it or leave it.

"Come on in." She tilted her head toward the house. "I'll get you something to drink. A huge glass of something to keep you occupied long enough for me to bathe."

Half an hour later, they stood at the back of the property. Wyatt planted his hands on his hips and surveyed the valley. "What a view. You can see downriver for miles. And the Appalachian Mountains, wow."

"People say there's no better view in Ohio than from Harmar Hill, and I agree. I love coming out here and just absorbing the sight."

They stood for a few minutes, inspecting the valley, commenting on the boats whipping the water into fleeting trails of meringue, Ellie pointing out the various buildings around town. Back on the patio, they seated themselves on the chaises and promptly began speaking at the same time.

"Sorry," Wyatt said. "You first."

Ellie took in a long measure of her iced tea. "I felt bad about the way I responded to you that evening, at the gala. It wasn't the end of the world that you didn't show up on the bridge that day."

She couldn't fault herself for her feelings that night. They had, after all, come from a place of amassed betrayal and pain. But she'd impulsively overreacted and sternly determined there would be no second chance for

Wyatt.

"It's okay. I hurt you, and I don't blame you for not trusting me after that. But I had every intention of coming back, and I'm sorry to have stood you up."

Ellie nodded. She believed him, and it would be ridiculous to base her impression of him on one incident.

"I told you before, I've never stopped thinking about you." He swirled the ice cubes in his glass, then looked back at her. "And I would love nothing more than having the chance to be with you and get to know you. Do you think there's a possibility of that?"

"Mmm." Ellie twisted her mouth to one side and gazed upward as if mulling over her answer, before looking back to Wyatt with a coy grin. "Alright, I suppose so."

Wyatt's laugh trailed through the air like musical notes on a scale. "You suppose so? Is that a yes?"

"Yes, it's a yes." *Yes, yes, yes.* In the few hours she'd known him, he'd left an imprint on her heart. How often did that happen in life? This man meant something to her. Exactly what, she wasn't yet sure, but she needed to find out.

"You don't know how happy that makes me." He smiled and bit his lip. "Really happy, Ellie. How about we start with dinner this evening?"

"Dinner out? Wyatt, that's so expensive, and..." She glanced down at her simple house dress and pawed at her hair, still damp from its washing. "I'm a bit of a mess. How about I make us something?"

"Well, okay, sure, that sounds terrific."

After dinner, they strolled through the neighborhoods of Harmar Hill before finishing the evening on the patio, answering infinite questions about each other and watching the river turn pink.

"You know, I've seen this house a thousand times. The stately yellow house on the hill. First thing you see when you come around the bend. And you were in it all this time. Some of the time, anyway." He eyed Ellie. "How come I never knew that? How did I never sense that you existed?"

Had she sensed that *he* existed? Was he the man she'd longed for that night back in Oak Park, the man she'd hoped was out there somewhere? Maybe. Maybe tonight, finally, that man stood in place of the longing and the apprehension and the aloneness.

"I don't know," Ellie said. "Apparently, I had to slug you to get you to notice me."

Wyatt laughed. "The only slug I was ever happy to take. So, Ellie, how long until you head back to Chicago?"

"I'm not sure. I'm going through my aunt's things. I'll be here for a while yet."

"Have you ever thought of staying here in Marietta permanently?" Wyatt stood, his eyes swept across the valley, he spread his arms. "I mean, look at this place."

Live here? She had the freedom to live anywhere, sure. But moving to Marietta would have to be for the right reasons. She would never make a major move like that for a man she barely knew. And how would it feel living in some other house, in the shadow of this wonderful home? Ellie joined Wyatt at the edge of the patio.

"Oh, I absolutely love it here. But Oak Park is my home. I've built a reputation with my stained-glass business, and there's plenty of work—or will be again, I hope. I have friends there. I love my house; it's where we raised the children."

"Sure, I understand. Just something to think about, maybe? But whatever you decide or don't decide, wherever you are is where I want to be." He took her hand and squeezed it. "We'll make this work. You spend time here, I spend time up there. You can even visit me in Biloxi if you want, when I'm not out on the river. I'm telling you, Ellie, I'm onboard with this."

It was past ten when he said he should get going. In the foyer, his hand slipped around her waist from behind. He nudged her hair aside and trickled soft kisses from her shoulder to her ear. Nudging her face toward him, he touched his lips to the corner of hers. Ellie turned to face him. With his eyes never leaving hers, his hands glided over her shoulders, her neck. His fingers wove behind her ears, through her hair. "Oh, Ellie," he whispered.

His raw expression of want pulled at her heart the way the moon's gravity tugged at the sea, its waters responding with rhapsodic waves. Raising her face to his, she melted in his warmth, and his kiss smoldered on her lips long after he left.

Chapter Twenty-Two

"Pickle isn't a bad cook," Wyatt said, "but a home-cooked meal in an actual home, now that's a rarity. And now I'm having my second this week."

"A rarity? Really?"

"You sound surprised." He arched an eyebrow.

"Seems like you'd meet a lot of people, given that you travel so much. You really never get a home-cooked meal?"

"Oh, yeah, lots of people shout out to us as we drift by and invite us in for dinner."

Ellie swung her spoon, trying to land a playful swat on his behind. He caught her hand before impact and laughed.

"Don't be such a smart aleck. You do dock sometimes. I know that from personal experience."

"We do dock sometimes, yes."

"And you meet people."

"Are you asking me if I've had home-cooked meals in other beautiful women's homes?"

Ellie stirred the gravy simmering on the stovetop. When was this Depression ever going to end? When would people be able to eat real food again and not just beans and breads and flimsy gravy made from bouillon instead of a scrumptious chunk of beef?

"I did not ask that." She flashed a scowl over her shoulder as she cut out biscuits from dough with an upside-down glass. "I have no reason to care how many bland meals you've choked down in the tackily decorated homes of the many desperate women who've lured you in off the river."

"Wow. That's pretty descriptive. Ever thought about writing a novel?"

"Yeah, a sordid romance novel. You have any more material I can use?" She popped the tray of biscuits into the oven, then tossed a tiny lump of leftover biscuit dough at him.

He snatched the dough off his face, pitched it onto the counter, and gathered her into his arms. After sweeping her into the sitting room, he deposited her on the settee and planted himself smack-dab against her. "You're a mouthy little thing, aren't you?"

"I have to be, with you," she said when she could finally speak through her laughter.

"I can shut you up, you know."

"And just how do you think you're going to do —"

His lips were on hers in an instant, then trailed over her cheek, her eyelids, back to her mouth. Wrapping her arms around his shoulders, she clasped him close, and for an extended, glorious moment, they sat inert, lips bonded, clutching each other, suspended in time. Nothing else existed. Nothing but Wyatt.

"Wyatt, the food!"

"Damn." He jumped up, and Ellie followed, hot on his heels, to the kitchen, toward a plume of gray smoke wafting from the oven.

Ellie grabbed a potholder and pulled open the oven door. "Oh, no! The biscuits are burnt to a crisp. I can't believe I wasted good food." Her shoulders slumped, and she looked at Wyatt, whose hand covered his mouth in an obvious attempt at stifling a laugh.

"It's your fault, you know." She coughed and waved at the smoke.

"I take full responsibility." Wyatt went to the breakfast alcove and opened a window. "But what was that you were saying about all the bad meals I've had to choke down?"

She swatted the potholder at him. "Oh, Wyatt, how can you joke at a time like this?"

He wrested the potholder from her and pulled the steaming tray from the oven. "It isn't the end of the world, dear, and yes, it's my fault completely. Come on, I'll take you out to dinner."

"No. Now, I said I was going to make you dinner, and that's what I'm going to do. I think I have a couple of potatoes left in the pantry."

After an improvised dinner of boiled beans and mashed potatoes with gravy, they headed back into the sitting room. Wyatt sat on the settee and pulled Ellie into his lap. "Delicious dinner, Miss Ellie."

"You're fibbing, but thank you." She drew strands of his tousled hair through her fingertips. A sleepy breeze found its way through the open French doors.

"Now this is heaven," he said.

They laughed again about the burned biscuits and chatted about their first full afternoon together, which they'd spent walking around Marietta, popping into various shops, and enjoying a waffle cone filled with ice cream.

Both fell silent now, their breathing the only sound in the stilled evening. His eyes closed, and she leaned and touched her lips to his. How she ached for all of him. He enclosed her in his arms and gently rolled her off the settee, onto the floor, and lay alongside her, his mouth sweeping from her lips to her neck.

The ringing of the telephone seemed to have no effect on his concentration. "I don't hear anything, do you?"

"Mmm." Ellie forced her lips away from Wyatt's. "I'd better get that."

The boat's generator had stopped working, Hoopie told Wyatt, and the captain was needed back at the boat.

"I hope you don't mind that I gave him your telephone number. I need to always be available for my crew."

"Of course not," Ellie said.

He exhaled a heavy sigh. "Tomorrow?"

****

Wyatt devoted the next day to making minor repairs around the house. He hadn't announced his intention to do so, but Ellie awoke to a *tap-tap-tapping* and went outside to find him hammering at some loose porch railing on the house. My goodness, his presence around the house felt good. She hadn't realized until then how much she missed having a cohort in her life.

Late in the afternoon, Hanne returned from her trip to Wheeling and met Wyatt when he returned to pick up Ellie for dinner, having finally convinced her to let him take her to a restaurant. He and Hanne exchanged rapid-fire banter like old friends, and although he invited her to dinner, she wanted to rest after the long bus ride.

They caught Marv that evening on his way out of the Levee House.

"Miss Eleanor, don't you look lovely toni— Well, I'll be a monkey's uncle. Wyatt Dare." Marv grabbed Wyatt's hand and slapped him on the back. "I see you found the lovely Miss Eleanor. It's about time. Now, you treat her good, you hear me?"

"For sure." He winked at Ellie. "How you doing, Marv?"

"Fine, just fine. I wish I'd known you were coming in tonight. I'd 've stayed. Promised the wife I'd be home early for the sister-in-law's birthday. Listen, tell Ruby your first drink's on the house. I'd say your meal's on me, too, but I know you'd ignore that anyway." Marv shot an accusatory look at Wyatt.

Wyatt never seemed to relish talking about himself, but during dinner on the patio, Ellie found out he had grown up on the Gulf.

"I never cared for the idea of college, but when Clemson came calling, I couldn't turn that down."

"Clemson? What, a scholarship? Are you kidding?"

"Football. Full scholarship. Changed my life. I got my degree in economics, then went to work on the river and started investing every penny I could. I wanted to acquire my own tow."

"So you own your towboat? Very impressive. And you've always enjoyed the river life?"

"Oh, sure." He nodded toward the river. "It's always been in my soul. But once I got married and we had Eddie, I pulled back a bit. When I was a kid, my father was gone all the time, and not always due to work. When he did make it home, he was usually zozzled or hungover. I wasn't going to be that kind of father."

"That must have been difficult for your mother and you. And did you have any siblings?"

"I'm an only child, and that's a good thing. I wouldn't have wanted another kid to grow up the way I did. My mom wasn't blessed with much of a maternal instinct."

"That's terrible, Wyatt. It's so sad when a child doesn't have at least one good, solid parent. Are your parents still alive?"

"Mom died about six years ago. Cancer, from what they told me. I don't know. I hadn't heard from her in years. I tried to keep in touch, but she was always moving and never letting me know where she was. And I haven't heard from my dad since I was a junior in high school. Left one day and never came back."

He motioned to her empty glass. "Another glass of wine?"

"No, thank you."

He swallowed another measure of his beer. "Beautiful evening, isn't it? And you sure don't see many restaurants situated right on the water. The Levee House is one unique place."

The sun had nearly fused with the horizon, and on cue, the bulbs crisscrossing the patio awning flicked on. A few other tables of people remained on the patio. Ellie pulled her cardigan closer around her shoulders, and they sat listening to the placid splash of water against the bank.

They walked slowly on their way back to the auto after dinner, their hands tightly clasped. Wyatt seemed reluctant for the evening to end, and Ellie dreaded saying goodnight—he and his crew were pulling out in the morning. So when he asked if she'd like a tour of his boat, she didn't have to think twice.

She'd never before stepped foot on a towboat. Showing her around, Wyatt explained the workings of the wheelhouse and showed her the crew lounge and the well-appointed galley. How well cared-for the boat was, freshly painted, in good repair, its wood trim gleaming. Ropes, lanterns, and assorted tools all neatly occupied their designated spaces on hooks and in cabinets.

After the tour, Wyatt led Ellie back to the deck, settled onto a wooden Adirondack chair, and pulled her to his lap. After a few minutes of chatting between kisses, they both fell quiet, listening to the crickets, faint voices, and a distant foghorn that rose above the ripple of the river. Flickering starlight in the charcoal sky competed with the lights of homes along the shore. When Wyatt tipped his head back against the chair, Ellie's eyes feasted on his face, his determined jaw, his sensual lips, the way his wavy golden hair lay against his neck. This man eroded the shell of her heart the way the ocean tide grinded seashells into sand.

Finally, she spoke. "I think it's time I headed home, Captain. You have to get up early." Her mind surged ahead, to the two of them in the captain's quarters, on his bed, his lips on hers, his hands moving across her body. Good thing it was nighttime. Wyatt couldn't possibly see the blush she was sure tinted her face.

"When do I see you again?"

"As soon as you can come back."

His lips curved into a smile. "Oh, I will be back soon, you can count on it. Say, Ellie, I've got an idea."

"Hmm?"

"Have you ever slept on a boat?"

Ellie cleared her throat and fiddled with her fingers. "Wyatt—"

"No, no, no, what I mean is…" He pursed his lips. "Well, whattaya say we go on a little trip? I'd like you to see what I see every day. I want you to see how I live. It would all be very proper. You would have your own cabin, of course."

"Okay!" Ellie blurted out as her eyes blazed wide. She shook her head then and rubbed her forehead. When would she ever learn to wait at least a heartbeat before coming to decisions? "I mean, for how long? Where would we go?"

"We'll head down the Ohio to the Mississippi and take that all the way to the Gulf, and I'll show you where I'm from. We'll have a great time. You can stay in Hoopie's cabin. He can find someplace else to sleep. I'll need him to come along to help me pilot so I can spend as much time as possible with the beautiful Miss Ellie."

"That sounds simply amazing, but when were you thinking we would go? The auction is scheduled for mid-November."

"Then we'll go in mid-October. The leaves will be beautiful then. Pack your bags, honey. I'm coming back for you."

Chapter Twenty-Three

Shoving off in the rose-hued hush of dawn on a bracing October morning, Ellie, Wyatt, and Hoopie headed downriver for their three-week trip. Hanne had hugged Wyatt nearly as hard as she hugged Ellie when she sent them off with a basket of sandwiches, coleslaw, and pumpkin pie for their lunch that first day.

Autumn turned out to be the perfect season for a cruise on shimmering waters, beneath lush, overhanging trees, into the esoteric world of life on the river. How delightfully the river reflected the impact of the red, orange, and golden leaves. Although the sun still warmed the air, the sweltering temperatures had packed up and gone on their own trip.

Ellie loved seeing Wyatt at the wheel, in captain mode in the wheelhouse, handsome in his captain's hat and performing the other tasks of his livelihood, and he began teaching her all about the tow business. Because of the low water level this time of year, he explained, he depended on his radio for reports from other craft of hidden underwater dangers. The radio also alleviated boredom and loneliness. The various crews served as each other's news sources and their entertainment, their banter at times humorous and often off-color. When two crafts passed one another, their pilots and deckhands waved both arms overhead, the traditional river greeting.

They docked in Portsmouth that first evening,

having traveled 179 nautical miles, Wyatt had told Ellie, adding that his boat could travel up to approximately fifteen knots, about seventeen miles per hour, when not pushing cargo. In Portsmouth, they enjoyed a crab-leg dinner on the patio of a riverfront restaurant. Hoopie had stayed behind on the boat. "It's where he'd rather be," Wyatt told Ellie when she insisted he accompany them.

"Wait here," Wyatt told her when they returned to the towboat shortly after ten, and he disappeared to the level below.

Soon, a placid jazz tune, accompanied by waves of static, flowed from a speaker mounted to a wall. Returning to the deck, Wyatt placed two glasses of wine on a fold-down tabletop. He took Ellie in his arms, and they swayed to the music and savored the wine from their glasses and from each other's lips. Civilization seemed a galaxy away.

"I'm very happy you're here, Miss Ellie. It's a little more pleasant having you onboard than all those characters."

"You mean this is something that doesn't normally go on out here with you and your crew? The music, the dancing, a little wine?"

Wyatt grabbed her off her feet and headed for the railing in one motion. "No, but I've been known to toss a person overboard on occasion."

"I'm sorry! I'm sorry!" Ellie shrieked. Wyatt lowered her back to her feet, and she doubled over in laughter. People on a nearby docked boat glanced over, smiled, and raised their drinks in greeting.

"Mouthy little thing, aren't you?" Wyatt clinched her chin between thumb and forefinger, giving it a reproving wiggle, and his hand lingered, then stroked her cheek. His eyes swept over her face before he leaned close and his lips melded with hers.

She slid her arms around him and ran her hands over his back, his sturdy muscles flexing as he clutched her closer. With a moan, he brushed his lips over the length of her neck. By now his face had taken on a stubble, and the combination with his tender lips sent sparking currents through her body.

Ellie scanned the other boats bobbing at rest for the night. "I feel like we're putting on a show."

Wyatt lifted her off her feet and carried her through a door, into the crew lounge, where he lowered her to a sofa. "No one can see us now."

Their mouths met again, his hands tracing her waist and moving over her hips. Writhing at his touch, Ellie pulled him closer.

"Cap'n?" A rap at the door accompanied the brittle voice. "You there, Cap'n?"

Wyatt pulled himself away and swung open the door. "Yeh, Hoopie, what is it, man?"

Hoopie emerged from the shadows. "Got a problem with engine two. Might be lookin' at replacin' one of the cylinders."

"All right, let's go." Wyatt returned to Ellie and brushed a strand of her hair from her face. "I'm sorry."

She kissed him, hugged him tightly, then released him. "It's fine. Go."

"Damn." He touched his lips to hers. "This'll probably take a while. Get some rest, and I'll see you in the morning."

Once Ellie finally stopped daydreaming about Wyatt, she slept incredibly soundly, by virtue of the gentle sway of the boat, no doubt. And the space was comfortable and charming. Wyatt had outfitted Hoopie's cabin with crisp cotton sheets for her, along with a jar of dahlias on the nightstand.

Upon awakening the next morning, Ellie climbed from bed and peered out the small square window. The river hid beneath a drifting, ghostly mist. Fuchsia-edged clouds on the horizon foretold the impending sunrise.

Surreal, all of it. This universe of life on the river, so close in proximity for her entire life, had been achingly unknown to her until now. The rumble of the engine, propelling the towboat forward when all Ellie had ever discerned from the banks was silent, effortless gliding. The displaced water whooshing beneath them, then falling silent in their wake. The piercing caw of a foreign bird. These were the props, the sights and sounds of Wyatt's everyday life.

Half an hour later, the engine coughed to a start, meaning the menfolk were up. Ellie flipped strips of bacon in a sizzling skillet, then cracked open several eggs. Wyatt had told her he would do the cooking, when they didn't eat ashore, but she wanted to surprise him and Hoopie with a nice breakfast, especially since they'd probably been up very late working.

Wyatt's arms slipped around her waist, he touched his lips to the side of her neck. "If I hadn't been covered with grease a few hours ago, I would have been knocking on your door."

Turning, she wrapped her arms over his shoulders and kissed him. He pressed hard against her. She could very easily let the bacon burn to a crisp and drag him back to her cabin that very moment.

"That bacon I smell?"

"Damn, Ellie, I can't handle this," Wyatt whispered.

She giggled. "Eggs too, Hoopie. Are you hungry?"

"I could eat, I could eat." Hoopie took a long drag of his cigarette stub, then pitched it overboard.

"How late were you fellows up?"

"What was it, Hoopie? Two, two-thirty? It took longer than we thought it would to replace that cylinder."

Hoopie wasn't far from what Ellie had pictured. Steel-wool black hair accented with gray, a wad of chewing tobacco in his jaw, a diminutive and thin man. But what a worker, more energetic than anyone she'd ever known. He served as a fifth-generation riverman, he told Ellie over breakfast.

"After President Abraham Lincoln's *Emancipation Proclamation*, my granddaddy made it up north, got himself work as a deckhand. Every generation of my family been working the river ever since." Hoopie reached into his shirt pocket, withdrew a small tin, pinched out a wad of chewing tobacco, and tucked it into his cheek. "This boat, she's my home. I got no other home. Wouldn't want it no other way." He turned his head to the side and discreetly spit into a tin can.

Wyatt had told the truth when he said his crew never shut up. Hoopie, for one, was a talker, his ebony eyes flashing with fervor at each dramatic tale he told, most of which Ellie could tell Wyatt had heard before. A person couldn't help liking Hoopie, given his passion for his work, his simple honesty, his raspy chicken's cackle of a laugh.

The men took turns piloting the boat, plowing the turquoise byway into fleeting furrows. When Ellie wasn't co-piloting with Wyatt, in her denim pants and the oversized newsboy cap Wyatt tapped onto her head, she swept the deck, prepared meals, or read one of the books she'd brought, all the while soaking up as much of the liquid journey as she possibly could. A journey through a parallel universe with a culture all its own and an unexpected, exquisite beauty. And one night, Ellie slipped into the cabin next door and joined her man in his bed.

Shortly before dawn, she lay hushed and still, watching him sleep, as if the slightest shift might break the sweet spell. She wanted to wring every image and sensation out of their time together. When he awakened, he reached for her and without a word they joined again and moved together with the cadence of the boat, and afterward, his first words swirled and glimmered around the two of them. *I love you, Ellie.*

****

"Ellie, come here, sweetheart. Take a look."

Ellie propped the broom against the railing and joined Wyatt at the bow. "Wowee, is this it?" Ahead, the water forked.

"Sure is. The mighty Mississippi."

The straightlaced, blue-green Ohio River had flowed passively through alluring old cities like Cincinnati and Louisville but now gave way to the lusty, mucky brown Mississippi at Cairo, Illinois, at the confluence of the two rivers.

"I can't believe how distinct the two rivers are," Ellie said. "It's like they're running alongside each other in their own channels."

"The colors are products of the depth of each river and the amount of sediment in each," Wyatt told her. "And you'll notice as we head into the Mississippi that the two colors run side by side for several miles. Eventually, though, it all blends in."

The Big Muddy enticed Ellie with the clout of the countless books, legends, and blues songs it had inspired, bequeathed through generations. As they churned along, Wyatt would hand over his binoculars, motioning toward a bobbing white-tailed deer or pointing out an elegant white great egret. The earnest cry of the common loon soared across the hills, and at night, spirited tree frogs busted out in creaky harmony.

The lights of distant civilizations would grow ever closer on the horizon. Then the boat would slide past the cities and towns, some rich with old homes and preserved buildings, their historical integrity intact, others modernized into commercial buildings and the trendy Craftsman and Tudor-style homes. Still other towns seemed decaying relics, hanging on with a few clapboard homes, warehouses embellished with faded advertisements, and a sprinkling of grayed church steeples peeking above great parasols of trees.

More than once, fishermen waved or tipped their straw hats from the banks. And Ellie was sure that somewhere in Missouri she spotted Tom and Huck on a brittle dock, their bare toes skimming the water, squashed worms dangling on hooks at the ends of their cane poles. Sometimes the Mississippi spanned such widths that both banks couldn't be seen.

Gradually, the river revealed its southernmost, syrupy heritage. Lithe weeping willow trees swayed with the subtlest breeze. Spanish moss dripped from enormous live oak trees. Antebellum mansions rose high on hilltops, their fronts always facing the river that once had served as their inhabitants' highway. Then there were the sunsets, more spectacular on the river than on land, with the plunging sun aiming sparkling beams across the water and the oranges blazing deeper, the golds gleaming warmer, then giving way to the dark and the cicadas and the screech owls.

Tying off in Memphis, the voyagers ended up staying there two nights, there was so much to absorb. They walked the haggard bricks of Beale Street and listened to the blues, authentic in its misery, in musty juke joints humid with residual tears. The farther south they traveled, the more excitement Ellie sensed building in Wyatt. She, as well, couldn't wait to see Biloxi, Mississippi, the place where Wyatt had been born and grown up. She couldn't wait to learn more about him through the lens of his hometown, although by now she knew him well, she thought. Quite well.

Chapter Twenty-Four

"Nice meeting you." Eddie's hand gripped Ellie's. A good-looking young man, a couple inches taller than his father, same eyes and smile but dark-haired, and his wife Paige was lovely and sweet.

Wyatt's interactions with his son were warm and relaxed. Instinctively, Ellie took a back seat. Wyatt and Eddie had missed each other and needed to reconnect. And when Wyatt invited her to go fishing with them the next day, she declined. Having his father all to himself would mean a lot to the young man. Instead, she took the opportunity to explore Biloxi.

The town reminded her in many ways of Marietta, both situated on a river and brimming with beautiful, historical buildings and homes. But as she wove her way through the streets, she soon felt the coastal ambience that saturated the city. The waters of the Gulf of Mexico outlined the city in olive green. Old brick buildings contrasted with sherbet-colored beach villas, strips of sand, and a sprinkling of palm trees. This was the town that had given birth to Wyatt, raised him, formed him, and Ellie sensed him in everything she saw and heard and felt.

The next evening, she and Wyatt met two of his lifelong buddies, Luke and Freddy, along with Luke's wife, Shaylene, for dinner at Luke and Shaylene's home.

"So, Ellie, how'd you end up with this character?"

Luke took a swig of his beer.

"She lured me in off the river with her siren call. And she fed me a delicious meal. Right, honey?"

"Just like many, many other women have done. Right, darling?" Ellie placed a basket of hushpuppies and a bowl of black-eyed peas on the table and directed a syrupy-sweet smile at Wyatt.

"Has he told you the real reason he's always out on the river?" Freddy asked. "You know, the felony? The fleeing-the-law thing?"

Wyatt gave his buddy a shove. "You'll pay for that later, Fast Freddy."

Their back-and-forth teasing reminded Ellie of Benny and his friends. Why did grown men always seem to revert to their high school selves when they got together?

After Shaylene added a platter of steaming crab legs and shrimp to the table, the women took their seats.

"So tell me about the teenaged Wyatt, the little boy Wyatt," Ellie said. "What was this character like back in the day?"

"Complete pain in the ass." Freddy shook his head and plucked seafood from the platter with his fingers, ignoring the tongs.

"But a decent football player, I suppose." Luke slapped Wyatt on the back. "When he wasn't out horsing around on the water."

"I'm sure all three of you did your share of horsing around," Ellie said.

"Oh, honey, I could tell you stories." Shaylene leaned across the table. "We'll talk later," she said before breaking into spirited laughter.

"Did you grow up with these guys?"

"Sure did, and lived to tell the tale. And don't listen to these two goofballs, honey. This one here is *the* best." She tilted her head toward Wyatt. "You won't find a nicer fellow anywhere."

"Come on, Shaylene, tell her the truth," Freddy said. "It's for her own good. Pass those hushpuppies this way, would ya, honey?"

"Okay, you want the truth, Ellie?" Shaylene asked. "Every girl in school was madly in love with Wyatt Dare." She flashed a quick smile toward Luke. "Except for me, of course. Wyatt was the star of the football team, prom king, you name it. And just nice as could be to everyone. Didn't matter who they were, he was just nice. Still is."

"Okay, he's not all bad." Luke thrust a shrimp into his mouth. "In between prison stints, he's done some decent things for the old hometown."

Ellie paused in digging a hunk of crab meat from its shell and directed a quizzical look at Wyatt. "What sort of things?"

"I have no idea what he's talking about," Wyatt said before a swallow of beer.

On their fourth day in town, Wyatt guided her into an old, brick three-story building on the coast that housed restaurants and shops selling artwork, hand-rolled cigars, locally made chocolates, and clothing made of finely woven cotton. Their footsteps clapped on wooden floorboards, and Ellie feasted her eyes on the various doors adorned with wrought iron and leaded glass.

"It's just lovely, very unique."

"Thank you."

"Thank you? You mean..." Did Wyatt actually own this place?

"The place sat empty for years. Old warehouse. I hated to see it crumble. About eight years ago I bought it, renovated it, brought in the tenants. It's been a good thing for the city."

Ellie screeched to a halt, grabbing Wyatt's arm to arrest his brisk pace. "Wait a minute. You never mentioned this. I thought you were a towboat captain."

He laughed. "That's my day job." He grabbed Ellie's hand and resumed his stride. "Of course, since the economy took a dive, it's been a struggle to keep the place afloat. You'll notice that many of the shops are selling utilitarian items and necessities along with their specialties. Grains, fabrics, basic clothing. It's the only way they've been able to survive, and not all have survived. You'll see a few empty spaces as we walk through."

"Wyatt, I'm shocked. This is major, and you never said a word about it."

"I guess I don't like tooting my own horn. But I like doing things for the old hometown, and this was my most recent project."

Ellie's mouth dropped open. "The most recent? What else have you done?"

"Come on." He led her to another old building, two blocks north. The sign planted on the lawn read *Youth Club of Biloxi*. Wyatt had donated the small building, he said, because he wanted kids enduring tough childhoods, like his own, to have a chance.

"They can come here after school, shoot some hoops, do some crafting, make friends, have a good meal. Keeps them off the streets."

Ellie had difficulty formulating words. "I'm just... I'm so proud of you, Wyatt. Really. You are amazing."

"Come on. There's one more thing I want to show you." He walked her a few blocks to a huge storage building on an inlet, where he flipped through a ring of keys that had been jangling in his pocket, then unlocked a door and flipped on a light. Half a dozen towboats perched on risers.

"Don't tell me. These are yours."

"They are. These are either waiting to go back out, or they're in line for maintenance or repairs."

"You didn't tell me you owned more than the one boat. And each of these has a crew?"

"I have about a dozen crews at any given time. When one tow needs repairs, it comes in and another goes out. I have nine out right now."

"I am simply shocked," Ellie said.

Some of the towboats, he told her, extended up to two hundred feet long and forty-five feet wide and could handle up to fifteen hundred tons of cargo, fifteen times more than a railroad car and sixty times more than a truck trailer could carry. The average river tow, he said, consisted of fifteen barges, linked together three abreast.

He grabbed her hand. "Come on, one more thing to see." Across the concrete floor, he pushed a massive, sliding wooden door aside. Once inside the room, he flipped on a light switch. A small old paddlewheel riverboat rested on yet another platform.

Ellie gasped. "Oh my! Is this yours?"

Wyatt glided a hand over its hull, then circled the boat, inspecting its sanded surfaces. "Bought her several years ago. Eddie and I work on it when we can find the time."

"My goodness. So you're restoring it? These old riverboats are rare. I remember Marv once telling me there aren't many of them left. Marietta has one, the *Valley Gem* sternwheeler. It's a tourist boat now."

"Yeh, sure, I've seen it. I was damned lucky to get this one. She was built right here in Biloxi in 1842. She was a beauty in her time. Sat for years in storage. Then someone bought her, fixed her up—if that's what you want to call what they did to her—and opened her up for tourist rides. The guy made it seaworthy, but the things he did to it..." Wyatt shook his head. "All in the name of making a buck, not historical integrity. You see here." He took Ellie's hand and led her up a ladder and onto the boat. He pointed out the dented aluminum strips mounted on the wooden railings, the warped linoleum covering the floors.

"Now, here's what she once looked like." Wyatt pulled a folder from a wooden bin attached to a wall and removed several photographs. "The Biloxi library let me borrow these."

The photographs appeared taken around the mid-nineteenth century. In one of them, people sat at a table in a dining room basking in embossed floral wallpaper, gleaming wood trim, and a crystal chandelier. Ellie's eyes widened at the stained-glass panels accenting the windows. Another photo showed people on deck, the women clothed in elaborate long dresses, parasols stemming from their gloved hands. Yet another showed a group of top-hatted men playing cards at a table, cigars dangling from their mouths, in a room lined with shelves of books.

"My goal is to get the boat back to its original appearance," Wyatt said. "It's costing a pretty penny and taking a lot of time, but it'll be worth it. Do you think you could help me out with some stained glass?"

"I would love to create some panels for this boat. I would make them as close to the originals as possible. Oh, Wyatt, I'm so excited. It's going to be beautiful when you're finished with it. What will you do with it?" She took a seat on the captain's chair.

"This will be our vacation home, mine and Eddie's. And yours." He shot a smile at her. "We'll take it out into the Gulf and watch the fireworks on the fourth of July, we'll take it over to New Orleans for Mardi Gras, wherever we want."

****

Their first night back on the towboat, lanterns swaying on their hooks blazed through the dusky mist but couldn't cut through the gloom that had settled over Ellie. Every mile upstream seemed to push Wyatt and her farther and farther apart. What different lives they lived, and so far away from each other. It was all so much more apparent, now that she'd seen what his life was like and visited his habitats. Would his interest in her withstand their long, frequent separations? Would they be able to make this work? Was this thing even real? They had talked more than once during the trip about a future together, but the doubts seemed to pile up more with every knot they traveled.

On their last evening aboard, Ellie sat on Wyatt's lap, the two of them wrapped close in a thick quilt on deck. Crisp, cooler air had replaced the South's dense atmosphere. A chorus of tree frogs *ribbit*ed, and a dark, V-shaped regiment of Canadian geese squawked overhead.

"Sweetheart?"

Why was she afraid to answer him? To even look into his eyes?

"Ellie, look at me." He nudged her chin so her eyes had nothing to see but him. "Why so quiet? What's bothering you?"

Wanting him so badly scared her. What if this had all been a fairy tale, a honeymoon of sorts, with no basis in reality? She pressed a palm to her forehead. Her head almost ached with the weight of her fears. "Everything has been so good, and now it's back to reality."

"This *is* reality. Just have a little faith, okay?"

She traced the pattern of the quilt with a finger and nodded.

"I told you I would cut down on my work, and I'll come see you in Oak Park as often as I can. We can meet in Marietta sometimes. Maybe we could both move there at some point. I want to be with you, Ellie." He peered sidelong at her through squinted eyes, as if sizing up her reaction. "You're not saying anything."

"Wyatt, I don't want you to make any major changes so soon, not for me. Anything you do should be because it's right for you. I think"—she searched for the right words—"I don't think we should manipulate our lives for each other this early."

He pulled her closer. "I'm not saying we have to rush things. But, honey, you're crazy if you think anything I do to be with you would have to be forced. You're my girl. I love you. We *will* be together. You do want this, don't you?"

"Of course I do. I love you so much, Wyatt. I want to be with you forever."

"Then we *will* be together, come hell or high water."

Chapter Twenty-Five

"Have you lost your mind, woman? That spectacular specimen of a man wants you, says he'll move to Marietta for you, and you can't pull yourself away from Illinois?" Deb paced the sitting room, shaking her head, flailing her arms. "What is wrong with you?"

"Sit down, Deb. It's her life."

Deb continued her tirade, ignoring Anita. "What is keeping you in Chicago? Your work? You can work anywhere. Your friends? Hello?" She pointed her thumbs at herself.

Ellie propped herself against the French doors, watching silvery droplets drizzle down from cantankerous clouds. The river always reflected the mood of the sky, and today that mood was gray, like her own. After bringing her home from their wonderful journey, Wyatt had headed back down that river three days ago.

He'd spent one night at Ellie's house before leaving, and that evening, the gals had met him and Ellie at Harmar Tavern. They'd all been as impressed by him as Ellie knew they would be—Deb, of course, having already met him, at the gala back in the spring.

How Ellie missed Wyatt now. She brushed her hands over her arms, remembering all the nights she'd luxuriated close to him, when the two of them whispered their desires to each other in the steamy air, their bodies like one, their mouths fused together, their passion building and building into molten crescendos night after night.

"Ellie?" Deb tapped her on the shoulder. "Are you with us or still somewhere off down that river?"

"Hmm?" Ellie spun around. "I don't know, Deb. I don't know how it will work out, but Oak Park is my home. I can't simply walk away. Not yet." Ellie returned to the settee and pulled her legs up alongside herself.

Thankfully, Ellie's friends had all been available tonight to come over. Friday nights could be lonely when a person was missing someone. And Ellie had helped Hanne move into her cottage during the past two days, so the house would have been particularly quiet tonight. Ellie had made pizza for the gals, and now they relaxed with drinks and the assorted cookies she'd baked.

"And I wouldn't want Wyatt to jump through any hoops and make any major changes for me and then, down the road, maybe resent me for being the reason for those changes."

"I'll tell you what, kid." Deb tapped an oatmeal cookie toward Ellie, "if you don't want him, I'll take him."

"Keep your paws off him," Ellie said. "Look, we're both committed to this, but we're not going to rush into anything."

"I thought you didn't want a man, Deb." Anita snatched the bottle of wine from the coffee table and refilled her goblet.

"I'll choose to ignore that remark." Deb plopped onto the floor and leaned back on her elbows. "Ellie, when you come to your senses, let me know. I'll come up and help you move."

"I'll help too," Charlene said.

Anita bit into a chocolate chip cookie. "How much does he make, anyway? I mean, the guy runs a tow."

"That's just like you, Anita. It's all about the dough, isn't it?" Deb said.

"Seriously, Ellie," Anita said, "you need to think about what this man can bring to the table."

"Well, what you need on your table and what I need on mine are two different things," Ellie said. "By the way, did I mention Wyatt owns a fleet of towboats and several buildings in Biloxi?"

"Wait, what?" Deb hoisted herself forward. "He owns what?"

Ellie told them about Wyatt's enterprises, as well as his generosity to charities.

Anita intently chewed on her cookie, longer than was necessary.

"Ooh, Ellie." Charlene rubbed her scrunched-up shoulders. "Could the man be any more perfect?"

"So where'd he get his money?" Anita asked. "Inherit it?"

"How about we talk about you, Anita?" Deb stretched back onto the floor, her head propped on linked hands. "You're so full of questions tonight. Who are you making whoopee with this week?"

Anita's expression soured. "None of your beeswax, Deb. And why aren't you with Vinnie, if he was so swell?"

Deb winced. "Well, I... Look, Vinnie was a good man. If you'd try dating someone single for once in your life, you might be able to discern what a good man is and isn't."

Anita issued a loud laugh. "You are hardly the

woman to be giving dating advice, Deb."

"Girls, come on." Charlene clutched at the sides of her head. "Enough of the bickering, okay? Let's have a nice evening."

"Right." Ellie stood and smacked her hands together. "How about we play a game? I picked up that popular new board game in town the other day. I forget what it's called, but you go around the board trying to buy up properties and hotels and stuff."

Deb shook her head. "You got anything else? We sell that game at the store, but I've heard it's too complicated and takes way too long to play. It'll be off the shelves in no time."

The gals opted for a game of cards instead. As usual, the evening went late and turned into a sleepover, the four sleeping in the sitting room on mounds of thick quilts like they did as little girls. Thank goodness for her friends, especially now with Aunt Lillian gone. Their gabbing, laughter, and even their bickering filled the house with a familiar hum and a welcome comfort.

****

When Hanne came up to the house for lunch a few days later, the drab palette of another rainy day extended into the normally cheery kitchen. Mother Nature was doing her part in contributing to the bleak atmosphere. The auction was fast approaching. Soon Aunt Lillian's possessions would be gone. The house itself would be gone. The notion stabbed at Ellie's heart.

"It is not going to be easy, missy." Hanne buzzed around setting the table, as comfortably as if she'd never left. "Lord knows we both have spent many wonderful years in this home."

"It never occurred to me that this house might not be

a part of my life one day." Ellie shuffled over to a kitchen window.

The river lay beneath a gray haze. The entire valley seemed to be mourning the impending sale of the iconic house that had long reigned supreme over the land.

Ellie returned to the stove, turned off the flame, and dished out potato pancakes from the cast-iron skillet. "They sure don't make nice, heavy pieces like this anymore." She paused with the spatula midair and glanced around the kitchen. They didn't make houses like this anymore either.

What had she been thinking? Putting the house on the market. And making the decision so quickly, so readily. Giving up this house on the premise that it would seem a sad place in Aunt Lillian's absence would be a mistake. A big mistake, and it would dishonor the home.

Marv had told Ellie that evening at the Levee House that the sadness would eventually flow along, like the river. The wistful memories and grief would reemerge at random moments regardless of where Ellie spent her time. But pushing the house away would fracture her last tangible link to her aunt. The space between these walls held so much happiness and years of cherished memories. But that space awaited new memories and continued joy. Joy that had become scarce for her, living alone now, in Oak Park.

"Hanne, I'm keeping it!"

Hanne went to Ellie and patted her shoulder. "Well, your aunt would want you to have it, dear. You have had many meals out of that skillet."

"No, I mean I'm going to keep the house." Ellie tossed the spatula onto the counter and flung her arms wide. "I'm going to keep everything!"

Hanne cocked her head, propped her hands on her hips, and frowned. "Sweetie, you are not thinking straight. You are tired and you are sad and—"

"No. Hanne, listen. There really is no reason to sell this place. I love it. It's my second home. I don't know why I thought it would be tough to keep it. Of course, I'll always miss Aunt Lillian, but I'll miss her no matter where I live. I'm going to sell my house and move here. I'll be closer to Benny and Jessie. You and I will be able to see each other often. Oh my goodness, Hanne, I'm moving here!"

She'd rushed into the decision to sell the house, when her grief of losing Aunt Lillian was fresh. And she'd based it purely on emotion. Vintage Ellie. But it seemed so clear now. Keeping the house was the right thing to do.

"Well, that would be wonderful. But I do not see how you will stop the auction at this point, missy. It is only a few days away."

"Where's that business card?" Ellie hurried to the desk tucked into a corner of the kitchen and shuffled through a folder. "I'm phoning the auctioneer to tell him I've changed my mind. I know you've done a lot of work getting ready for the auction, and I'm sorry. But I'm moving in, Hanne." She hugged Hanne, did a little dance, and picked up the telephone.

During the next several days, Ellie and Hanne disassembled tables full of household items and put them away. Deb and Charlene came to help, thrilled that their friend would be living here permanently, in the house that had been nearly as much a part of their lives as Ellie's. Having been told of her plans, Benny and Jessie also supported her without question. Ellie shuddered at how close she'd come to losing the house, the site of decades of laughter and conversation and tears and comfort and growing up and adventure and love. This was home.

Late that afternoon, Ellie wrapped herself in her chunky cardigan and strolled to the back of the property. A chilly day, but temperatures weren't so cold that she couldn't enjoy these last few afternoons outside. She'd always milked summer for every last drop of fresh air, sunshine, and warmth she could wring out of it, wearing cutout shoes as long as possible and resisting coats until forced to acquiesce. When everyone else declared summer over with the onset of school, she'd always refused to comply.

She soaked up the view over the valley, stunning year-round but spectacular now, with the leaves lingering late this year, clutching to branches with all their brittle might. Waves of red, umber, and burnt orange billowed like cumulus clouds across the landscape and reflected in the river like an oil painting. The river itself seemed to know it was supposed to flow at a slower pace. But for the stray fishing boat, the only craft out now were on commercial missions.

No sooner did she enter the kitchen than the telephone rang.

"Hello, gorgeous. What are you up to?"

Ellie's heartbeat quickened, as it did every time she heard Wyatt's sonorous voice. He'd phoned at least once each week since they'd parted, and she'd been barely able to stand waiting for his call this week. How happy he would be to hear her news.

"Hello, Captain. Just getting back inside the house. I was outside taking in the valley in autumn. It's so beautiful. I wish you were here."

"I wish I were there too, honey. How are you doing? I know this is a tough week for you, with the auction coming up."

Ellie paced the kitchen floor, as far as the telephone cord would allow. "Actually, there isn't going to be an auction."

"What? Why?"

"I've decided to keep the house. And live here, permanently. I'm going to sell my house and move to Marietta."

Silence.

Oh no. Ellie paused and supported herself against the counter. Could it be that this news didn't please him, after all? "Are you there? Wyatt?"

"I'm here. I'm just...speechless. You're moving to Marietta?" Wyatt let out a laugh of pure delight. "Are you kidding me, Ellie? How did that happen?"

Ellie exhaled and laughed and resumed her pacing. "I had an enlightening, I suppose. I just realized I couldn't give up the place. The children live close by, I have good friends here, I love Marietta, and I love this house. It just all makes sense."

"Aw, honey, I can't believe it. We're actually going to be together. I've got a good lead on some warehouse space in Marietta, for my riverboat. And Eddie is ready to take over the management of part of my tow business. He's top notch, and he's always expressed a desire to take on more responsibility. He'll have some ownership now, too. And I'll be able to lighten up on my workload."

"You mean... Wyatt, you've already made all those plans?"

"Well, tentative plans, sure. Ellie, did you think I

wasn't serious? I mean, I would never try to rush you into anything you weren't ready for, but I told you I would do whatever it takes to be with you. And I knew I had the best chance of being with you if I put down some roots in Marietta, Ohio."

Ellie caught a sob before it erupted, her hand went to her chest. "That's wonderful, Wyatt."

"I'll come back as soon as I can, honey, and you can help me find a place to live. Something small, not far from Harmar Hill."

"All right, yes, that sounds terrific, darling. How soon can you get here?"

"Well, I have a couple trips I need to finish up, and then I want to meet face to face with my two biggest accounts, to let them know what's going on. I'll need to finalize the arrangements for the business, the legalities. How does early spring sound?"

"Too far away, but I'll be waiting for you, my love."

Chapter Twenty-Six

"First the Duke of Windsor, now you. Why is everyone running away from home?"

"Aww, Betts, we'll be just a short drive away from each other. I'll be coming back so often you'll get sick of me. And you will bring your bottom down to Marietta at least a couple times a year, no excuses."

"Well, I don't know why I'm helping you. I don't want you to go, girlfriend. Are you sure about moving to some godforsaken little town in the depths of rural Ohio? And selling the house? Have you really given it some serious thought?"

Betty's concerns were legitimate. Ellie had listed the house once before, right after Mason moved out. How could she live in the house after he deserted her, leaving her there to survive on nothing but memories? Thankfully, the first offer that rolled in had startled some sense into her, and she'd promptly taken the house off the market. She hadn't been ready to leave her home. When would she ever learn not to make such hasty, emotion-driven decisions? But this decision continued feeling right.

Ellie pulled off another length of tape and pressed it into place around a window. "I'm sad too, Betts. You know that. But yes, I'm sure of what I'm doing."

"Well, things just won't be the same here without you." Betty swished her roller brush through the tray of off-white paint, then onto the biscotti-gold dining room wall. "And I don't know how any woman could pull herself away from Wyatt long enough to spend time with her friend or anyone else. The man is magnificent, Ellie. He really is."

Ellie had invited Wyatt for a visit while Benny and Jessie were home, so he'd flown up after Christmas and checked into a hotel for a few days, and Ellie and Wyatt had met Betty in Chicago for dinner one evening. The children seemed to like him too, Benny saying he was an upright guy, Jessie declaring him a dreamboat, and both saying they only wanted their mom to be happy.

"He is pretty great, isn't he?"

"The best, which you deserve, Ells. And I will never recover from the remorse of having pushed you to see that cad Gregory. Major blunder on my part."

"You had no way of knowing what he was really like."

"Well, thank heaven you're not the type to put up with any hogwash and you got away from him. And what about Mason? Is he still phoning you?"

"I haven't heard from Mason in months." Why had the mention of his name clawed at her heart just a bit? "I guess he finally gave up."

****

Once the house was listed, the impending move became real. Ellie couldn't wait for spring and to be with Wyatt. But she didn't want to leave the house sitting empty until it sold, and that was taking longer than anticipated. In spite of its beauty, architecture, and historical significance as one of the original homes in Oak Park, showings were sparse during winter, and the few offers had been lower than she wanted to accept. So she stayed put and tried to curb her longings. Thankfully, she had her stained-glass work to occupy herself.

Wyatt also had his challenges this winter, Ellie came to learn. Thick ice could cause structural damage to the boat hulls, frigid temperatures might freeze the water pipes, and maintaining full crews in the cold months proved challenging. All of which collaborated to restrain his productivity.

Once Ellie finally completed the stained-glass project, in mid-February, she flew to Biloxi to spend a week with Wyatt after he insisted on purchasing her airplane ticket. On that first morning in their coastal hotel room, she awoke to his touch. He moved more powerfully than ever before, devouring her with what seemed a compulsion. His eyes left hers only to drift over her body or to shut briefly at the pleasure. After, he lay close at her side.

"I need you, Ellie. I can't be away from you that long again."

Ellie kissed his lips, his face. Such a beautiful, honest face, so expressive of his love for her. "I feel the same, darling. I can't wait to be with you permanently."

"Well, it won't be long. No more of this far-apart nonsense." He pulled her into the bend of his arm, and she burrowed her face against his neck, indulging in his scent.

He smacked her bottom when he rolled out of bed a few minutes later. "Come on. It's our last day in Biloxi. Let's make the most of it."

A short drive over to Gulfport after breakfast, followed by a brief ferry ride, took them to Ship Island. They spent the morning strolling the boardwalk and the beach and indulging in sugar-dusted beignets and thick strawberry milkshakes at a weathered, clapboard-sided soda fountain. Ellie thrived in the sunshine and balmy temperatures, such a contrast to Illinois this time of year.

They dined that evening at a rooftop restaurant peppered with yellow-striped umbrellas and immersed in squawking seagulls. From there, they could see the blue-green waters of the Gulf of Mexico ripple to shore, then swoosh out again. As dusk descended, lights around town switched on one by one, as if choreographed.

After dinner, they strolled the short way to the coast, kicked off their shoes, and walked barefoot on the still-warm sand of the beach. Wyatt had rolled up his trousers, and Ellie lifted the hem of her cotton dress. Pink and coral and lavender airbrushed the sky. But even more beautiful was Wyatt in his light-blue, button-down shirt. Much more than handsome, his face reflected the strength and passion she'd come to know in him. The breeze mussed his already unruly hair, and his hazel eyes squinted against the low sun. With his hand clutching hers, they stepped along the coastline, their feet sinking into the gritty sand, cool waves splashing their legs.

Wyatt led her to a bar in an old beachfront building. Inside, wooden planks squeaked and submitted slightly under their feet, and magenta and turquoise neon signs advertising one or another brand of beer buzzed on the walls. A band of five talented young men about Benny's age twanged out a very southern country music tune. According to Wyatt, he and his buddies had begun frequenting the place as soon as they were old enough, maybe even a bit sooner. This was one of his favorite hangouts back in the day. Biloxi's answer to the Low Falutin.

People crammed into every square inch of the place,

so Ellie and Wyatt took their drinks outside. Beneath white lights dripping from the magnolia and cypress trees bordering the patio, patrons talked, laughed, and drank as the sun completed its descent into the Gulf, leaving behind a smear of gold, eggplant, and burnt orange. Taking Ellie's hand, Wyatt led her onto the sun-bleached pier stretching into the Gulf in front of the bar. Other couples leaned against the wooden rail, clinging to each other. An old man in a Greek fisherman's cap swung his fishing pole sidelong, casting his line into the dark waters. Had he come out tonight for want of fish or humanity?

At the far end of the pier, Wyatt kissed Ellie. His resolute love and the salty Gulf air wrapped her in a warm, promising mist. Water sloshed below them, seagulls squealed above, and the flickering of a thousand lightning bugs dappled the black-velvet sky. And when the night couldn't get any more magical, a lovely song from the band drifted to the end of the pier. Wyatt and Ellie moved together to the tune, their chests pressed together, his thighs brushing hers.

Wyatt hummed along, never moving his eyes from hers, and when the song ended, he dipped her backward, then drew her back up and squeezed her tightly. "My beautiful gal," he whispered. "I will always feel a glow whenever I remember the way you look tonight," he said.

Ellie's heart billowed and surged like the ocean waves and tucked him deep inside, and she trembled in her need for him.

****

Jessie took the bus home during spring break, along with Benny, who was able to get away from his farm work for a few days. Ellie's heart slumped in a weighty heap at knowing this would be their last time together in the family home, for the house had sold. But hard as she tried to divert her eyes every time the tears welled up, Benny and Jessie must have noticed the torment. They, too, had to have felt some pain, but they promptly dispelled the momentousness of their mother's move.

"Home is wherever you are, Mom," they told her, repeatedly assuring her that it was the right decision and the best thing for her until she remembered that it was.

In early April, Ellie headed down the highway, a moving van full of the things she couldn't part with trailing behind. She would miss her cherished city terribly, but she would visit. She would come back to soak it all up again. And the city itself would come back. When the somberness of the Depression lifted, brilliance would once again glint off the many facets of the White City.

Wyatt had told her he would arrive in Marietta during the third week of the month. Maybe now Ellie could finally let down her guard and know that everything was going to be all right. No. That things were going to be wonderful.

Chapter Twenty-Seven

Rain drenched Marietta on Ellie's first day as a resident. A good day to stay inside unpacking, storing her clothes, arranging furniture. How nice that the things she'd brought—her antique bookcase with beveled glass doors, the vintage vanity from her bedroom, the cut-glass vase she'd received as a wedding gift—blended so well among Aunt Lillian's furnishings. She kept her own bedroom at the house, rather than moving into Aunt Lillian's master suite, which would go to Benny, and Jessie would stay in Hanne's old quarters, whenever they came home.

The wide landing at the end of the second-floor hallway had proved the perfect spot for Ellie's stained-glass studio. Two pretty cabinets stood against the side walls, full of her tools and solutions and bits and pieces of colored glass, with her sturdy wooden worktable in front of the bank of floor-to-ceiling mullioned windows. Not only did the windows provide abundant natural light, necessary for the miniscule functions of stained-glass work as well as for matching and coordinating various colors of glass, but from here Ellie could see nearly the entire valley, a good stretch of the river, and the Appalachian Mountains beyond. The balcony outside would provide the perfect space for breaks in her work, and she'd added a decorative folding screen to conceal the worktable when she wasn't working.

After a few days of getting settled, Ellie headed into town to pick up groceries and other necessities. The river reached frighteningly high on the banks. The rain hadn't stopped since she'd arrived. Everywhere, everyone was talking about the incessant rain and the level of the river. The most Marietta had seen since the great flood of 1913, they said, with more forecasted. Ellie's heart quivered at the sight of the bloated river. The homes and businesses in the valley were at tremendous risk. Thankfully, her house sat high above the river. She couldn't wait to get back home.

Home. The word seemed foreign, given that her home had changed within the period of a few days. Of course she felt infinitely comfortable in the house, and its former incarnation as Aunt Lillian's home would gradually and willingly evolve into really being her place.

Before heading back up the hill, Ellie sent off a telegram to Mason to tell him she'd sold the house and moved to Ohio. Although he likely already had heard, it was only right that she inform him since they had children together.

Mason's reply the following day seemed shaded by melancholy and regret and inferred that he also knew about Wyatt. *I wish you the best. I wish it were you and me.*

And that was that. Mason Todd, father of her children, the man she'd wanted to spend the rest of her days with, shifted from her rearview mirror to completely out of her line of vision. And she was okay with that. He'd betrayed her, and consequently their marriage had ended. That was that, and she was all right with it. She would have to be.

Four days later, with the rain still pummeling the valley and the river swelling like bread dough, many residents of the lower areas of Marietta began to leave town or seek shelter with friends or relatives atop Harmar Hill. Ellie dialed up Hanne and didn't have to prod her very much to return to the house high above the river. She soon arrived lugging a suitcase and two bags of groceries, distraught over the recent crash of the *Hindenburg* airship, particularly since it had originated in her homeland.

"It is tragic, simply tragic," she squeaked out through tears. "I am telling you what, I don't know what this world is coming to. All sorts of terrible things are happening. I am very worried for my family back in the old country. I am not so sure the Führer has their best interests at heart. One would think he wants war. Oh, Eleanor, everything is such a mess."

"I know, Hanne, I know. But it's going to be fine." Ellie pulled her into a long hug. "You're here now, we're here together, and everything will be fine."

Deb phoned to say she'd be heading up. No need to ask permission.

"Have you talked to Charlene or Anita?" Ellie asked.

"Anita thinks she'll be okay. She's a bit on edge, but her house sits pretty high up, you know. And Charlene and Alan got the store all boarded up. They said I could come out and stay with them, but of course I'd rather be up there with you. That place is my second home, you know."

This wasn't the first time the sturdy old house had harbored refugees from the valley during a flood. A yellowed, framed newspaper article on the wall in Uncle Edward's library described the home's history, including the haven it had provided in 1884 during what was described as a flood of biblical proportions. Before Aunt Lillian and Uncle Edward, only two families had owned the mansion, built in 1880 by Captain Samuel Wilkes, a riverboat pilot and prominent citizen. More than a home to the Wilkes family, the house had also served during their residency as a meeting place for men's political discussions and women's tea parties and garden clubs. The next family to purchase the home had opened an inn, and Aunt Lillian and Uncle Edward had owned it since Ellie could remember.

Within the hour, a knock at the door, followed by a commanding *hello*, brought Anita, dripping wet, lugging a suitcase and a grocery bag.

"Anita! I was going to phone you, but Deb said you were staying home."

"I cannot take another night alone with all this rain. My word, have you ever seen the river this high?" Anita headed for the kitchen, reached into the paper sack, and placed three bottles of her favorite wine on the counter, the only thing she'd brought, as it turned out. "Thank God Prohibition ended when it did," she added.

Ellie laughed. "I'm glad you're here. Come on. You're soaked. I've got a nice fire going in the fireplace."

Ellie led her to the sitting room, then peered out the window for the hundredth time today. Bulging, murky clouds continued flinging blankets of rain onto the suffocating town. If this rain kept up, the river would overflow its banks by morning. Marietta seemed a soggy remnant of itself, with the only activity being efforts to protect homes and businesses. Store proprietors pounded nails into wooden planks crisscrossing windows, homeowners shoved outdoor furniture into sheds. Along the banks, men slid boats onto trailers hitched to pickup trucks and pulled them from the water.

Soon, Deb arrived at the house and promptly unloaded an array of deli meats and cheeses, several bottles of beer, and her pet cat. Vito was a gentle white-and-gray American Shorthair, and Ellie welcomed the adorable distraction from the impending disaster.

"Ladies and gentlemen." Deb spread her arms and stepped in a circular pattern. "Let the games begin. Summer Olympics, water sports."

Ellie's guests devoured the baked lasagna, Caesar salad, and homemade Italian bread she made for dinner. Later they gathered around the fireplace, gazing at the fluttering flames, and chatting late into the night, mostly about the inflamed river and about Aunt Lillian, sharing their many fond memories of her.

When Ellie noticed a few yawns, she stood, tossed a pillow at the sacked-out Deb, and declared it bedtime. Upstairs, she pulled quilts from the linen closet in the hallway. What was it about the older generation and quilts? Aunt Lillian, like most ladies of her era, possessed a seemingly endless supply of cushy, cottony, hand-stitched quilts. But thank goodness, as they certainly came in handy now. Ellie then doled out bedroom assignments. Vito padded along behind Deb, on their way to their room, with the air of a distinguished guest at Le Ritz Paris.

Before falling into her own bed, Ellie peeked out the French doors. Rain thrashed the black patent leather menace that was the river. Lightning flashed in an incessant strobe, and thunder rumbled ever closer. How could the man she loved be out in this terrifying chaos? According to radio reports, the rains fell as heavy throughout West Virginia and Kentucky as in Marietta. Wyatt had phoned the day before yesterday, from somewhere in Tennessee, saying he was on his way to be with her, pushing one last string of barges upstream in his role as captain. After this trip, he would make only the occasional run.

"Don't worry, sweetheart," he'd said. "Given this heavy rain, I'll be docking soon, and we have motel rooms lined up outside Louisville."

"Don't take any chances, Wyatt," she had told him. "I love you so much and I can't wait to see you, but if I need to wait a little longer, I will."

Scurrying to the bed, Ellie leapt in and whispered a prayer for Wyatt and his crew, and for all the people who might lose their homes and businesses—if not more—before this nightmare was over. With the rasping downpour swathing the house and pattering onto the roof, she flipped on the bedside light and opened a book to try to settle the storm going on in her mind and her stomach.

****

The bedside clock showed just after seven, but Ellie had awakened to the darkness of midnight. The halos of light that usually glowed around the edges of the roller blinds were absent. Hurrying to the French doors, she flung them open and stepped onto the balcony. When rain peppered her face, she drew back and kneaded her arms against the chill, shaken to her core by the apocalyptic scene.

The river had surged over its banks, and the entire

valley swirled like a saucer of stirred chocolate milk. In the lower-lying areas, only white church steeples, treetops, and house chimneys rose above the muddy rapids. The streets no longer existed, and supporting beams were the only evidence of bridges. Ellie's gaze shot to what had been the town's coastline, and she gasped. Charlene's five-and-dime! Its ground floor was nearly immersed, and the poor Levee House Cafe had been all but swallowed by the river!

Trembling, Ellie went for the telephone. No service. *Dammit.* She just wanted to connect with Charlene and with Marv, to see if they were all right, to commiserate on their flooded businesses, if they even knew. And this meant that Wyatt wouldn't be able to call her. Hopefully he wasn't still out on that river. Hopefully he was safe and sound in a motel.

The rain continued its soggy invasion for the next three days and nights. Brushstrokes of black and gray loomed menacingly above the plundered little town, and it seemed to gasp for air. In its nearly 150 years, it had survived early power struggles, pioneer hardships, the Civil War. But how would it ever make it through this? By the fourth day, the water reached near the roofs of many of the vulnerable downtown buildings, including the five-and-dime, and, God help it, the Levee House Cafe had completely disappeared. What looked like shrubs dotting the water were treetops, and the old railroad bridge leading to Harmar Village was nowhere to be seen.

How fitting that the weather matched Ellie's mood, a kindergartner's scribble in cerulean and charcoal, if he were lucky enough to have the box of forty-eight crayons. The sky spanned wider here than in Chicago.

Sometimes there, you forgot there was a sky, dominated as it was by towering buildings. Here, now, there was no chance it would be disregarded. It rained and raged and entrapped the little town under a dome of terror, like a snow globe but with pelts of gunmetal rain instead of drifting white snowflakes.

Ellie and her guests feasted on huge pots of chili and platters of fried chicken. How wonderful to be able to afford a little meat again—one small treat amid all the tragedy. They tried not to let the flood consume their minds, distracting themselves by playing cards and board games and listening to the radio, although the staticky music, soap operas, and comedy shows had given way to nearly nonstop flood coverage. The flood, they learned, had stricken everywhere from Pittsburgh to Cairo, Illinois, the entire length of the Ohio River. Dislodged fuel tanks sustained damage in the roiling river and exploded, triggering massive fires. Countless businesses and homes had been lost so far, rendering hundreds of thousands of souls homeless, and millions were without power. Thankfully, the electricity on Harmar Hill remained in service, so Ellie and her guests had light, as well as heat during the chilly nights.

Vito, in his own inadvertent, lackadaisical way, provided much needed comfort, seeming perfectly comfortable basking in the attention he commanded and making sure no lap stayed empty for long. Appearing out of nowhere, he would leap up and settle in with a *ptttttrr*, and it made no difference to him whose lap he commandeered.

Marv stopped by early one morning, shedding his dripping overcoat and hat in the back hall. He lived a few miles away, to the north and west of Harmar Hill, also on high ground.

"How about some pancakes, Marv?" Hanne asked.

"No, thank you. Just had my fill of Janet's ham and eggs. I will take a cup o' joe, if you've got some made." Marv pulled out a chair at the kitchen table and seated himself. "How you ladies holding up?"

From his breakfast bowl, Vito conducted a quick visual inspection of the stranger, then resumed nibbling. Hanne joined Marv, Ellie, and Deb at the table, where they alternated between peering out at the deluged valley and gazing into steaming cups of coffee and tea. The guests had settled into a routine of eating breakfast in shifts. First Hanne, Ellie, and sometimes Deb, with Anita eventually appearing around mid-morning.

"We're doing all right. We're very fortunate, given what everyone down there is going through." Ellie nodded toward the window. "But how are you doing, Marv? I can't imagine what you're feeling right now."

Marv considered the lake that used to be Marietta and rested a hand on his chin. This was a man who cared for his restaurant like a member of his family. "I'm born and raised here," he said, "and I have to say I never thought I'd see the day." He tasted his coffee. "I've seen some flooding in my time. Some of it really bad. But I don't know if the old town is gonna be able to come back this time. Don't know if the old Levee House'll be able to bounce back this time."

"Oh, Marv, I sure hope so," Ellie said. "Darned rain."

"Well, I knew the risk when I opened the place," Marv said. "When you're situated right on the river, you've gotta expect some flooding now and then."

"You once worked on the river, didn't you?" Deb

leaned and picked up Vito.

"Why, I spent the better part of twenty years on that river. Only when my aching bones told me to hang up the ol' captain's hat did I come ashore and buy the Levee House." Marv stood and went to the kitchen door leading to the patio, for a better look at the valley.

"What kind of boat did you have?" Deb asked.

"Ah, the *April Rain*. She was a beauty. An old steamboat. She and I had many a fine voyage together. Made the tourist run between Marietta and Cincinnati. Never got tired of it." Marv paced back and forth, punctuating his words with hand gestures. "You know, the first steamboat on the Ohio River caused quite a stir."

"Why?" Ellie asked. "What was the big deal?"

"It was 1811, the year of Halley's Comet." Marv returned to his chair. "Back then, people weren't as educated about astronomy as they are now, particularly not about things like comets. Well, when that ball of fire appeared, streaking across the firmament, they were scared half to death, thought it was the end of the world. Then, no sooner had it passed by and a sense of security returned, a powerful earthquake hit. Why, the combination of those two events brought about the widely held belief that the end of the world was a-coming."

"More coffee, Marv?"

"Please. Well, people studied their Bibles." Marv blew at his steaming mug. "Thank you, Hanne. They got their behinds to church in droves. Anything for a little comfort and maybe some answers. And in time, things settled down, people went about their lives. But one day, in that very same year, a sound came from the river unlike anything ever heard before. Well, the people, they rushed to the banks, and there on the river was a sight to behold. What they saw"—Marv paused for dramatic effect, casting his eyes from one rapt listener to the next—"was a huge iron beast creeping upriver, breathing great puffs of smoke." Marv's voice grew louder, his arms circled about. "Spewing fire, making a terrible whooshing sound. The people were terrified, certain that this horrible monster was responsible for the bright orb that had slashed through the sky and for the violent shaking of the Earth. The Native Americans called it the fire canoe and tried to chase the beast away in their own canoes. People dropped to their knees and wailed to the heavens in prayer. But finally, once the demon vessel passed and the peacefulness of the valley returned, the people came to learn that what they'd seen was none other than the *New Orleans*, the first steamboat to sail the Mississippi and Ohio Rivers."

Ellie and her houseguests had listened in fascination. Deb spoke first. "Is that true?"

"Oh, yes, yes. It's absolutely true. Look it up in the encyclopedia." Marv finished the last of his coffee and glanced at his watch. "Well, Janet has a honey-do list for me." He stood and extended his cheek for Ellie's kiss before retrieving from the back hall his overcoat and his jaunty boater hat with its red-and-black ribbon. "Now, you gals let me know if there's anything you need," he called back. "Course, telephone service is out, but you know where I live." Sticking his head back into the kitchen, he peered out the window. "I'm afraid things are gonna get worse out there before they get better."

Chapter Twenty-Eight

Marv had been right; the rain didn't relent for two more days. Then, finally, sunshine pushing through the onset of dawn raised spirits in the house on Harmar Hill, although the damage in its more than two-week absence had been done. The scraps of diversion the house's occupants had managed to find had lost their appeal, and conversation had diminished, replaced by snippets of tense interaction. Anita tried repeatedly to light up a cigarette in the house, with Ellie repeatedly guiding her out the nearest door. Most of the guests had adopted the habit of afternoon naps to pass the endless hours.

Out on the balcony, Ellie peered through the binoculars that always perched on a windowsill of the sitting room. The water level seemed to have dropped a bit. Some of the submerged buildings bobbed their heads above the muddy water. But no sign of life except for the occasional boat.

Ellie had continued struggling to maintain the notion that Wyatt had spent most of his life on the river, that he knew how to handle anything it could throw at him. He *had* to be safe. Yet she constantly fought off encroaching doubt and terror. Then she spotted it.

"Deb! Deb, come here!"

Deb hurried out to the balcony. "What?"

Ellie handed her the binoculars. "That towboat lying sideways against Buckley Island!" Her words rushed out. "See it there, at the tip of the island, on the south side?"

"Uh-huh. What about it?"

"That's Wyatt's boat! Oh, my goodness. Deb, look at it."

The boat listed on its side, bobbing in the water, a ragged gash sliced into its mud-caked hull. Ellie's stomach somersaulted, her heart ricocheted in her chest.

"Are you sure it's his? They all look the same, if you ask me."

"I'm sure. His boat has a metallic gold stripe. I'd know it anywhere." Ellie slumped to her knees, propping her arms on the balcony and dropping her head against them.

"Oh, Deb, what if he's—"

"Aww, come on now, kid." Deb tugged at her arm. "I'm sure he's fine."

"Then why hasn't he contacted me? If his boat is here, where is he? God, Deb, what—"

"Shh, shh. Come on, now." Deb pulled Ellie to her feet and laid an arm across her shoulders. "Look, the boat isn't in horrible condition, it didn't sink. And Wyatt's an experienced river man. He's probably working hard to secure his freight or something like that. He'll get in touch with you as soon as he's able to."

Ellie locked eyes onto Deb. "How far down there do you think we could get?"

"What? You're not thinking of trying to drive down there, are you? And what do you mean *we*?"

"I can't just sit here when Wyatt might be hurt. Stay here if you want, but I've got to do something."

"Well, that's just nuts, Ellie," declared Deb. "The streets are impassable."

"I've got to try, Deb. I'm going to drive down as far as I can go. Maybe I can get a hold of the authorities or someone with a boat. I can't just sit here wondering."

"What's going on?" Anita joined them on the balcony.

"Ellie thinks she sees Wyatt's boat, and she wants us to go rescue him." Deb paced the balcony, her arms flailing. "What do you think we're gonna do, Ellie, huh? Drive part way down the hillside, hike the rest of the way, then dogpaddle over to the island? We are not Army soldiers, you know."

"Well, maybe if we try to be positive and helpful, we'll figure something out," Anita said.

"You figure it out, then, Einstein. And by the way, you're one to talk about being positive and helpful. You haven't lifted a finger this whole time. All you do is sit around on your ass bitching about anything and everything."

"Maybe I'm sick of being around you. Maybe I'm sick of being cooped up in this damned house. I can't even talk with Tad to see if he's okay."

"I'm sure your eighteen-year-old boy-toy is just fine," Deb spewed.

Anita lifted her chin, turned, and tramped into the house.

"I'm sure his mommy is taking good care of him," Deb yelled after her.

Ellie returned to the sitting room, slumped into a chair, and dropped her head onto her hands. Deb was right. Reaching Wyatt's boat was impossible. What would be the point of driving partway down the hill?

"What is going on in here?" Hanne appeared in the doorway. "People hollering and stomping around like a herd of elephants."

Ellie kneaded her forehead. "Anita and Deb had another row."

"Well, this whole thing has been difficult on everyone," Hanne said. "Patience is being worn thin. Hopefully very soon we can all get back to norm—"

A faint clunk sounded from somewhere in the house, and with it the hum of appliances fell silent.

"Great. Now our electricity is out." Ellie covered her face with her hands and surrendered to the tears.

Hanne went to Ellie and rubbed her shoulders. "Listen, Eleanor, don't you worry. I have prepared many meals without *electrical* in my lifetime. Nobody here is going to starve."

Ellie wrested herself free of Hanne's hands, stood, and paced. "I'm sick of this. I don't know whether Wyatt is dead or alive." She wiped at her eyes with a sleeve. "Now we have no electricity, which means everything in the icebox is going to spoil. We won't be able to flush the toilets. I give up. I'm going to bed."

By morning, resolve had gained control of Ellie's gloomy mood. "I'm driving down there," she announced as she forged into the kitchen. She'd checked out the valley from her bedroom balcony, and the river had become somewhat distinguishable from its recent incarnation as a lake. Several small motorboats and rowboats headed this way and that, like ants in a colony. With much of the water having receded, portions of streets were visible, black satin ribbons winding through saturated ground.

Deb had barely rolled her eyes and opened her mouth when Ellie's glare cut off whatever remark she intended to make. Instead, Deb finished buttering her toast, propped herself against the counter, and took a hefty bite.

Ellie pulled the pitcher of orange juice from the icebox and went for a glass. Vito traced a figure eight around her legs, seeming to sense she planned a mission. "It'll be all right, Vito. I know you're worried, too."

Hanne's lips thinned to a taut line, her forehead crinkled. "I wish you would not do that, Eleanor. But you make sure you turn around and head back up the minute you run into water, do you hear me?"

"Where you going?" Anita traipsed into the kitchen and headed straight for the coffee pot.

"I'm going to drive down the hill, see if I can find out anything."

Anita planted herself in a chair at the table and blew at her cup of coffee.

As Ellie began backing out of the driveway a few minutes later, a loud *hey* halted her. There was Deb hurrying down the front steps of the house. She plodded to the motorcar, jerked open the door, and spilled in without a word.

Ellie maneuvered the hairpin curve of the road down Harmar Hill, her heart pumping faster with each rotation of the car's tires, inching them closer and closer to the apocalypse. Deb sat silent, arms crossed, no doubt struggling to stifle her vehement objection to what she considered a foolish and pointless mission. But Ellie couldn't simply stay up there safely in the house when Wyatt might be… She shivered off the notion and concentrated on her driving.

No sooner than they made it down the hill and into Harmar Village than a massive blob of mud halted the auto. Ellie backed into a driveway, turned the vehicle around, and had to fight against gunning it back up the hill, away from the abyss. Struggling for a deep breath to calm her terror, she made a right at the next street and followed it until high water dotted with bobbing branches and other debris stopped them.

"Oh, Deb, just look at the Village. Look at poor Harmar Tavern. Everything is ruined," Ellie said.

Backtracking, she finally turned onto the street leading to the bridge connecting Harmar Village to Marietta.

"Oh, come on, Ellie. Are you kidding me? You can't possibly be planning on going over that bridge."

When Deb didn't get a response from Ellie, she produced a dramatic sigh. "You do know we're about to have our asses sucked into the river?" Deb cracked her hands together. "That's where we're gonna be, floating right down that river."

Ellie ignored Deb's dramatics.

"Why do I let you talk me into this crap?"

Ellie herself couldn't believe she was doing this. Her mother had instilled a fear of water in her as a child. *You're out too far, Eleanor, come back in. Oh, be careful, Eleanor.* Being in boats large enough to provide a secure feeling was fine, but she'd always avoided immersing herself in water. Then, when Benny was old enough for swimming lessons, she summoned her courage and overcame her embarrassment enough to first take lessons of her own. She hadn't wanted him to inherit her fear of water, wanted to be able to take him swimming and jump in after him if necessary. She managed now in water, but this swollen, roiling river was bloated to within inches of the bridge.

"I can't do this." Her eyes flitted to the rearview

mirror. She shifted the vehicle into reverse, twisted herself around, and motioned for the vehicle behind her to back up.

"Ellie, they can't back up." Deb said. "What the hell are you doing?"

"I'm not... I can't... The water is almost up to the bridge." Ellie's forehead crinkled, her heartbeat played hopscotch. She pivoted herself around again and swooshed an arm at the driver behind her. "Darn it, why won't he back up?" She squeezed the bulb of her horn, then squeezed it again. *Aooguh! Aooguh!*

"Ellie, stop it. You're being ridiculous. We have to drive over a bridge if you're bound and determined to get to Marietta. It's the only way."

The driver of the car behind them sounded his own horn. *Aooguh!*

The bridge would collapse. Her car would plunge into the cold, muddy river, and she and Deb would be swallowed within seconds. She should have listened to Deb and never come down here. She and her damned impulsiveness. But Wyatt might be in a worse situation. He might be lying on the splintered deck of his boat right now, in agony and bleeding to death. Ellie had to try to get to him, or to someone who might be able to help him. Sucking in a shaky breath, she urged the gear shift into drive and paced her vehicle onto the bridge at a timid creep, as if moving faster would cause the water to spill over the bridge, like a cup of tea if the person carrying it walked too fast.

"Damn, that water's high," Deb said.

"This is... I can't... Oh, my goodness."

Deb gripped the dashboard, her knuckles white. "Let's get the hell off this bridge, Ells. Floor it, woman."

And they managed to laugh as Ellie sped across the bridge toward salvation. Soon, she turned onto Front Street and directed her car toward downtown. She crept along for half a block, then stopped and shifted into park. The street sloped toward the river from there, and the water was too deep to go any farther.

"Darn it. We're so close." Ellie dropped her head onto the steering wheel. Then, straightening her spine and squaring her shoulders, she backed into an alley and headed in the other direction. Inching her way through shallow water, she made her way toward first the police station, then the fire station. Both sat desolate in the grimy flood waters, so no way could Ellie make it close to either of them.

"There's got to be one soul somewhere who can help me," she pleaded.

"Wait." Deb twisted around in her seat. "Back up. It looked like someone at the gasoline station on whatever street that was we just passed. I can't tell where the hell we are."

Ellie backed up and steered the car to the filling station, where a man was trudging around in tall rubber boots, surveying the water-logged building. Deb wound down her window and called across the lot.

"Excuse me, Mac, have you got a working telephone?"

"Nope." The bearded man sloshed toward Ellie's car. "Service is out. Where you headed, ma'am?"

"I'm just trying to get some help for someone who was out on a towboat. The boat is listing against Buckley Island, but we haven't heard from the captain."

"You're gonna have trouble getting any help right now. Maybe in a couple days, when the water's receded some more. Ain't much anyone can do right now. Best thing you can do, ma'am, is get yourself on back home."

Ellie dammed the tears clouding her eyes and turned back toward the bridge and Harmar Hill and home. *Where are you, Wyatt?*

Chapter Twenty-Nine

Anita's muffled but shrill shout punctured Ellie's bedroom walls, jolting her awake the next morning. "The telephone is working! And we've got electricity! Hey, everyone, we're back among the living."

Exhausted by their foray into town yesterday and the flood and all the worries and the constant hum of houseguests, Ellie moaned and nuzzled deeper into her bed. Would it be so bad to yank the covers over her head and stay there all day?

Then Anita's words took hold. Electricity. Telephone service! Lurching up, Ellie grabbed the bedside telephone but got nothing but busy signals for the police and fire departments. Great. The utilities had been restored, the rain had stopped, but Ellie and her houseguests were as isolated as before. She wanted to scream. If only she could just get some answers. Plummeting back onto the bed, she buried her face in her pillow.

"Ellie? Ellie, you awake?" The edge of Ellie's bed dipped with Anita's slight form. "I got through to the fire station."

Ellie flipped upright. "You did?"

"They're putting Wyatt's boat into their queue, but they've had so many telephone calls already and they're just today able to start dispatching the fire department. They're really stretched beyond their resources. Police and fire departments from other towns are sending in squads. Lots of people are stranded and several have been reported missing. But they know about Wyatt, and they'll get to his situation as soon as they can."

Ellie seized her friend into a hug. "Thank you, Anita. And what about Tad? Is he all right?"

"Tad?" Anita shrugged. "Don't know. Haven't tried him yet."

Ellie smiled. Anita's good heart, although sometimes hidden beneath a stoic veneer, was intact, having prompted her to report Ellie's concerns for Wyatt before trying to reach her own boyfriend.

Throughout the day, Ellie's subsequent telephone calls to the fire department, when she got through, were met with caring but harried responses. They simply hadn't come to Wyatt's situation on their triage list yet. The certainty that Wyatt was dead simmered somewhere deep inside Ellie, but the prospect of letting it become real kept it from boiling over. Wyatt *had* to be all right. Darned flood for putting him in danger, for doing this to her beloved Marietta. It had been drowned, destroyed, annihilated, and now an eerie vapor hung in the air over the little town, like the remnants of perished energy.

****

Ellie's guests lumbered about gathering their belongings and lugging their bags down the staircase. Hanne had fed them a mammoth breakfast, her last hurrah in her old kitchen. French toast and fried sausages and a German egg dish and fruit salad. She'd brewed coffee and squeezed oranges. Now it was time for everyone to get back to their homes, back to their lives.

Vito, who'd dozed in an orb of sunshine on the sitting room floor through all the packing, sniffed his way through an inventory of the suitcases and bags piled in the foyer. In spite of her anticipation of a quiet, orderly house, Ellie would miss everyone and told them all they were welcome any time. Hugs were exchanged, and Anita was the first one out the door, after barely tossing out a *See ya, don't take any wooden nickels*. Deb stayed until after she'd helped clean up the kitchen and strip the beds.

In between the washing of the many sets of sheets and the remaking of beds that afternoon, with Hanne's help, Ellie tried not to think the worst about Wyatt. Tried not to let herself really consider what might have happened to him, instead relegating her terror to her subconscious. He was strong, experienced, willful. He was all right, and he would come back to her.

After picking at a quasi-dinner that evening, Ellie drove down to the cemetery. Heaven knew she needed to get out of the house, and she wanted to visit Aunt Lillian's grave. What condition would the place be in after the flood, given its location so close to the river?

The grass that had survived the inundation wilted under a film of dirt, and the flowers had been reduced to mush. Gravestones were stained a muddy brown. At Aunt Lillian's gravesite, Ellie knelt and wiped dried mud and debris from the stone. It seemed like yesterday and yet it seemed a lifetime ago that her aunt had died. Ellie gazed at Aunt Lillian's name. Of all the places she'd seen that remarkable lady's name—engraved on various plaques, calligraphed on numerous certificates, printed in countless newspaper articles—this rendering loomed with a harsh permanence.

Ellie sat back on her calves. Such a beautiful, sunny day. If the ground weren't so crusted with dirt, she would have stretched out flat on the grass. She couldn't remember the last time she'd done that. As a little girl, she would lie in the yard on a still day when you could barely detect the clouds moving, but in no time at all, they would evolve into shapes, and an animal or a heart or a face would form. Like those shifting clouds, so much had changed in Ellie's life these past few years. The notion sank her heart, as it always did when she thought of the people gone from her life and about her status quo having been forever changed. After a few minutes, she pushed herself to her feet and brushed off her dress. It was then that her eye caught the name etched into a nearby headstone. Her gasp nearly choked her.

Chapter Thirty

James C. Farlow. Died May 6, 1936. Only two days after Aunt Lillian's burial. Ellie kneeled at the marker and ran a hand along the cold granite. He'd seemed fine the last time she saw him, but of course, anything could have happened. The thing was, Ellie felt that she knew what had happened. James had died of a broken heart.

And here he was buried in Marietta, very near to Aunt Lillian's grave. He'd had a wife who'd died, but the headstone made no mention of her. Obviously, James had made sure his final resting place was as close as possible to that of the love of his life, his Lillie.

****

Marietta fought to recover from its own tragedy. Traffic once again coursed through the streets, and boards were pried off windows. For the clean-up, massive refuse containers brought in from neighboring cities sat at nearly every doorstep. Red Cross trucks dotted the town, delivering household staples and medical supplies. To help with the humanitarian recovery, Ellie and Deb signed up at the community center to deliver donated food, clothing, and other necessities to those displaced or otherwise in need. Deb didn't believe Anita's claim that she had a bad cold.

"She's lazy. That's all there is to it." Deb added a box of canned food to the nearly full trunk of her automobile. "She's lazy, and she's probably holed up in some motel out off the highway with yet another random guy. Have you heard from her?"

Ellie shook her head. "No, I haven't. I've phoned her a couple times to see how she's feeling, but she didn't answer."

"She uses you for a place to stay, then disappears. That's Anita for you." Deb slammed her trunk closed. "Well, you know, I long ago quit hanging out with her. The only time I see her is when you come to town. She's a piece of work."

"Aww, Deb, she's a good person."

Sure, Anita could be quite harsh, but she also could be very caring. Although Deb didn't have much use for Anita, Ellie valued her friendship so always chose to take her spicy antics in good humor.

Ellie appreciated the mental distraction and the physical labor involved with the work she and Deb were doing. The first post-flood issue of *The Marietta Gazette* told of the devastation that the disaster had caused in the cities and towns along the Ohio River. Over 500 homes lost or damaged, businesses destroyed, 385 lives lost. Unbelievably, Marietta had endured nearly half its area covered in flood waters, which had reached twenty feet deep in some places. President Roosevelt had dispatched the largest Coast Guard relief effort ever, with units from the Atlantic and Gulf coasts, as well as the Great Lakes, arriving to aid in the endless work. Now called the Great Ohio River Flood, it was deemed one of the worst floods in U.S. history.

As horrible as things were, and as much as she willed herself to believe that Wyatt was alright, Ellie's imagination worked overtime. She'd always heard of the many dangers of work on the river. Boats could strike ice or underwater debris and sink, boilers could catch fire or explode. Thanks to technology, modern day river work was safer than ever before, Wyatt had told her, but still not without risk, especially in times of flooding.

Finally, it occurred to Ellie to try to contact Wyatt's son Eddie. But upon dialing the long-distance operator and asking for a telephone number for him, she was told that no listing could be found. She didn't know the last names of his crewmates or his buddies in Biloxi. If something had happened to Wyatt, how would she know? Panic invaded her entire being, her stomach tumbled, her heart lay mauled.

She would go to Biloxi. She would find Wyatt's son, his friends, someone, anyone who could tell her what had happened to him. No matter what she might find out, she needed to know. After phoning the bus station and reserving a ticket, she packed a couple changes of clothes and barely slept that night.

The teakettle bubbled to a whistle the next morning, and Ellie's slice of bread popped from the toaster at the same time the doorbell rang. Not a good time for company. Her bus was scheduled to depart in two hours. She hurried down the hallway and peeked through a sidelight.

The man grasped a duffel bag. A sling cradled his other arm. Leaning closer and blinking, Ellie struggled to grasp the sight, and in an instant, all the terror that had built inside her these past few weeks collapsed like scaffolding. She flung open the door.

Wyatt dropped the duffel bag, pulled her to him with his free arm, hugged her, kissed her mouth, her face. "Ellie. My Ellie. Are you alright? I couldn't get ahold of you. I'm so sorry I wasn't here with you through all this—"

Ellie deluged his mouth with a torrent of kisses through laughter and tears. "Wyatt, oh, my goodness, I can't believe you're here." She took his good arm and pulled him inside.

"I've been so worried about you, honey. Is everything okay with you?"

"I'm fine, but where have you been? What happened to your arm?" She led him to the kitchen. "I can't believe you're here! Would you like something to eat? Are you thirsty?"

"I'm a little hungry. A glass of water would be nice."

In the kitchen, she motioned for him to sit, then poured a glass of water. "I'll make you something to eat. Oh, Wyatt, I was so worried about you. Where were you? What happened?" She took a package of sausages from the icebox and set two of them to cooking on the stove.

"Oh, it's been quite a time." He scraped fingers through his hair. "We were able to dock in Louisville just before the river reached the flood stage and the waters developed into rapids. I got the crew off and into motel rooms outside of town, so we could wait out the flooding. After a few days, the rain eased a bit, and by the next day, the river had settled somewhat, so we set out again, with all the crew in agreement."

But soon the rain had come again, in torrents, and it became too dangerous to continue, Wyatt told her. So he made the decision to dock several miles south of Parkersburg. But just before they made it in, the towboat hit debris and dropped its rudder, rendering the boat unsteerable. When the current swept the craft sideways, Wyatt managed to unhitch it from the barges so the cargo might have a chance of surviving. The towboat promptly crashed into the bank, sustained a gash, and began to take on water. Wyatt and his crew had no choice but to abandon ship.

"Oh, no, Wyatt." Ellie finished scrambling three eggs and dumped them into the heated skillet.

"We all made it into one of the life rafts, but things weren't looking good. Being in a raft in those conditions…" Wyatt shook his head. "Before long, the raft got caught in rapids, and there was no controlling it after that. We smashed into the shoreline and started to sink. Of course, everyone had their life vests on, but my guys were…" Wyatt shook his head again and swiped at his wet eyes. "They were getting tossed around like corks. There just was no way to navigate our way to the shore. We were in the water for hours, freezing, fighting to keep above the waves, fighting to keep from swallowing mouthfuls of water. Finally, a craft heading north spotted us and managed to pull us all onboard." He lowered his head. "But Hoopie didn't make it."

Ellie's hand shot to her mouth, she sank onto a chair. "You lost Hoopie?"

"Hypothermia." Wyatt blew out a long breath, his eyes closed, his head fell back. "Whew." He stood and paced the floor of the kitchen. "I just can't believe it. Hoopie worked his behind off to save that tow. He always withstood everything the river could throw in front of him. But this time…" Wyatt wiped at his eyes.

"I'm so sorry, darling." Ellie went to him and wrapped him in her arms. "I know how much Hoopie meant to you. He was one of a kind. Did you lose anyone else?"

"Everyone else is all right now. We all spent a few

days in the hospital, but everyone's fine. I was right down the river from you, honey, in Parkersburg, but I was out of it. Unconscious."

"Oh, Wyatt. Why? Did you have hypothermia too?"

"That and pneumonia. Almost got me. I don't remember them pulling me out of the water."

Tears spilled from Ellie's eyes. He held her close and whispered that everything was all right now.

"And your arm?" Ellie returned to the stove, poked at the sausages and stirred the eggs.

"Fracture of the radius." He motioned toward his forearm. "I don't know, it happened sometime after we lost the rudder." Returning to his chair, he shook his head. "I heard someone towed it up to Buckley Island."

"I saw it there. I was scared to death for you."

"What about you, honey? How were things here?"

Ellie filled a plate for Wyatt, then seated herself next to him at the table and told him about the houseful of friends who'd stayed with her during the flood, about driving down into the valley to see if she could find him, about the loss of electricity and telephone service.

"You've had a helluva time. I'm sorry I wasn't here for you, Ellie." Wyatt shoveled the food into his mouth. "I regained consciousness the day before yesterday and got here as soon as I could. They forbade me from checking out, but to hell with that. I needed to get to my baby."

"Well, I was getting ready to leave for the bus station when you knocked on my door. I was going to go to Biloxi to try to find out what happened to you. Oh, Wyatt, I had no way to reach you, I couldn't phone you, I couldn't—"

"It's okay, honey, I'm okay now. I'll make sure you

have the telephone number and address for my boat warehouse in Biloxi. That's the best way to reach me. My office there can radio me on the boat most of the time." He stood and took his dishes to the sink. "Thank you for the breakfast, honey. Best meal I've ever had, I'll tell you that."

"I just can't believe you're here," she said. "But you probably aren't well enough to have left the hospital so soon. You look pale, and you've lost weight. Come on, let's get you settled into a nice warm bed." She held close to him as she led him down the hallway and up the stairs.

"I feel fine. I'm gonna grab a quick bath, though. Those sponge baths just don't do the trick."

"All right, and I'll phone and cancel my bus ticket."

A few minutes later, Wyatt emerged from Ellie's bathroom with a towel wrapped around his waist. His hair waved even more from the dampness, water drops glistened on his skin. Damn, he looked good. Thinner, with shadows under his eyes, but so handsome. He leaned against the door jamb between the bathroom and the bedroom, looked directly into Ellie's eyes, and let the towel drop.

After raising her eyebrows and a few seconds of stunned hesitation, Ellie smiled, then abruptly sobered. "Oh, Wyatt, I don't think... Aren't you tired?"

He shook his head.

She arose from the chaise and pulled down the roller blind on one window, then the next and the next. The room darkened, with enough light glinting through for her eyes to remain fixed on his. Unbuttoning her dress, she made her way with a slow step to his extended arm, then let the dress slip to the floor. In an instant, he pulled her tight against his body, his mouth pressed to hers.

Lifting her with his good arm, he placed her on the bed and lay alongside her.

Between kisses, he wove whispered words. "I want you so much, Ellie. I don't think you know how much I love you."

In one motion he spun her onto her back and placed himself on top of her. "Agghhh!"

"Wyatt, your arm!"

He laughed and rolled onto his back.

"Are you alright?"

"Well, I obviously was thinking of something other than my arm." He turned onto his side. "Back that pretty bottom over here, baby."

She slid close to him, trembling under the kisses he dabbed onto her neck, dissolving under his touch. Running a hand over her hip, he clenched at her chemise, and they soon melded into each other like soldered iron.

****

After a few days, once Ellie felt confident Wyatt would be all right, and after she regained her own strength, she began helping Marv and Janet with cleanup at the Levee House Cafe. Once the major clearing out had been completed, muddy floors needed scrubbing, walls needed repainted. Pots and pans and dishes had to be washed. The flood had caused dreadful damage to the old waterfront place, but good for Marv to not throw in the towel. Always the optimist, "Whatever damage the water did can be undone," he had declared.

Marv also pointed out to Ellie the battered stained-glass panels of some of the town's churches. "They'll be needing some repair work, you know," he said with a wink. Ellie would gladly offer to help as soon as some of the more crucial work was complete.

To Ellie's amazement, Wyatt helped around town, salvaging or rebuilding fences and sheds, clearing branches and other debris, doing as much as he could with a broken arm. He and Ellie both worked from morning until early evening, pausing for lunch provided by the congregations of various churches. Endless work, it seemed. The flood had ravaged dozens of homes and businesses, some of which would be saved, but others lay in massive heaps of splintered wood. The days proved exhausting but satisfying.

****

Ellie and Wyatt picked at their breakfast, their appetites obliterated at the special announcement that had interrupted the regular morning news broadcast. Amelia Earhart's airplane had disappeared during her attempt at flying the entire way around the world. After several minutes of listening to the repeated coverage, Ellie went to the radio and switched it off. So many trials and tribulations these past few years. What a blessing to be getting away for a few days. After weeks of nonstop clean-up work in town, she and Wyatt planned to leave after breakfast for a long weekend at a resort in the mountains of Virginia. No sooner did she return to her chair than the telephone rang.

"Mom. Something happened to Dad."

Ellie barely recognized the voice through the convulsive sobs. "Benny? What's wrong?"

"Dad was in an automobile accident early this morning."

Chapter Thirty-One

"He's gone, Mom. He's gone."

Ellie's hand darted to her mouth, tears spilled from her eyes. She fell into a chair, trembling, trying to comprehend.

"No! Oh, Benny, what happened?"

"He was driving home from the airport. He'd been in St. Louis on business for a couple days. I don't know, I guess someone tried to pass him and clipped his auto, and he spun into a tractor-trailer."

Ellie scratched at her head, kneaded an arm. "Honey, I...I'm so sorry. I'll come up. I'll come right away. Does Jessie know?"

"No, I needed to talk to you first. I just can't believe it, Mom. I just talked with him yesterday. At least he didn't suffer. They said that he...that it happened instantly."

"Well, that's a blessing. I am so sorry, honey. Where are you now?"

"I just left the hospital. I don't know, I guess I'll go home."

"I'm coming up. And I'll phone Jessie."

"Can you come up today, Mom?"

"Yes. Yes, I'm on my way."

"I'll go ahead and call Jessie at her dormitory. She'll have a lot of questions about the accident and stuff."

"I love you, Benny. I'm just so sorry, sweetie. I'll be

there soon." Ellie dropped the telephone receiver and stared into nothingness.

"Ellie? What is it? What's wrong?" Wyatt kneeled at Ellie's side.

"It's Mason. He was in a car accident. He's dead." Ellie leapt from the chair and paced the floor. "Benny is a mess. I need to go to Columbus."

"Aww, Ellie, that's awful. I'm so sorry. May I drive you there?"

Ellie shook her head on her way out of the kitchen. She wanted to go alone. She wanted to fully be there for the children, without distraction. "I need to get my suitcase." At least it was already packed.

"Honey, are you sure you're up for the drive?" Wyatt followed her up the stairs. "I can take you, then come on back to Marietta, if you want. And I'll come get you whenever you say."

"No. Thank you, Wyatt. I just…I just need to get to my children."

Ellie struggled to see through her tears on the two-hour drive to Columbus. Benny and Jessie didn't deserve this. First the break-up of their parents' marriage, now this. Although their relationship with their father had become strained during the divorce, it eventually strengthened again, and the three had seemed closer than ever in the past year.

Ellie took a suite at a downtown hotel so she and the children could all be together. Benny seemed grateful at getting out of his tiny room at the boarding house for a few nights, and Jessie burrowed close to her mother. Although the days passed in a lumbering, obscure haze, Ellie helped the children through the funeral planning and stood at their sides during the calling hours and the service in Columbus, Mason's hometown. Hanne and Deb had ridden up with Charlene and Alan. Nobody had been able to reach Anita.

"She'd probably be too bowlegged to walk into the funeral home, anyway," Deb spat out.

Ellie concealed a laugh, and Charlene blushed. But Anita finally had shown up, ten minutes into the service. Never good at directions, she'd gotten lost, Ellie later learned.

Ellie couldn't hug Benny and Jessie enough when she left to return to Marietta, and on her drive back, the levee of strength she'd maintained during the past few days gave way, and grief for the man she had loved with all her heart for more than two decades washed over her.

****

"Thanks, honey." Wyatt took the tall glass of ice water from Ellie, finished it off in seconds, and wiped his forehead with the back of an arm. "I probably shouldn't have picked such a hot week to replace the gutters. Whew."

Ellie had come home three days ago to find Wyatt hard at work. They had spoken about the gutters needing replaced, but she hadn't known he planned on taking care of it himself.

"I appreciate your doing this. Do you have much more to do?"

"All done." Wyatt gathered his tools and folded the ladder.

Ellie turned to go back inside the house.

"I missed you last night."

She replied without looking at him. "I couldn't sleep again. I didn't want to wake you."

She had left their bed every night since her return

from Columbus and finished the night in a different bedroom. Shutting off her thoughts enough to fall asleep was proving a challenge. And she hadn't been much more sociable toward Wyatt during the daytime, spending most of her time taking walks, trying to read, napping. Nothing felt right. She didn't want to be home but didn't feel like going anywhere, didn't want to be with anybody but didn't want to be alone. Since Mason died, so many thoughts and feelings zigzagged through her mind, and she couldn't seem to corral any of them into something that made sense.

"What can I do to help?" Wyatt asked now.

"Nothing. I'll be all right." If she couldn't interpret the incapacitating shadow that had formed and now hovered over her, how could she explain it to him?

"How about if I get these things put away, grab a bath, and take my girl out for a nice dinner?"

"I'm not hungry. I'm going to phone the children." She turned and went inside.

She had abandoned him. There was no other way to describe her treatment of Wyatt just now, her treatment of him these past few days. But she simply could not muster the least bit of consideration outside of whatever was going on inside her. She wanted to scream.

Wyatt's tender, low voice broke through her deep sleep the next morning. "Ellie. Sweetheart." His hand on her shoulder gently rocked her.

"What time is it?"

"About eight-thirty. I brought you some toast and orange juice."

"Thank you." Ellie sat up and wiped at her eyes.

Wyatt lowered himself onto the bed of the guest room and handed the tray to her. "Honey, I'm going to fly to Biloxi. It's time I checked on the fleet, took an inventory of my supplies. And I'll pack up the rest of my clothes and stuff and have them shipped up. I won't be gone long."

"You're leaving?"

"For a little while. I'll be back soon."

She sipped her orange juice, avoiding his eyes.

"Are you all right with that? Would you rather I stay?"

"No. Go." She banged her glass onto the tray, spilling the juice. She set the tray aside, tossed off the covers and edged herself off the bed. "I'm going to take a bath."

"Okay, well, I'll be downstairs. Let's talk about this."

Ellie slammed the bathroom door shut at the same moment the tears overflowed her eyes. Now *he* was leaving. Like Mason had left her. Like Mason had left her for good this time. He'd been long gone from her life way before this. So why were the effects of his death lingering like this? Doubts and questions and regrets pummeled her.

When she lumbered into the kitchen forty-five exhausting minutes later, Wyatt extended a cup of steaming tea toward her.

"Hot off the press," he said. "How are you feeling, honey?"

She ignored the tea. "I'm going to water the flowers."

He followed her into the garage, where she picked up the watering can. After filling the can at the brass spigot on the back of the house, she began watering the last of the summer's flowers.

Wyatt reached for her arm. "Ellie, let's talk. Please."

She flung the can to the ground and marched toward the back of the yard, feeling his heat behind her.

"Will you just tell me how you're feeling? Please. I don't have to go. I just thought you needed some time to yourself."

"Oh, I have time to myself. I've always had plenty of time to myself, so go ahead and leave." She flung herself around to face him. "Have a nice trip." She turned away again.

He walked around and faced her. "Talk to me, Ellie. I know things have been really tough for you, but please don't shut me out."

The sun slipped behind a cloud, its billowy shadow extinguishing the rosy-melon glow of the morning. A breeze nudged Ellie, as if trying to prod a reaction from her, to snap her to her senses.

"You're hurting, and it's understandable. You and your husband were married for a long time. He was the father of your children. But I don't know what to say, I don't know what to do. I thought you might need some space."

"I don't need anything, Wyatt. If you want to go, go."

Looking away from the fierce resolve that seemed to scuffle with reluctant resignation in his eyes, Ellie focused on the far reaches of the property, past where the lawn dipped toward the thicket of trees separating it from the steep bank. An array of bridges embossed the river. Faded red brick buildings and lily-white church steeples rose above the town, and dense masses of trees resembling fluffy green cotton provided the backdrop. The panoramic view was considered one of the most beautiful in Ohio. At this moment, it meant nothing.

"I don't want to leave. But maybe you need time alone to grieve, to get through this without me hanging around."

"Go. It doesn't matter. I'm always alone anyway. I never wanted him to leave me. I didn't want our family to break up. I didn't want to be here in this big house in Marietta without my family. I didn't want to be alone."

He looked like she'd kicked his very soul out of his body. Understandably. She'd pretty much dismissed his presence, had blurted out that she was alone, when all he'd been doing was trying to be there for her, to help her in any way he could. Her heart swelled with pain for him, like an over-inflated balloon about to burst. Yet she lacked the slightest capacity right now to say *I'm sorry* or to take him into her arms or to do one damned thing to take away the hurt she'd inflicted on him.

She stood looking anywhere but into his eyes, avoiding the reality of whatever this was that was happening, until the town below lay silent and the river stilled and the world stopped turning and there was nowhere to look but at him.

"Just go," she said.

"Ellie, I don't understand. It's as if…as if your heart has slammed shut. You really want me to leave?"

A nod.

His eyes bore into hers, seemed to search for a scrap of understanding, for some hint that she hadn't meant it. Time fell dormant, then finally his words emerged, haltingly and whispered. "All right. Call me when… Call me if you need me. I love you, Ellie."

She couldn't have seen him if she'd looked at him, and as he walked away, she let the torrent spill down her face.

****

Once the world creaked back to a tentative rotation and time again began ticking away, Ellie salvaged the remnants of herself and hobbled to her feet. She shoved her hair from her face and brushed away the bits of grass pasted to her arms. How long had she lain there, on this deserted patch of ground? Long enough for the world to have revolved away from the sun. Long enough, apparently, for Earth's gravity to pull the life from her, because the only thing she felt or thought or knew was the faint echo of a crippled heartbeat.

Ellie hugged her arms and looked to the darkening sky. She'd fallen asleep, obviously, but for all this time? Even amid all the darkness, the stars still twinkled. Damned stars. She'd taken Aunt Lillian's little fable about finding one's place according to where their three stars crossed too seriously. It had been intended simply as inspiration. Wyatt was gone, so he obviously hadn't been some fairytale second star. And she never had figured out what her would-be third star was.

Time to get her heart out of the stars and her head out of her behind. She'd been selfish. What about all the other people suffering in the wake of the devastating flood? What about all those who had it much worse than she during this never-ending Depression? Those were the people she needed to look to the stars for, not her own self-serving wants, so she closed her eyes and made a wish for everyone but herself.

Chapter Thirty-Two

The trees strutted their colorful leaves in front of the mirror that was the river, doubling the blazing spectacle. Slumping in a chaise on the patio, Ellie viewed the scene through heavy-lidded eyes. Gold, rust, and wine-colored mums bloomed around her property, many of which she'd helped her aunt plant in past years. Although she'd always loved autumn in Marietta, the burnished tapestry of earthy hues was now woven with a thread of dejection. She missed the rituals of past years, and the crisp air and smell of burning leaves brought it all back.

After raking leaves into huge mountains, she and Aunt Lillian would run and jump into them, not caring that they had caused themselves more work. They would pick apples at the orchard just outside of Marietta, then come home and peel and chop them, toss them with sugar and cinnamon, and fill the waiting pie shells. Early on, Ellie had learned how to crimp the edges of the crusts, carve slits to vent the steam, and place cut-out pastry leaves on top. She could almost smell the spicy cinnamon and sweet apples baking. They would spread an old blanket on the leaf-covered yard and hold an afternoon tea party with Hanne's freshly baked cookies. Ellie would read to her aunt, and they would chat. Sometimes Hanne and Charlene or Anita would join them, Deb never having been much for tea parties.

Ellie felt blessed at Lillian Blaylock having been a

part of her life, filling it with steadfast love and support. Tightly woven, their relationship had been pieced together from many scraps of chats and lazy afternoons and bound by the sturdy thread of family, much like a cherished quilt. Tears fell at the notion that no more pieces would ever be added to their quilt. Tears fell for Mason's life lost, for the finite end to their life together, for her children's hearts. Tears fell for the man Ellie now loved with every element of her existence and had sent away. Another spur-of-the-moment act. What in the world was wrong with her? All were people who had once shone bright in her world, but their radiance was now residual, like the light of stars long ago burnt out. And now Ellie passed the minutes and the hours and the days in a stupor, each measure of time indistinguishable from the next. A swirl of autumn breeze against her face provided the only evidence that she was alive.

Eventually, Deb forced her out of the house after prying out of her that Wyatt was gone. Ellie hadn't told her why, only that it hadn't worked out. She hadn't wanted to rehash the whole, ugly thing with Deb. In her numb state, she didn't understand it herself.

After they placed their dinner orders at the Bellevue Hotel restaurant, Deb leaned over the table and leveled stern eyes at Ellie. "Look, kid," she said, "Why don't you call the man and tell him to come back? You're obviously miserable. It's like you're half dead. Just get on the horn and tell him to get his ass back up here."

"I don't know." Ellie swirled her glass of wine and gazed out one of the room's massive windows, each of which were topped with panes arranged in a fan shape and which afforded spectacular views. On the horizon, the bleeding sun gradually ebbed, then collapsed into the river, where its crimson wounds were soothed into pinks and lavenders.

"So what happened with him?"

"I really don't want to talk about it."

"What aren't you telling me? Did he do something?"

"No. I just don't want to talk about it."

"Okay, I'll drop it."

The waitress brought their entrees, and Deb dug in, while Ellie picked at her entrée, gazing outside, gazing around the room. Such a lovely place, decorated in the Art Deco style, with a hand-painted ceiling, crystal chandeliers, and a geometric-patterned tile floor, along with a touch of a nautical theme, in homage to the riverboat era of the previous century.

"But I will say this," Deb blurted out. "Sometimes we women need to take the bull by the horns and make things happen." She grinned in a self-satisfied sort of way.

"All right, what's going on? And, by the way, you look amazing."

Deb had lost a few pounds. Her brown hair was longer and swirled into gentle waves, and her lips shone with a rare slick of pale lipstick. She looked good. In fact, she looked pretty.

"Thank you, ma'am." Deb swished the stir stick around in her martini and continued grinning.

"And you've been smiling nonstop. What is going on?"

"Well." Deb hesitated, seemingly for dramatic effect. "I've been hanging out some with Vinnie."

"What? You're hanging out with your ex-husband?"

"Yep, Vinnie the ex."

A stab of envy pierced Ellie's heart, but she was

happy for Deb.

"Oh, my goodness, when did this happen?"

"Look, it's not a big deal. I dialed him up a few weeks ago."

"What brought that on?"

"I wanted him to know I was seeing someone, so I made up some reason to call him."

"You were seeing someone? Who? Deb, when did all this happen?"

"I *wasn't* seeing anyone. I just told him that. And just as I planned, he got jealous." Deb laughed. "He demanded to know who, and I told him he was a very successful businessman from Parkersburg." Deb barely finished her sentence through the laughter. "I told him that he proposed and that I was considering it." Deb sawed off another bite of her pork chop.

Ellie couldn't help but join Deb in the laughter. "Why are you lying to poor Vinnie? And why did you want to make him jealous?Thank you," she said to the waitress, who had delivered another round of drinks.

"I don't know. For some reason, I'd been thinking about him a lot. Anyway, when I told him someone proposed to me, he couldn't stand it," Deb continued. "He wanted to know if we could get together sometime and talk. I told him"—Deb wiped tears from her cheeks, struggling to contain her laughter enough to continue her sordid story—"I told him that if I married this fellow, we'd probably be moving to his villa in the south of France."

"His villa. In the south of France." Ellie shook her head but couldn't help laughing.

Deb laughed even harder. People at nearby tables glanced at them.

"He said"—Deb was hysterical—"He said, 'Now look, Debbie, you don't need to go running off to France with some asshole. You'd never be happy there. All they do is paint and eat bread and snails, for chrissake. Now, let's talk about this, okay?'"

"So you talked." Ellie had composed herself enough to speak. My goodness, it had felt wonderful to laugh, though.

"Not until I was good and ready to talk. I let the telephone ring off the hook for a few days." Deb burst out laughing again.

"Pull yourself together, Deb. You're out of control. Why did you treat Vinnie that way? He was always so good to you."

Deb sniffed and wiped her eyes. "I know he was, but you can't make it too easy for a fellow. It didn't kill him to work a little to get me back."

"So you're back together?"

"Yup. And the poor cuss I was engaged to is probably crying his eyes out on top of the Eiffel Tower right about now. And painting gloomy scenes of stormy skies over Paris and gorging himself on snails."

Ellie rolled her eyes, then leaned across the table and squeezed Deb's hand. "Well, it's about time you got back with Vinnie. He's such a good man, and I knew you missed the fellow. Are you happy?"

"Well, let's see… In the past two weeks, he's taken me out four times, he's sent me a bouquet of flowers, twice. And we've been screwing like dogs in heat. Yeh, I'm happy."

"You're vulgar, too."

"I think it's gonna work this time, you know? I think I was scared before. You know how my old man took off when I was a kid. Then that asshole I dated in college ended up dumping me for that walking skeleton. When Vinnie came along, I think I figured he wouldn't stick around either." Deb took a swig of her martini. "I was young and stupid. But damn, I missed that man."

"Well, I've always liked Vinnie."

"Look, Ells, remember what I said, okay? Sometimes you've gotta make things happen. Call that man. There's no point in being miserable."

"Well, this isn't about me." Ellie raised her goblet. "Here's to you and Vinnie."

Chapter Thirty-Three

"You've got the place looking lovely, Hanne. Are you happy here?"

The two sat at the table in the bay window of Hanne's cottage, tackling a plate of freshly baked brownies.

"Oh, *ja*, it is fine, and Ruth has got me into all sorts of activities at the community center in the neighborhood. Cards on Wednesday afternoons, exercises three mornings a week. They even have dances each month."

"Dances? How fun! Have you been doing a little Charleston, Hanne?"

"My lord, *nein*. I would throw a hip out. But the music is good."

"It sounds like you're having some good times." Ellie took another bite of her brownie.

"I am telling you what, it is getting to be just a little bit too much good times. I am going to have to sit Ruth down for another talk. I think that woman is *deliberatively* wearing me out on purpose. I am being asked to dance by the gentlemen more than she is, you know." Hanne scrunched her shoulders in delight and covered her grin with a hand.

Ellie laughed. "I'm so happy you're having fun. But it sure is quiet up on the hill without you. And, mmm, I've missed your baking."

"Speaking of the hill, take a look out here." Hanne stood, removed her spectacles, and parted the slats of the window blind above the table. "Do you see it?"

"Oh, my goodness, you can see Aunt Lillian's house from here! That is amazing."

"I can sit right here and look at it. And I have to say"—Hanne's voice wavered—"It makes me feel like this little place of mine is a part of that big old house. Like it is a little guest house in the back yard. And that makes me feel like your aunt is still with me, and we are still sitting together here at this good, old kitchen table."

After Hanne had wistfully dragged a hand over Aunt Lillian's kitchen table shortly before moving out, Ellie had insisted she take the table and chair set with her.

"Aww, Hanne, you know she's still with you," Ellie said now. "She'll always be with you. I think I'll have a refill on the tea. Would you like some more?"

"*Ja*, please. And what about you? How are things going with that handsome fellow of yours?"

Ellie filled their cups and spooned a bit of sugar into hers. How could she explain why she'd thrown Wyatt away? Had she sunken into some sort of temporary insanity brought on by the trauma of Mason's death? She seemed to mourn Mason and the family she'd had with him more than Wyatt. Why? It simply did not make sense, when Mason had left her long ago and she'd loved Wyatt so much. Did she still love Wyatt? If she did, her love for him lay suppressed under the lava smoldering from the eruption of her life.

"He's in Biloxi right now, taking care of some business. Listen, why don't you come up to the house for lunch on Sunday? I want to try out a new squash soup recipe. I don't remember the last time I cooked a meal.

And I thought I'd bake a loaf of crusty bread and an apple pie."

"What can I bring?"

"You are not bringing a thing." Ellie stood and gathered the cups and plates. "You've spent a lifetime cooking for everyone else. This time, you're going to relax and enjoy."

"Well, that is very sweet of you, missy. I am so glad we are still friends. It means so much to me."

"Family, Hanne. We're family."

****

"It's like my feelings about Wyatt have just shut down. I loved him so much, but now I don't even feel bad about him being gone. I just feel, I don't know, neutral about him."

Ellie had made an appointment at the local mental health center. Her icy heart had cut Wyatt loose like a glacier, perfectly willing to let him drift away from her life. When Mason died, her soul seemed to have traveled back in time, searching for her old life, yearning for it, mourning it. She'd spent so much time trying to make sense of it all that her brain felt like cornmeal that had been cooked into an insipid lump. Her heart had ached so deeply and for so long, it seemed a crippled ghost of itself. She needed someone to help her figure out what was going on.

"Yet, it's killing me about Mason. I keep wishing for the old days, when the children were still at home and the four of us were a family."

The kids had told Ellie more than once that their father had indeed dumped Louisa and that he'd frequently asked about Ellie, that he'd seemed lonely. Would they ever have gotten back together? Should they have?

The therapist, Helen, placed a saucer with its cup of steaming tea on the table next to Ellie's chair, then took her own chair. Pushing a strand of blonde hair behind an ear, she turned merciful, Wedgewood-blue eyes to Ellie. "Tell me about Mason. What did he do for a living?"

"He was such a hard worker. He grew up poor and started working as a kid, trying to make a buck any way he could. Then he put himself through college, which is where we met. After graduation, he began working at an almshouse. He cared very much for the indigent and enjoyed helping make their living conditions there comfortable. Eventually, he worked his way up to chief administrator of a conglomerate of almshouses."

Ellie savored her tea and shifted in her chair. "But after a few years, he saw needs in the senior citizen residents which he considered as important as the basics of shelter and food. The need for companionship, the need for feeling useful. So he walked away from his position to start a non-profit devoted to providing those things. He employed mostly high school and college students. The students would provide camaraderie to the elderly folks living in the almshouses, but they also would work with them to create art or record their memories in journals. It benefited the elderly, and it built empathy in the young people.

Ellie gazed at the ceiling and shook her head, a slight smile on her lips. "It was a marvelous thing, what Mason did with his life. Things were tough for a while, financially, but I made good money once I built up a presence with my work."

Helen repositioned her crossed legs. "It sounds as if Mason was a very caring person. Tell me about your marriage."

"It was a partnership. It was fun. We were very close, very supportive of each other. We talked, we listened, we encouraged each other. And when the children came along, we took such a mutual interest and pride in them. It was like nothing could break the bond we all had. We were a genuinely happy family. It was always the four of us." Ellie's voice trembled, then faltered as she broke into sobs.

Helen handed her a box of tissues and waited.

"It's like, when he died, it was the end of an era. It's like the definitive end of my past life. The life I lived for over two decades. I loved being a wife and a mother. I loved our life. And it makes me so angry that he wrecked it all, that he let our beautiful life end." Ellie's voice rose in volume. "And for what?"

"What did he do to end it?"

Ellie managed to explain one of the most painful periods of her life succinctly and swiftly.

Helen listened and nodded, seeming to thoroughly assimilate before speaking. "Loss, especially the loss of something so wonderful, is difficult for us to accept. So we sometimes hang on, to some extent, to what we had, and we don't always realize we're hanging on to it. We may move on, recover, and do quite well in our new life."

"I did move on. I fell in love again. I was finally happy about my new life. So why this…this fresh wound? Why all this longing now, when I thought I was past that?" Ellie took another tissue and blotted her eyes.

"Sometimes things happen to bring that longing for those wonderful times to the forefront. In your case, it was Mason's death. Perhaps you've believed and hoped, on some level, that you and Mason might get back together, that the four of you might be a family again. And there's nothing wrong with that. Like I said, loss is a difficult thing to fully accept."

"He didn't..." Ellie struggled to say the words. "He didn't want the divorce. He was remorseful, when I found out about the other woman, and he begged me for another chance, but I told him it was over and I made him move out."

I'll regret it until the day I die. Mason had once said those words to Ellie. Would she torture herself with regret until the day she died?

"He was a terrific man who made one mistake, and I rejected him." Ellie dissolved into tears again.

"Because your trust in him had been compromised. Try not to torment yourself about turning him down. You reacted honestly. You acted in the way you believed you needed to act. It takes two to make a marriage, Ellie."

Ellie pondered Helen's words. "But I'm always making abrupt decisions. My friends tell me I'm impulsive. And that stupid decision ended my marriage, ended our family."

"Mason's actions, not yours, broke your marriage."

Helen's words and her calm and confident manner began to comfort Ellie. She wadded another tissue, took a fresh one, and mopped at the tears flooding her face, the tension in her neck and shoulders easing a bit.

"A part of you may always wish for those days, understandably. They were wonderful days, and they will always be a part of your life. But that doesn't mean you can't live more terrific days now and in the days and years to come."

Chapter Thirty-Four

Ellie packed up the apple pie left from yesterday's lunch at the house with Hanne, along with a quart of vanilla ice cream, and dropped in at Charlene's house. Alan was away on business, and Ellie didn't need all that extra pie on her hips.

Sitting at Charlene's patio table, the two of them basked in the late afternoon sun as it cast snippets of light through the canopy of oak and maple trees. Brown-tipped Shasta daisies drooped, and roses withered in Charlene's meticulous but fading autumn gardens. Along the top of the wooden fence, hyper-intent squirrels darted with the skills of a high-wire circus act, sending gnawed fragments of acorn shells clicking onto the stone patio.

Charlene blew at her tea, which she'd brewed to go with the pie. "I'm so glad you came out. We haven't had a chance to talk much since the flood. How is everything?"

Ellie shook her head. "Wyatt is gone."

There it was, clear and lethal. And then it all spilled out. The way she'd rejected Wyatt, her unexpected, profound feelings after Mason died, the confusion, and the aimless existence she'd been living. That she had talked with someone at the mental health center and felt better but hadn't yet reached the point of making peace with it all and moving past it all.

"I don't know, Char." Ellie let her head drop back against the cushioned chair. "Maybe if I'd given Mason a second chance, he would be alive today. People told me not to divorce him, they told me that men sometimes stray, that I shouldn't wreck my family over it. They warned me that I'd be ruining my life, and they were right. I'm alone and I'll be alone the rest of my life." Ellie words tumbled out now, craggy and sopping with tears, like whitewater rapids over rocks. "I should have looked the other way and hung onto my husband and—"

"He crushed you, Ellie. He's the one who ruined your marriage, not you. And don't fault yourself for not wanting to put your heart on the line with him again."

With Ellie's sigh, she felt as if every breath she could ever again take left her body. "I know. Then why is everything so wrong? My life is a mess. I should never have moved down here. I should have gone ahead with the auction of Aunt Lillian's house and stayed in Oak Park. In fact, that's what I'm going to do." Ellie sprang to her feet and paced the patio. "I'm going to sell the house and I'm going to move back to Oak... No, I'm going to get an apartment in Chicago, far away from the memories of Mason and Oak Park."

Charlene went to Ellie, caught her by the shoulders, and planted her face to face with herself. "Ellie, stop. Take a breath. Think about what you're saying."

Ellie shimmied herself free of Charlene's hands. "I don't need to think about it. Yes, I've made some snap decisions in my life, and, yes, I should have thought some of them through better, but I'm doing this, Charlene. I just... I need to get away from here. I need to..."

Ellie halted, then shuffled back to her chair and

withered onto it. Propping an elbow on an arm of the chair, she rubbed her forehead. "Get away. Hmph." She picked up her fork and swirled it around the ice cream puddling on her plate. "What am I getting away from? I left Mason behind in Chicago, and I've left Wyatt behind here. They're already gone. And what would I be going back to if I moved to Chicago?"

"Give yourself some time, Ellie." Charlene's voice was fluid and weightless in the air, like the bubbles they blew as little girls. She returned to her chair and leaned close to Ellie. "You've been through so much these past few years. Take the time to figure out what you really want."

A drowsy breeze whorled through the trees, prompting a deluge of crisp red and orange and golden leaves all around them. Tugging at her cardigan, Ellie sank deeper into its warmth. Sitting amid fly-bys of fluttering Blue Jays and ebony-winged Yellow Finches, she and Charlene watched the western sky take on the colors of sunset.

Aunt Lillian had told Ellie she would find her place where her three stars crossed. Maybe that place wasn't dependent on anyone else or anything else. Maybe it was dependent only on her, on what she wanted, what she needed. Perhaps she herself was one of those three stars. The first star would always be Benny and Jessie. Another, she realized, was still the love she hoped to find again one day. But, dammit, maybe she was the third star.

****

That night, Ellie lay alert deep into the early hours trying, as she'd tried every single day and night of these past weeks, to reconcile her reaction to Mason's death, to understand why she'd pushed Wyatt away. And sometime between the distant strike of midnight and the blush of dawn, she allowed to herself that her grief for the man she had loved for the majority of her life, the father of her children, was justified. His death had unearthed buried hopes and reopened wounds and led to her rejection of Wyatt. All things Helen had suggested, but Ellie had needed to learn them on her own.

After a few hours' sleep, she awoke to crystal stripes of sunlight filtering into her bedroom and reacted by stretching her arms and legs. The usual shedding of sleep seemed this morning to reveal a clearer mind and a soothed heart, freed from the chaos that had burdened them for too long. Maybe she'd reached a place of peace concerning Mason. And maybe the unfathomable sorrow of having lost Wyatt would someday go dormant, roused only when she might let down her guard and he would re-emerge into her consciousness.

After dressing, Ellie took a cup of tea out onto the patio. The river flowed tranquilly now, secure in the vibrant autumn sweater fitted snugly around its shoulders. Two men balanced on ladders, draping a white banner emblazoned with big red letters across Front Street. *Welcome to the Ohio River Sternwheel Festival.* Boats would soon begin arriving, with the majority of the festivities taking place over the weekend. Having always loved the annual Sternwheel Festival, Ellie would go again this year, her heart perhaps not in it, but she would go. She would immerse herself in the music and the chattering people and the merriment.

She'd learned from Aunt Lillian to never miss opportunities to take in all of life. To allow the strains of a lovely classical melody to caress your soul into serenity. To marvel at the architecture of Paris when others saw only scraps of litter skittering along the sidewalks. To savor that one strawberry as fervidly as the slice of cheesecake it embellished. She had learned through a lifetime of observing that beloved, iconic person in her life. She recalled overhearing her mother and her aunt talking not long after Uncle Edward died, when Ellie was too immature to absorb the lesson she now firmly grasped.

"How do you do it, Lillian?" Ellie's mother had asked. "You're always so positive. You still seem to find so much joy in life."

"Oh, I allow myself the occasional well-placed pity party," Aunt Lillian had responded with a slight smile. "But it helps to indulge in the little things. I'll go into town only for an ice cream cone, and I'm not ashamed to admit that at times it's a large cone. I might stop to chat with an elderly lady resting on a bench, and she might delight me with an unexpected point of view or a funny story. I'll get a manicure, have a few chocolates with my cup of brewed tea. The little things can help a person get through the big things."

And Ellie would get through this. She'd made mistakes, but she was human. She would pick herself up, dust herself off, and she would be happy in her new life, here in Marietta. This was her place, with or without Wyatt. As a child, she had considered Marietta her secret place, hidden from the rest of the world, accessible only beyond magical, winding roads. Her cozy haven then, her delightful home now. She would see more of her children, spend time with her friends, and carry on Aunt Lillian's charitable work. She would work to repair the damaged stained-glass of the churches. And she would allow herself time to repair and reinforce and polish herself, the way she restored the glass. Then to catch the soothing glint of the stars and take it within.

She *was* that third star. What she wanted and needed was that third star. And the place where her three stars intersected was right here in Marietta.

Her dear Marietta once again stood on both feet, sparkling with renewed life, unafraid of what might someday again knock it to its knees. Its people had cleaned up after the flood and gotten on with their lives, staring down the possibility of one day being hurt again.

Ellie's eyes swept the horizon, where the river met the hills in a distant blue land of hopes and possibilities. How many endless days had Annabelle Wilkes, whose husband had built Ellie's house, stood on this ridge watching and waiting for him? The couple had lived here alone, having had no children, and their devotion to each other was legendary. On his way back to Marietta near the end of a month-long journey on the riverboat he had named for his wife, Captain Wilkes contracted pneumonia and died at the age of forty-two, one day before his wife expected him home. Annabelle's body was found three weeks later, her black dress snagged on the tip of a dead tree branch extending into the Muskingum River. According to legend, her fate had been of her own choosing.

James also had likely given up on life, when all hope of being with the woman he loved finally crumbled. And Aunt Lillian had deprived herself of passionate love for nearly her entire life, never able to overcome what she thought were the shameful circumstances of long ago.

Making her way to the back of the property, Ellie's gaze swept to the southern horizon, to the blue-gray peaks of the Allegheny Mountains, over which drifting clouds formed misty, ever-changing impressions. Sweet memories materialized in her mind. That pier on the Gulf in Biloxi, Mississippi. Herself secure in his arms, luxuriating in his kisses. The swoosh of waves, the rhythm of the song that had drifted out onto the pier, his heartbeat. Ellie's eyes fell closed, and she wrapped herself in her arms and swayed at the memory.

From the moment he'd told her he loved her, on his boat during their wondrous river journey, she'd never really doubted it. He'd been willing to move to Marietta, to anywhere, for her. The man had even donned an uncomfortable tuxedo for her, for heaven's sake. And she'd turned him away, out of some unreasonable longing for something that was in the past. When he'd given her hope for the future. Had given her love. Had proven himself to be one of her three stars. What a fool she'd been. Yes, she understood now why she'd rejected Wyatt, but what a mistake that had been. She simply could kick herself.

Now the echoes of all those times with Wyatt carried as if by telepathy, from another time and place far beyond those mountains, up to her now on Harmar Hill, and it all came back. All pulsed and swelled in her chest until the dam holding back love burst and she cried out in a surge of longing. Wyatt Dare loved her, and she loved him. God help her, she loved him with all her heart. Chills nipped at Ellie's skin.

She sped across the yard, into the house, straight to the desk in the corner of the kitchen, and shuffled through a pile of papers. And there was the telephone number Wyatt had scrawled out, the number for his warehouse. Grabbing the telephone, Ellie tapped the switch hook a few times.

"Operator, I'd like to place a long-distance call, please."

After several rings, the operator intervened. "I'm sorry, ma'am, no answer."

Ellie tossed the telephone aside and grabbed her pocketbook from the desk. Minutes later, she bent over the shoulder of the telegraph office clerk in downtown Marietta, her voice quivering as she dictated a telegram.

"Head has cleared. Heart is open. I'm sorry. I want us. Hope you do too."

Chapter Thirty-Five

Ellie drove into town three times in the next few days. In her typically abrupt way, she'd decided to redecorate. Every piece of ornate furniture in the house, the dark, weighty draperies trimming each window, the knickknacks and crystal collections and fringe—all were a reflection of the life Aunt Lillian had lived, of her exquisite taste. And Ellie loved it all. These were props in the story of her own life. But the house was Ellie's now, and she needed to make it her home, needed to design the scenery for her continuing life story.

She picked up several gallons of paint at Charlene's five-and-dime and would get help with stripping dark, floral wallpaper and coating the walls in airier shades. Because Aunt Lillian had filled the house with lovely, quality pieces, mostly antiques, much of the furniture would stay, but Ellie would have some of them reupholstered in mellow solid colors.

The sitting room should evoke all that was the valley below, she'd decided. The olive-green settee, both Aunt Lillian's and Ellie's favorite piece of all, would remain as is, complementing the foliage of the valley and mimicking the color of the river on particularly stormy days. In deference to the river's sunny-day hue, Ellie chose a pale aqua silk for the sofa and a wide stripe in tones of olive, aqua, and rose on an ivory background for the two side chairs. The soft rose paint she'd chosen for the fireplace wall would reflect the aura cast by the setting sun. Gradually, she would get to the other rooms, but this room was special. This was the space where so much of her life had played out, and this was the room where she knew she would continue spending the most time, visiting with family and friends, reading, living. *Maybe with Wyatt.*

Anita showed up at the house late one afternoon bearing a pretty gift bag.

"I heard you're doing some redecorating," she said. "Maybe you can find a spot for this."

Ellie took the bag and sifted through the tissue paper to find a beautifully framed photograph of herself, Anita, Deb, and Charlene as little girls, their faces full of glee, along with Aunt Lillian midair, her long, dark hair flying.

Ellie's hand went to her mouth. "Oh, my goodness, I've never seen this photo before. Where did you get it?"

"My dad took it. Remember how he would walk over to tell me it was time to come home for dinner? One time, he had his camera with him. He'd just bought it, his first camera. Anyway, Mom ran across the photo recently, and I had it copied for you."

"I don't remember your father taking the photograph, but I remember that day so well," Ellie said. "Aunt Lillian never cared how much we marked up her sidewalk with stones, but that day she came out and played hopscotch with us. Look how young she was." Ellie dabbed at a tear and hugged Anita. "Thank you so much. This is incredible."

"How are the kids doing, after losing their father?" Anita propped herself against the foyer wall.

"Come on in. Would you like something to drink?"

Anita shook her head. "I've got a date."

"With?"

"You don't know him."

"I hope it goes well." Ellie lowered herself to a step of the staircase. "The children are doing as well as can be expected. I feel so bad for them."

"Yeh, it's really awful what happened to Mason."

"I've found myself really missing him, too," Ellie said.

"Understandable. You had a lot of years together. And what about that hunky riverman? How are things going with him?"

Ellie shook her head and twisted one side of her mouth in disgust. "Hmph. I wrecked things with him. He's gone."

"Oh, my word." Anita straightened herself to attention. "What happened?"

"I don't know. I was so mixed up after Mason died." Ellie combed a hand through her hair. "I treated Wyatt like dirt, and now I'll probably never see him again."

Anita's head dipped and her eyes softened in sympathy. "You know, Ellie, I haven't been very nice, or supportive, about your man issues." She swept the toe of an elegant, two-toned pump back and forth over the marble flooring. "Sorry about that."

"It's all right," Ellie said. "Looks as if my man issues are over anyway."

"How do you do it?" Anita leaned against the wall again and crossed her arms. "How do you go without having a man in your life?"

"I don't know. I haven't ever been without a man for very long. The few years after Mason left was the longest."

"Few years?" Anita smacked a hand to her forehead.

"My word, I would simply die. I cannot stand one weekend without a date." Her hands flailed. "And I think I've put up with a lot more crap from men over the years than I should have, just so I wouldn't have to be alone."

"We all have our needs. I'm not happy about being alone now, but I'll be fine, and you're strong, Anita. You'd be all right, too, being alone for a while. It would be much better than being with the wrong man."

"You know that night at the Levee House when I was running my mouth about Gregory treating you the way he did, saying it didn't sound like abuse and all that crap?"

Ellie nodded.

Anita fiddled with her strand of pearls. "I had a guy once who liked to smack me around."

Ellie leapt to her feet and planted her hands on her hips. "Who? Why didn't you tell me?"

Anita shrugged. "Nobody you knew. And it didn't seem like a big deal. He never used his fists. But I see now, after you told us about Gregory, and seeing the way you thought enough of yourself to not put up with that baloney, that I didn't deserve being treated that way either. I'm finished with being a patsy. This fellow tonight, he seems like a really good guy. About my age, divorced. I'm rather excited about him."

"That's terrific, Anita. You do deserve a man who treats you well. Let me know how it goes."

"Will do, and I've gotta get going. He's picking me up in an hour. But listen, I just wanted to say I'm sorry for all the crap I've given you about your situations. It was just me being a bitch. And thank you for making me see I deserve a good man."

Ellie pulled Anita into a tight hug. "Thanks again for

the photograph. I'm going to go right now and find the perfect place for it."

After propping the photo on a side table in the sitting room, Ellie had one last thing to do to complete the redecoration. She went to Aunt Lillian's old bedroom, retrieved an item from the closet shelf, and unwrapped the blanket. She would have Aunt Lillian's stained-glass panel of the riverboat *Anne* installed as soon as possible, where her aunt had propped it.

****

Catching the next morning's light, the chandelier's crystal pendants sprinkled it about Ellie's bedroom, urging her eyes open. She always left the roller blinds open just enough that the morning light awakened her, never wanting to sleep late here. She stretched, plumped her pillow, and snuggled between the soft sheets that layered her bed like a luscious torte.

Four days. No telephone call. No knock at the door of the house on Harmar Hill. With each day, hope had receded further into a dark tunnel leading from possibility, through dismay, to emptiness. She shouldn't have sent that telegram. He wasn't coming back. Obviously, he was done with her, and who could blame him after she'd treated him like an annoyance and coldly rejected him? Then had the nerve to send that pathetic message, practically begging him to come back. Her face flushed hot at the humiliation. Why could she never think things through before acting?

She would have to let the reality of Wyatt fade like an old photograph. How long until the revelation that he hadn't monopolized any particular moment of her thoughts and longings? How long until the crushing ache would subside?

Chapter Thirty-Six

Ellie tossed on a pretty new dress, the first item of clothing she'd purchased since the Great Depression began. One of those deliciously fashionable, bias-cut numbers, in amethyst splashed with white polka dots, accented with a thin white belt and flared at the hemline. After straightening the seams of her hosiery and grabbing her new cinnamon-colored cardigan, she headed downstairs, smiling at the memory of playing dress-up with her friends so long ago. They would descend the curved staircase, step by grand step, dressed as southern belles in her paternal grandmother's billowy silk and satin gowns, which Aunt Lillian had kept in a closet.

Soon Ellie strolled along the riverfront, soaking in all that was Marietta. Cooler temperatures and a cloudless blue sky had crafted a perfect day for the Sternwheel Festival. With brilliant sunshine warming the autumn air, crisp oak and birch leaves swirled around her like monarch butterflies. Fading pink coneflowers and blossoming russet-colored sedum adorned narrow flower beds abutting clapboard homes.

Ellie admired the many sternwheelers parked along the banks, although some flaunted unnatural colors and garish decorations—a gigantic, artificial fish hanging here, a shocking-pink mermaid tacked up there. Others were more fortunate in their tasteful restoration. The aroma of barbequed chicken and candied apples permeated the air, and locals as well as tourists from miles away filled the little town. And there was Marv, on a rare day off from the Levee House, strolling alongside his wife.

"Eleanor, good lord, young lady, where have you been hiding? I don't think I've seen you in a good two weeks."

"Oh, goodness, I've been working a lot up at the house, doing a little redecorating."

"Hard to believe what happened here a few short months ago." Marv propped his hands on his hips. "I said it before, but I'll say it again. Thank you for helping us with the clean-up. It meant the world to us."

Janet agreed and expressed her own thanks. "We're opening back up Monday morning," she added.

"It was the least I could do," Ellie said. "You've always been there for me. What a horrible time for all of us. I hope to never see anything like that again."

"You won't. A flood like that won't happen again in your lifetime. Last winter was a bear, then the rain this spring. More than we've seen in fifty years. No, Marietta is safe and sound." Marv's words were comforting.

"You two stop by the house soon, to see what I've done."

"That we will, my dear." Marv leaned in to collect his kiss on the cheek.

Continuing her stroll, Ellie paused to talk and catch up with the many people she knew. Everyone expressed pleasant surprise at her having moved to Marietta and joy that the iconic yellow mansion on Harmar Hill would stay in Lillian Blaylock's family, God rest her soul.

Ellie stopped for a chat with the hand-holding

Charlene and Alan, who thanked Ellie for her help with getting the five-and-dime back on its feet. Several minutes later, Ellie spotted Anita, propped by an elbow on a blanket on the levee, licking at a dripping ice cream cone while locking eyes with a very attentive man. Ellie grinned, shook her head, and continued her stroll, eventually finding her way across the bridge, to Harmar Village.

Named for Revolutionary War General Josiah Harmar, the little village wore its timeworn brick streets like a proud peacock, and many of its buildings dated to the late 1700s. Ellie passed a general store, which carried everything under the sun, and a Victorian-style gift shop, its display windows all white and lacy. And, of course, the beloved, age-old Harmar Tavern, all cleaned up and thriving again, although—like most other businesses that weekend—it had shut down for the Festival.

By late afternoon, Ellie had crossed back over Harmar Bridge to the mainland, where she bought a coney dog from a street vendor to calm her rumbling stomach. Claiming an unoccupied bench, she perused the scene. The lowering sun gilded the valley in a tranquil glow, but the riverbanks were alive with the sparkling festival. The neon lights of the vendors and the deck lights of the sternwheelers glinted across the water.

Soon, Deb and Vinnie came strolling along, arm in arm. Ellie had never seen Deb with such a spring in her step. She hadn't known Deb was capable of a spring in her step.

Ellie stood and hugged her pal.

"Where the hell have you been, woman? You been hibernating or what?"

"Hello to you too, Deb. Vinnie, it's wonderful to see

you."

Vinnie, never quiet nor shy, crushed Ellie in his arms, lifted her, and swung her around. "Hey, you good-lookin' doll, gorgeous as ever," he declared to everyone within a three-mile radius.

Ellie laughed. "Same ol' Vinnie."

"Seriously, I haven't heard from you," Deb said. "You okay? What've you been doing with yourself?"

"Just finishing with the redecorating up at the house. I'm fine, everything's fine." Ellie waved a hand toward the town. "Isn't it marvelous to see everything getting back to normal?"

"God, yes. What a nightmare. But did you hear they're not reopening the Low Falutin?" Deb asked.

"What? No way." Ellie glanced downstream, toward the spot where the remnants of their beloved honky-tonk slumped. "Too much damage?"

"Yeh. The place is destroyed. We were just over there. The wood floors look like toothpicks."

"That's so sad." Ellie and her friends had frequented the Low Falutin for over two decades. The watering hole had been like an old friend with whom they'd shared many nights of laughing, dancing, talking, polishing off platters of deep-fried onion rings, and meeting cute fellows in the early days.

"But what about you, Ells? Have you heard from him?"

Ellie started at the abrupt query. She'd finally told Deb about sending Wyatt away, sharing her profound regret at what she considered yet another impulsive move. Mercifully, Deb had skipped the reprimand and directive Ellie was sure she'd dole out and told her only that she was sorry.

"I sent him a telegram a few days ago."

"And?"

Ellie shrugged and shook her head.

"Well, rats. Sorry, kid."

"It's all right. Vinnie, you and Deb need to come up to the house for dinner. The place has been way too quiet since everyone ditched me after the flood."

"Hell yeah, sweetheart, just say the word."

"You staying for the concert?" Deb asked. "Come on, we're gonna try to find a place to sit. Come with us."

The orchestra would be playing from a barge. As early as yesterday morning, people had begun setting up chairs and spreading blankets on the banks to claim their spots. Many others would listen from their boats, clustered close to the barge like bees buzzing around a hive.

"I may catch some of the music. I'm going to walk around a little more, though. It's so nice out. You two have fun."

"Okay, well, we'll get together soon." Deb tugged Vinnie off toward the levee. "Have your people contact my people," she tossed back to Ellie.

Ellie headed back toward Harmar Bridge, which a constant stream of people crisscrossed. Others leaned against the railing, checking out all the goings-on. Stepping onto the bridge, Ellie surveyed the scene. Sternwheelers and motorboats that had docked for the night swayed sleepily. Recently put back into service, the sternwheeler *Valley Gem* rested, building steam for another day of tourist excursions tomorrow. Although it had long ago fulfilled its commercial duties, the old boat still had purpose.

In one of Marv's many stories over the years, he'd

told Ellie that thousands of steamboats once transported millions of passengers and tons of freight from port to port by way of the rivers. Then midway through the nineteenth century, when locomotives took over much of the transportation, many of the steamboats were converted into tourist vessels or showboats carrying acting troupes and circuses to the river towns. Most were eventually abandoned to decay, were lost in fires, or sank and remained on river bottoms. Marietta was lucky that the *Valley Gem* had survived and landed here.

Leaning against the wooden rail, Ellie closed her eyes and raised her face to the lingering warmth of the sun. The soundtrack of the festival echoed from every direction—the clanging of bells, animated conversation and laughter, a distant melody. People meandered off the bridge to take their places on the banks for the concert. Rubbing her arms, Ellie silently thanked herself for wearing the thick cardigan. The distant melody grew louder. A calliope. A rare sound. *How charming.*

Beneath the bridge and through the rolling hills of Marietta and beyond, the seductive river flowed musky and dense with mystery and longing. The gleaming white-yellow sun barely peaked above the horizon, casting wispy layers of sunset colors across the lower sky and onto the river. Above it all, the approach of nighttime unveiled a million flickering stars. The calliope music intensified, and it seemed to be coming from somewhere downriver. Ellie squinted at the fluid horizon.

From around the bend, near the confluence of the two rivers, a white riverboat emerged, a luminous pearl plucked from its oyster shell, the fanciful notes of the calliope skipping from its deck. Its window trim and paddlewheel blazed red, the American flag fluttered high above its pilothouse, and white clouds of steam billowed from the smokestack. As the boat moved closer, only two people were visible onboard, so it probably wasn't a tourist vessel. A rare, exquisite sight.

Everyone seemed to pause to watch the work of art drift into town and wave to it. Just short of Harmar Bridge, the vessel inched closer toward shore, as if searching for a place to dock, its calliope pleading to call somebody *sweetheart*. Rich, shiny wood paneled its sides, and the sun's ebbing rays lit a pewter bell and glinted off brass railings.

On the barge, members of the orchestra placed chairs, tuned instruments, and assembled drum kits. The riverbank morphed into an ever-expanding patchwork quilt, pieced together with colorful blankets. Children ran about, tumbling, laughing. People snacked on all manner of carnival treats and sipped, or guzzled, from paper cups.

As the melody of the calliope ended, the riverboat continued gliding toward the bridge in tranquil dignity, then backed into a vacant space along the shore. Ellie squinted and blinked, struggling to focus her eyes on the boat in the fading light.

Then, suddenly, the people left on the bridge faded into shadows, the laughter and music and steam whistles of the festival all receded into a muffled murmur. And in a heartbeat, Ellie found herself transported, as if on a swirl of glittery fairy dust, to the end of the bridge, nearer to the boat, and the impossible sight drew the air from her lungs. On the stern, the name bestowed upon the exquisite old boat blazed in scarlet script...

Eleanor.

And he stood on deck, saying something to the other

man, pointing, giving instructions. Then he turned and somehow spotted her. When exactly he disembarked, she didn't notice. How he made his way to Harmar Bridge and climbed its steps, she wouldn't remember. All she knew was that Wyatt was there, standing in front of her.

She'd taken Aunt Lillian's advice and figured out what her passions were, her three stars. And her journey to discern those three stars, a journey with as many twists and turns as the river, had brought her here, to the place where her three stars crossed.

And now here he was, and his eyes told her that the two of them stood together at the confluence of forever.

A word about the author...

Dottie scratched out her first fiction as a little kid transfixed by the books she read all those lazy summer days on the front porch swing.

Two of her short stories have been published in The Ernest Hemingway Foundation of Oak Park's literary journal, Hemingway Shorts, having placed among the top ten entries in its annual short story contests.

Where the Stars Cross is her first novel.

dottiesines.com

Thank you for purchasing
this publication of The Wild Rose Press, Inc.

For questions or more information
contact us at
info@thewildrosepress.com.

The Wild Rose Press, Inc.